Janet Elizabeth Simpson

FALLING

BOOKS BY ANNE SIMPSON

FICTION
Canterbury Beach (2001)
Falling (2008)

POETRY
Light Falls Through You (2000)
Loop (2003)
Quick (2007)

FALLING

ANNE SIMPSON

McCLELLAND & STEWART

Library and Archives Canada Cataloguing in Publication

Simpson, Anne, 1956–
Falling / Anne Simpson.

ISBN 978-0-7710-8090-6

I. Title.

PS8587.I54533F34 2008   C813'.6   C2007-905936-8

We acknowledge the financial support of the Government of Canada through the
Book Publishing Industry Development Program and that of the Government of
Ontario through the Ontario Media Development Corporation's Ontario Book
Initiative. We further acknowledge the support of the Canada Council for the Arts
and the Ontario Arts Council for our publishing program.

The epigraph on p. vii is from the poem "I Will Return" by Pablo Neruda, from
Isla Negra: A Notebook, edited by Dennis Maloney (White Pine Press, 2000).

Typeset in Baskerville by M&S, Toronto
Printed and bound in Canada

ANCIENT FOREST
FRIENDLY

McClelland & Stewart Ltd.
75 Sherbourne Street
Toronto, Ontario
M5A 2P9
www.mcclelland.com

1 2 3 4 5   12 11 10 09 08

Some other time, man or woman, traveller,
later, when I am not alive,
look here, look for me
between stone and ocean,
in the light storming
through the foam.
Look here, look for me,
for here I will return, without saying a thing . . .

– PABLO NERUDA

FALLING

THE GIRL ON THE FOUR-WHEELER turned sharply at the top of the bank and felt the vehicle drop heavily beneath her. There was no time to correct the mistake, though she tried, and the four-wheeler fell, toppling to one side, slowly, all four hundred and eighty-eight pounds of it, as it slid down the bank, landing in the stream and trapping her body underneath. Her cry could have been that of an Arctic tern, high above, its wings an open pair of scissors against the blue.

Struggling to free herself, she could only bring her head above water briefly before her exertions wedged the vehicle more firmly in the thick, wet sand.

Damian, she shrieked, raising her head out of the water a second time.

Panicking, she moved her head wildly from side to side, choking, trying to get air, which made her take in water. She heard an overwhelming beating in her ears.

Her body was splayed in the stream. She struggled several more times, with less vigour, and then she didn't move. Though she was face down, one of her hands lay with the palm up so the water moved over her fingertips.

At the other end of the beach, where the rocks piled and tumbled like upended shelves and tables, Damian was dozing. He'd been swimming, and his bathing suit was still damp. The sun was warm on his body – it showed his pelvic bones in relief, touched his features with light – and it had made him sleepy. Each time he exhaled, there was the suggestion of a snore. He hadn't slept well the night before, and now dreams came fleetingly.

He might have been carved in stone, except for the almost imperceptible movement of his chest, rising and falling. A fly landed lightly on his leg, and he reached out a hand to brush it off. Disconnected images flickered in and out of his consciousness until he heard the distant cry of a bird and opened his eyes. After a while he got up, and stretched to one side, the other side. He had a man's body, with a broad, tanned chest, though his blond hair was as fine and sleek as a girl's, and would have fallen past his shoulders if it had been loose. He picked up his towel and stood at the edge of the rocks.

The sea glinted and moved and shifted before him, becoming a hard, steely colour where it met the softer edge of sky. A roll of waves fell gently and retreated, leaving the sand darkened, velvety brown, as they drew away. The tides of the Northumberland Strait weren't as high as those of the Fundy, and seemed almost lazy by comparison, and although the water was as warm as that off the coast of the Carolinas, the jellyfish had already come and gone: there were no more of their purplish, nearly translucent bodies, some as large as purses, to be seen on the beach. The light was beginning to slant across the land in early morning and late evening, which meant autumn was coming.

Far off, so far as to be dreamlike, was a line of blue hills on the western coast of Cape Breton. To the north were the headlands of Cape George, but Ballantyne's Cove was beyond the nearest cliff, with its reddened, exposed soils. On the water, some distance out, and apparently equidistant between the coasts on either side, was a white sailboat, but its sails were furled. There was no wind. The sky was clear, devoid of any clouds, and it promised to be hot all day.

Damian got up and moved over the rocks with a kind of animal grace, dropping from this shelf of stone to that one, over a small crevice where some broken beer bottles lay, and at the edge of the rocks he leapt down to the sand below. He paused and ran his hand over initials carved in the stone: Hey man! It's 15°C – Oct. 21, 2000. J + E.

Out of the corner of his eye he saw something yellow, sticking up out of the sand. He couldn't figure it out for a moment. It was all wrong. Lisa's kayak. But why –

Lisa, he shouted.

He ran, sprinting so fast that his heels made little tails of sand fly up. He yelled again, more loudly this time. When he reached the ATV, overturned in a stream on the beach, he howled – a long, drawn-out cry. But he'd already waded into the water to raise his sister's head out of the stream, which he managed clumsily. He was shaking so badly he could hardly keep her head steady. Water dribbled out of her mouth. He opened it, checked it with his fingers, and started resuscitation. He worked as swiftly as he could, holding her head up, realizing, in a distant, shocked way, that it wasn't doing any good, but continuing relentlessly.

On a ridge above the beach, a man came out of a house after hearing someone howl. A cry for help. All he needed was a glimpse of the overturned vehicle and a boy cradling someone in the depression where the stream ran out to the ocean. He went inside to make a phone call and then grabbed some plastic picnic cushions and ran to the beach, down the path between wild rose bushes with a glossy black dog racing ahead. He followed the tracks of the four-wheeler to where the trailer and two kayaks had come unhitched. Going over the bank, he fell, regained his balance, and plunged down the sandy slope.

Damian was still doing mouth-to-mouth; he hadn't tried to move Lisa. But she wasn't breathing. Her hands didn't seem to belong to her. The twine bracelet he'd made, with the shells and blue beads, was still on her wrist. And how strange it was that the striped beach bag had been thrown on the sand a few feet away, flung to safety.

He moaned, unaware of the man who had arrived at his side, gasping for breath, and the dog, sending up a flurry of sand as it made circles around them, running in and out of the water and spraying them as it went.

We need to do CPR, said the man.

Damian looked up at him. She's my sister.

Put these cushions under her head, the man instructed. Then maybe we can pull her free. I'll see if I can hold up the end of this thing – you get the other end.

Damian nodded.

It was the man, not Damian, who stuffed a plastic cushion under Lisa's head, carefully but swiftly. Damian had to be persuaded to let go of his sister for a few moments while they each took an end of the ATV and, with a great effort, hauled it to one side, freeing her.

· Careful, said the man. Brace her head and neck.

They carried her up from the stream and set her down on dry, level sand. Her body was heavy and wet, and her head was turned to one side.

The man immediately began CPR. There was nothing delicate about the way he pushed down on Lisa's chest, quickly, confidently. He pumped her chest thirty times, gave her two breaths, and continued pumping. Sweat appeared on his forehead, but he didn't stop to wipe it. There was only an occasional grunt as he kept up the CPR, and, intermittently, the barking of the dog.

Time wasn't moving in the usual way: it could have sped up, or reversed, or made some peculiar twist. The man thought that a year could have passed before he saw the paramedics running across the beach with the spinal board. They'd come along the path from the wharf road, the one with the old barbed-wire fence across it, then down the steep path. When they arrived they were breathless; they moved in closely while the man continued to do CPR. The red-haired paramedic quickly set up a portable defibrillator and prepared a bag-valve mask.

How long had she been under water?

Damian shook his head.

And CPR – how long had they been doing it?

The red-haired paramedic placed the mask over Lisa's mouth and nose as he asked the question, and the man, relieved of doing CPR, glanced at his watch and told them it had been about fifteen minutes since he'd made the phone call.

Swiftly, they transferred Lisa to the spinal board. They scarcely seemed to shift her, so efficient were their movements. It was almost as if they rolled her onto it, bracing her as they did so, immobilizing her head with a C-collar and strapping her body in place. They cut her bathing suit straps neatly and peeled back the material, wiping her chest dry before placing electrode pads on her skin and hooking her up to the heart monitor on the portable defibrillator.

One of the paramedics took the mask off Lisa's face.

All clear, he said, but Damian was still holding his sister's arm.

Stay back from her – okay? All clear. Shock delivered.

Lisa's body jumped violently when the paramedic shocked her. He held up his hand so none of them would touch her as he checked the heart monitor.

He shocked her twice more, then stopped. He picked up the bright red defibrillator that resembled a child's toy but left the electrode pads on Lisa's chest. The skin of her chest was white, in contrast to her tanned arms, and her breasts were exposed, yet chaste in their girlishness.

What are you doing? asked Damian.

Right now – giving her oxygen. And epinephrine –

But what about her heart?

We're still monitoring her heart. The paramedic squeezed the oxygen bag attached to the tube he'd inserted into Lisa's mouth. He spoke rapidly to his partner. And we'll keep up CPR, he assured Damian.

The paramedics lifted the board and began carrying Lisa across the beach, instructing the man to do CPR as they went. He pumped Lisa's chest as he walked alongside; it was awkward, but he did his best. Damian tucked in her hand so it wouldn't hang over the edge of the board.

The dog no longer barked, but ran close beside them. They made a curious procession, winding over the rocks at the end of the beach and up the path, fringed with soft grasses, blond and dry at the end of summer, and clusters of mauve asters and goldenrod. The man was breathing hard; at times the path was simply too steep or too narrow for him to continue CPR. At the barbed-wire fence they halted, while the dog, tail wagging, nosed through the asters and found a stick.

It took a few moments to get the board, with Lisa on it, over the twisted fence, which had been pulled down so people could step over it. After the board was passed over the fence, the red-haired paramedic took over from the man and continued CPR. The dog did not come, but as they went across the patch of gravel at the side of the wharf road, the man whistled, and the dog came leaping over the fence, carrying the stick in its mouth. Damian, behind the others, was shivering. He had put on a T-shirt from which the sleeves had been ripped. His lips were blue, but he had no idea he was cold.

They put Lisa into the ambulance and the red-haired paramedic kept doing CPR. Damian climbed inside and crouched, shivering. He watched the paramedic dully. Despite everything that was being done for Lisa, something was missing. There would have been more urgency if –

But he couldn't face thinking it.

At the back of the ambulance, the other paramedic turned to the man. He can't come with us.

Let him, said the man.

The paramedic shook his head as he shut the ambulance doors.

And make sure he gets a blanket, said the man. It's the least you can do.

The man watched them go, then turned and went back along the path, stepping over the barbed wire. The dog had gone ahead, but the man picked his way carefully down the steep path, sending a scattering of pebbles to the rocks below. The ocean was as calm as it had been earlier, and the sky was the same wide-open blue, and this was astonishing to him. There were tears in his eyes and he had some difficulty getting over the rocks and down to the beach. He slipped several times, despite his caution. Then, once he was on the sand again, he saw the footprints they'd made on the way to the ambulance. He stood helplessly, crying. He wiped his cheeks roughly with his hands and kept going directly to the place where it had happened. There was the four-wheeler and its trailer, with the kayaks tossed this way and that. He'd get these things off the beach, but he couldn't bring himself to do it just then.

Yet he knew which cottage had been rented; he knew where he would take the four-wheeler, trailer, and kayaks. It was one of the smaller cottages, the one with the roof that needed to be reshingled, and it was rented each summer to a woman from Halifax. A MacKenzie, he thought. Yes, that was right. And these two, the boy and the girl, must be her children. He felt his throat constrict. She wouldn't know yet about her daughter.

The thought came to him that if he'd just looked out the window sooner, if he'd got up for another cup of coffee – but of course he hadn't. He walked to the edge of the water, thinking of the girl's suffering, and how no one had known of it.

At last he turned and went up to his house, where there was no one to greet him. He brushed his hand across the thinning hair on the top of his head. Every summer for as long as he could remember he'd come from Halifax to spend a few weeks at Cribbon's, in a house that reminded him of the place, not far from here, where he'd spent summers as a child. It was curious that he hadn't known the boy or the girl, but he had always kept to himself, just as they must have kept to themselves.

Now he would have to live with the fact that he had not been able to help. He had seen several people die during his life, but never one as young as this. This thought depleted him, and he went up the path and then the steps of his house slowly, stopping at the top. The dog was with him, eager to get past and go inside, and in a moment he was by the door, his tail batting against it. But the man didn't go inside. He stood on the deck, looking out at the deceptively tranquil water. He waited for a moment, as if to get his bearings.

Cecily, he said, and his voice broke. He sat down heavily on a plastic deck chair, putting his hands firmly on the armrests and shutting his eyes.

He continued to sit where he was, his eyes closed.

The dog whimpered, and the man opened his eyes. He knew that it was going to be hard on the boy, a terrible thing that he would take into himself. It would do things to him. But there was no changing it. It was like a stone falling in water. A stone dropping with a little sound – *plink* – and a ring around the place where it had vanished, and another, and another.

He supposed he might have been more of a help to the boy. He knew he had the capacity to do such things, to offer a word when people were in trouble, and that this time he hadn't managed it. He'd been a judge for more than twenty-five years. He'd gained a tolerance and kindness that went beyond professional tact. It had taken him longer to come to conclusions in the last decade than it had in the beginning, but he thought that these latter decisions had been a cut above the rest of his work. He'd been invited to sit on the Supreme Court, but Cecily had been sick then, and he'd declined the offer and retired.

Now he recalled that he hadn't asked the boy his name, because it hadn't been relevant. But he'd been so young, and so had the girl.

The dog whimpered again.

All right, Max, said the man finally, rising out of the chair. All right. He gave in and opened the door.

Through the windows of the ambulance, everything was as clear to Damian as if he were looking through binoculars, so close that it was unreal, but later he would not remember it quite this way.

It was a perfect late-summer morning, with sunlight falling generously across the slopes of Sugarloaf. It lay across a cornfield, where the stalks of corn were tall and leafy, with silky tassels, and it lay across the meadows below. It flecked the water of a small pond. It shone on the marmalade-coloured fur of a cat lying in the sun on the deck behind a house. The hour was not yet noon, but already the air shimmered with heat.

On the harbour road, the ambulance was nearing the hospital. It appeared and disappeared, threading through stands of trees, mostly spruce and birch, on either side of the road, a tiny, white shape on the sinuous road that wound in and out along the water and then away from it. Occasionally the ambulance gleamed in the sunlight as it rounded a curve, going past a farm on one side, then a farm on the other, where a cattle barn was being raised. At a new house past the farm, a woman finished putting out her second load of laundry and gave the line a last, quick jerk to send it out farther.

Below the road, the water of the harbour was serenely blue. A bald eagle could be seen making a slow circle through the air above an island off William's Point. A man cutting the grass at the small golf course at the end of the point stopped his tractor mower and got off to light a cigarette. He dragged deeply on it, scanning the water and the broad shoulder of Sugarloaf. Someone was paddling a green canoe beyond the islands just below him. Across the water to the west, the man could see a flash of white on the road near Lanark, but he didn't know it was an ambulance. He threw the cigarette down into the grass and stepped on the butt.

After the ambulance passed the abattoir and the north end of the Landing, a trail that traced the edge of the harbour wetlands, it turned into the hospital. The angelus was ringing at the convent, a large brick building that lay on the slope above the hospital, just as the ambulance drew up at Emergency. The paramedics jumped out and quickly took the body on the spinal board inside. Damian followed.

Though it was hot, he still had the blanket around his shoulders like a cloak.

It was over, Damian thought. How quickly life went out of someone. This was his first time seeing it, and he knew, without absorbing any of it fully, that he would never be able to forget it. He would walk through these doors and something would come crashing down. The years would come to him; he could see them as if they were shapes in the distance, but this single event would mark the rest of his life. He was alive, and Lisa was not.

He hesitated for a moment. It was dark beyond the doors, but once he got inside his eyes would adjust to the light. This went through his mind as he paused, though he paused for no more than a second or two. One of the paramedics glanced back at him, and he knew he had to follow. He took one step, then another, but as he moved it seemed to him that he moved through one year, another, a third. He went across the threshold and felt the unbearable weight come down on him.

Then the glass doors closed behind him, and he was lost to view.

THEY COULD HEAR THE ROAR of Niagara Falls when they got out of the car.

Damian stretched, but Ingrid set off immediately down the wooden stairway, lured by the thundering sound that came up through the leaves of the darkly crowded maples. He caught up with his mother at the bottom of the steps in a parking lot set with rows of jewel-bright cars. Beyond was a green swath of lawn and clicking sprinklers near the old power plant, and tour buses making a slow funereal procession along the road by the river. A great plume of mist lifted into the air as powerfully as a raised fist, forming and dissolving into a shifting, changing shape that softened and folded into air above.

You shouldn't be seeing it like this, murmured Ingrid.

Damian glanced at her: white hair pulled back from her face, straight nose, tanned skin. Her chin was lifted up slightly, as if she were trying to catch the scent of something.

How should I be seeing it? he asked.

I should have brought you here years ago – you and Lisa.

It had been a long drive, and now the heat made him dizzy. He closed his eyes and stood swaying as small, dancing shapes sparkled behind his eyelids. He wasn't keeping up with her train of thought.

Are you all right? she said.

I'm okay.

He was thinking of how his father had taken him, together with his sister, to see the waterfall at James River when they were young. It had been nothing like this; it had been merely a modest rush of water over some rocks. The path to the waterfall had been thick with spruce, but there were places where the trees weren't so dense and dark. They seemed to be filled with light, and his father called them hardwoods. He had scooped up Lisa and carried her over a puddle and set her down on her feet again, and it was then – just then – that a ruffed grouse made such a loud drumming that Damian, startled, fell back against a birch. Finally they had come to a very steep bank where someone had rigged ropes to guide people to the bottom.

It's fine, his father had said. We'll just go slowly and hold on to the ropes.

But his father wasn't with them now, Damian thought, as he walked across the parking lot with his mother. They were two sleepwalkers, walking a little apart, as if leaving space between them for another person. They'd arrived at Niagara Falls in the middle of the afternoon, but he had the feeling of having woken up in another country. A country of clamour. The exhaust from the buses was blue, and there were tinny voices on intercoms hawking tickets. A helicopter flew over once, twice, and at intervals a great balloon, striped with gold and scarlet, rose straight up, slowly, and descended just as slowly, settling on the American side of the Falls. Damian crossed the road, lagging behind his mother, and a leather-clad man on a motorcycle swerved to miss him. The man turned to raise a gloved hand, middle finger extended.

Now get together, said a man with a camera, facing a little group posing in front of a flowerbed, where exotic blooms of amaryllis stood, darkly crimson, behind them. The man pushed his cap back on his head and waited for people to move out of the way.

All righty, let's get this show on the road. No, get in closer, Dwayne. Closer. Okay, say *cheese*.

Ingrid said she'd meet Damian in half an hour in the same spot. Was he listening? She was going to buy a few bottles of water. Her white hair was beaded with diamond-fine droplets as the mist fell over it. He nodded, wanting to tell her about the droplets, but she'd already turned to leave, and he squeezed into a place at the railing beside a heavy-set woman. The Niagara River ran swiftly past, just beneath where he stood, and thinned to green transparency before falling over the ledge of stone. It began with water, thought Damian. Things began and ended with water.

I don't like vinegar on them, said the woman beside him.

Damian half turned to her, but she was speaking to her friend.

I like gravy, though. Donald can't stand it on fries, but I like it.

A person caught in that current might possibly have a chance of swimming to the bank, Damian considered. But the current would be unrelenting; it would sweep the swimmer away just at the moment he held out a hand for help. He'd be tossed over the edge.

He who hesitates is lost, his father called. Don't be afraid.

Damian knew he'd slide and fall straight into the dark, rushing river below. So Lisa went first. She was only five. She did what their father told her to do and laughed when she tumbled against him at the bottom. Damian's heart was thumping hard as he reached for the rope and held it with both hands. Thumping hard as a grouse. He clutched the rope and skidded down, holding on so tightly that the rope seemed to rip the skin from his hands.

His father caught him, rubbing the burns on his hands, and the three of them stood on the bank together. Damian's heart was still beating fast, but he was dazzled by the water pouring into the deep, black pool, a pool that was ringed around with a wall of rock topped with spruce trees. They gazed at the waterfall without speaking. Bright and dark. Then their father tore off his T-shirt and jeans, his socks and shoes, and made a swift, shallow dive into the pool. He came up, laughing, his hair plastered against his head.

God knows where Donald got to, anyway, said the woman. He said he was going for a leak, but it can't take that long.

Damian lifted his eyes to see, farther away, a place where the river dipped and rolled before it coursed over the Falls. It furled in vivid green, a constant wave that seemed to stay in one place, thick as a muscle. Just at the edge, the water became a froth of white.

The lip of the waterfalls made a long, rounded curve. In the middle distance was Goat Island, separating the American Falls from the Canadian. The American Falls were less impressive, with piles of rocks below. Lisa had told him that they'd once stopped the Falls for several months on that side, as if they'd been turning off a tap. They'd wanted to get rid of the talus at the base, though in the end they'd decided to leave it. But in halting the flow they'd found things they didn't expect. Bones. Twelve quarts of coins. More bones. All those people, Lisa had said, had thrown themselves in. They'd killed themselves.

How did she know that?

She'd done a project on it. The one she'd done for Mr. Craig.

A whole project on how many people killed themselves at the Falls?

He was stupid, she told him. He was a *stupid* idiot.

He remembered the tone of her voice. *Stupid.*

She'd always wanted to see Niagara Falls. When she was little, she'd had a paperweight that their Uncle Roger had sent to her one Christmas: if she shook it, little flakes of white fell over the miniature Falls. There was some looping white script on the top of the paperweight: *Niagara Falls, Canada*. Because she liked it so much, more things had arrived from their uncle, in mailing tubes, until she had posters of the Horseshoe Falls in Icy Glory, An Aerial View of the Falls, the *Maid of the Mist* Near the American Falls, the Spanish Aero Car Offers Thrills Over the Whirlpool, the Spectacular Blossom Festival, and Roger Hockridge Challenges the Falls Again. The poster of Roger Hockridge, Canada's Number One Daredevil With His Bomb Barrel, had been put up on the ceiling of her room. She liked looking at the round barrel, decorated with red maple leaves, bobbing at the edge of the Falls – a barrel that held Uncle Roger, the uncle they'd never met. It was the very poster Damian had ripped down and put up in his own room, because he didn't get the same one.

He'd got one of his uncle being carried on the shoulders of some grinning men, but not one of the Bomb Barrel.

Lisa also had pens with *Niagara Falls* scrolled along the sides in silver lettering. There was one made with clear plastic: when it was turned upside down, a spurt of blue-green liquid descended. When the pen was turned the other way, the blue-green waterfall drew back, up, and over the edge. Lisa took it to school when she was in grade seven and promptly lost it. Another pen was sent, but it didn't work as well as the first, because the liquid representing the Falls merely dripped when the pen was turned.

She knew the history of the Falls. She knew who had lived and who had died among the daredevils; she could rhyme off the names and death dates of the ones who hadn't made it. She'd read about how the Falls had been before the Europeans came, and after they'd arrived, when Father Hennepin knelt at the sight, his portable altar strapped to his back. She told Damian how the Iroquois had seen wolverines reaching out to snag carcasses of dead elk from the river, how rattlesnakes had sunned themselves on Table Rock when it hadn't been named Table Rock, back when it had been a huge, unbroken shelf, and how eagles had wheeled over the water in great flocks, lost in mist, almost as if she saw it exactly as it had been hundreds of years before. A sacred place – wild, fearsome, untouched.

Damian turned away from the railing, steadying himself by putting a hand on the top of a Hi-Spy Viewmaster II. It cost fifty cents for a minute, so he dug a couple of quarters out of his pocket and dropped them into the slot. He looked through the viewer into darkness. Nothing. He stayed where he was, listening intently, aware of the roaring that filled his ears. The sound of the nearer current was layered over the rush of water farther away, combined with the noise of the Falls themselves, a heavy curtain of sound.

He wasn't sure he wanted to be there at all. He had no idea why he'd brought it up with his mother. Wanting to scatter his sister's ashes in a place she'd hoped to visit had only been a half-baked idea he'd had, but his mother had fastened upon it. She'd made arrangements. She'd phoned her brother, though Damian knew that relations between them were cool. The next thing Damian knew, they were going to be spending several weeks with his Uncle Roger and his cousin Elvis, neither of whom he'd ever met. His mother had put off all her massage appointments for a month; it was the first time in years she'd taken so many weeks away from work. She had pulled down the blinds in the little house in the backyard – the Studio, as she called it. She had locked it up.

And, she added, a pencil poised above a list she was making in the kitchen, the Motel au Vieux Piloteux had been booked in Trois-Rivières, because they could make it there from Halifax on the first day – a long day, but it would break up the trip nicely.

It really was a good idea, his mother told him. Lisa would have wanted her ashes scattered on the Niagara River.

But as soon as she said it, they both knew it wasn't something Lisa would have wanted. If Lisa had been able to want anything, she'd have wanted to stay alive. They'd stood in the kitchen looking at each other. His mother was stricken, but Damian didn't put his arms around her; he simply turned and went out of the room.

Nevertheless, they had made the trip to Niagara Falls. It had been ten months almost to the day since it happened.

I'd like to see, piped a voice, and Damian looked down to see a girl with tight brown braids staring up at him. There was a small cap on her head. Please, she added.

Sure, he said. But it ate my money – you can't see anything.

A plump Mennonite woman reached out, putting a large, tanned hand on the child's shoulder. Damian dropped his eyes, making his way past a cluster of little girls, all wearing long dresses and sensible shoes.

You shouldn't speak to strangers, Leah.

He has hair like the angel Gabriel.

He's not the angel Gabriel.

Damian walked along the path by the river, feeling the force of the current moving toward him as he went against it. It gave him a sense of vertigo. Near the intake pool for the power plant was a smooth lawn that ended in a jumble of rock.

A man and woman were sitting there, and the man had his fingers tucked into one of the belt loops on the back of the woman's white jeans. He leaned over and kissed her on the ear, and she half-turned to him and murmured something. They got up and left: the woman brushing at a grass stain, the man chucking a paper coffee cup into the water. Damian watched as the cup was caught on the surface of the green water, light and buoyant, spinning comically before it vanished over the edge. He could feel the power of the water, yet at the same time it didn't seem so very powerful; it was close enough for him to dip his feet into the river.

The waterfall was shot through, here and there, with sunlight. Laughter. His father netted by shadows, by dappled lights, swimming strongly away from them, toward the waterfall, where he dunked under and came up – *Holy Christ, it's cold* – always moving away from them.

Come on, you two, his father had called. Damian, hop out of your clothes and jump in.

Lisa stripped down to her pink-and-green bathing suit and jumped in.

There! You did it!

How strange her small legs looked as she frog-kicked frantically toward her father.

It's cold, darling, he said as Lisa threw her arms around his neck.

Damian sat down on a flat rock by the Niagara River, and it occurred to him that he could go back to the car and get the box with the urn in it. He could throw handfuls of Lisa's ashes into the water, since it was what he had come here to do, after all – toss up handfuls of that remarkable dust that had once been a human being and watch it drift away.

Sometimes he thought the urn of ashes lived inside him. Lisa, the memory of Lisa, the ashes of Lisa, boxed in and taped shut. She could have been in her bedroom there, inside her little urn. She could have been sitting on her miniature bed, in her miniature room with the miniature posters all around her, the one of the Spanish Aero Car and the one of Uncle Roger's Bomb Barrel. There she was, sitting on the bed inside the box that was inside his brain. Her smile was fixed in the immovable smile of the dead. She was gently smiling or not quite smiling, a bit like Buddha. He carried her everywhere he went, but soon he'd have to let go. His eyes stung with tears. It always happened like this. Things went away, leaving him behind.

Here we are, said Ingrid as Damian parked the car under the shade of a chestnut tree in front of a rambling white house. Now don't worry when you meet Elvis. He's harmless.

I wasn't worried, said Damian.

And your Uncle Roger –

You've told me all this.

Someone's done a book about him, she said, getting out of the car and leaving the door open. A book about Roger. And they're coming here to film him for television.

She was proud of him, thought Damian. She was proud of her brother, but she'd never brought her children here.

Why didn't we ever come here to visit? he asked.

She was standing beside the open door and he could only see part of her. Well, she said, gesturing with the water bottle. I know I could have brought you – it had to do with Elvis's mother.

But she's been gone a long time, hasn't she?

Yes, I guess she has. But things between Roger and me –

He couldn't hear what she was saying. She drummed her fingers against the kayak on the roof rack.

Damian got out and yanked his knapsack from the backseat. It was the house where his mother had grown up, one that seemed to offer an expansive welcome, in the way of old mansions, with its ample front porch and ivy growing over the eaves and up the rounded wall of the turret. It might have stood there for a hundred years or more, like an oak tree growing on an unkempt lawn patched with crab-grass. Behind it was another, smaller house in the same style, half hidden by trees and a high box hedge that no one had clipped, so the leafy ends – thin, green arms – waved up to greet him.

His mother had already started taking the bags out of the trunk. She took out the heaviest one, her burgundy suitcase, before Damian could help her with it.

Someone was singing, and the voice, off-key, was accompanied by monotonous strumming. When Damian heaved his mother's suitcase forward, though the wheels on it didn't work, he was startled to see a young man blocking the path, wearing bell-bottoms and a shirt unbuttoned on a pale, freckled chest. He held a child's red guitar; his song started and stopped and started again. Uhhh-huh – honey – uhhh-huh –

He stared at Damian.

Who're you? He held up one hand with his fingers curiously clenched.

Oh, Elvis, you're so much taller, said Ingrid, coming up behind Damian. In each hand she held one of the freshly baked pies they'd bought on the way. When did I last see you? It must have been at Mother's funeral. That was five years ago. Elvis, this is Damian. Damian, Elvis.

She had been speaking very quickly; she stopped abruptly.

Who're you? he asked Ingrid.

I'm Ingrid, your Aunt Ingrid – your father's sister. Is he here?

Elvis slowly brought down his clenched hand and turned his back on her. He shifted from one foot to the other, and after a moment he started strumming the guitar again.

Elvis, we're going to find your father, Ingrid said, holding the pies flat.

Damian followed her up the steps. He wanted to walk all around that grand porch to the front of the house, where he thought he'd be able to look over the Niagara River, across the gorge, to New York State. The windows were huge, with panels of flowering vines in the transoms. Yellow glass, red glass, blue glass.

I guess I'll see if he's inside, she said.

Damian put down the suitcase and went around the porch. He'd been right; when he got to the front of the house he could see across the gorge, though he couldn't see the river below. He sat down on one of several old Adirondack chairs and shut his eyes. It was just as hot as it had been before, but there was a cool breeze, and it brought the scent of clover to him. Not far away was the sound of a lawn mower, droning back and forth, until it caught on something and there was a brief explosive sound. The leaves moved a little on the chest-nut tree, concealing a robin that was making a sweet sound over and over. *Phoebe, phoebe,* it called. It lulled him.

Elvis came up the stairs and put down his red guitar loudly across one of the chairs. Damian jumped.

When's your birthday? he asked.

May 31.

Your full name, date of birth, place of birth, said Elvis.

Why?

Name, date, place.

Damian Benjamin MacKenzie. 1987. Halifax, Nova Scotia.

Damian Benjamin MacKenzie, May 31, 1987, Halifax, Nova Scotia, repeated Elvis, dropping down into the chair next to Damian's.

Elvis Aaron Presley was born at 12:20 p.m. on January 8, 1935, in East Tupelo, Mississippi, he said confidentially.

He'd be old now, mused Damian. If he were alive.

Elvis got up abruptly, so his chair nearly tipped over. He picked up his guitar and went down the porch steps.

Damian could hear his mother inside the house calling up the stairs to his uncle. Roger. There you are.

There was a pause. His uncle greeted her.

Oh, it's good to see you, she said.

There was a sound of tapping.

I brought pies, his mother was saying. Apple and rhubarb, because I know you like rhubarb. We've got barbecued chicken. And I bought some potato salad on the way here, but it's probably still in the car, in this heat, with the mayonnaise going bad. I'll get Damian to bring it in.

There's no need to –

Damian, she called. Anyway, the chicken's already barbecued. All I have to do is pop it in the oven to warm it up. And I've got wine and –

Ingrid.

His voice was closer now, near the screened door that led onto the porch.

I'm so sorry about Lisa, he said. It's been a hard time for you.

There was a pause.

Yes, it's been hard, she said softly. Harder than anything.

In the silence that followed, Damian rose from the chair, kicking his foot against the uprights of the porch balustrade.

I'm sorry I didn't get to her funeral, said his uncle.

Oh, well, you had Elvis and everything. Anyway – well, anyway. I'll just get some food fired up here. You don't need to help. Go see Damian.

Go *see* him, muttered his uncle.

But Damian went lightly down the porch steps and walked to the car, where he took out the shopping bags.

When he came back, he saw his uncle on the flagstone path. A man with grey hair pulled back in a ponytail, a face darkened by sun. It didn't seem that his uncle was old, nor did it seem that he was young, but his cane made him seem indecisive, nosing in front of him like an animal. His uncle, thin and shambling, went after it, as if he was counting the stones in the path. One, two, three, four, five. He left the flagstone path and meandered to the bed of peonies, past their prime and lying in heaps of blown pink. He poked at the stalks with his cane, lifting them and letting them drop. Then he got down on his knees, putting the cane to one side and picking up a flower, its pale petals dropping on the grass; he put what was left of the bloom up to his face and drew it along his cheek. His eyes were half closed. His expression was like a child's, given over to pleasure. When he got up he made his way unsteadily to the chestnut tree, where he touched the rough bark of its trunk with his cane, mapping his way, and kept going toward the house.

Damian put the plastic bags down by the porch steps at the front of the house, and the smell of barbecued chicken wafted up from one of them. He was surprised his uncle wasn't more outlandish, that he wasn't wearing a tiger-skin loincloth like a circus performer, brandishing a whip in one massive hand and holding a stool in the other. He'd been a daredevil, after all. But his Uncle Roger turned out to be an ordinary man. No – he wasn't just ordinary. He was vulnerable. It was as if the wind could knock him down.

Hi, said Damian, holding out his hand as his uncle approached the steps. I'm Damian.

Hello, Damian.

His uncle tapped the cane against the bottom step. Damian dropped his hand, feeling stupid about having held it out to a blind man, and watched his uncle work his way to the top step, where he turned, carefully, and sat down in one of the chairs.

You met Elvis?

Yes, said Damian, picking up the bags and following him up the steps. His mother was going to come to the screened door soon, asking what he'd done with the chicken and the potato salad.

Roger swivelled the slender cane in front of him. Long drive?

Pretty long, said Damian.

Hot too, I guess. Sit down for a bit.

Damian set down the bags and sat on the broad wooden arm of a chair.

You're the artist, said his uncle.

You could say that.

Roger folded up his cane. Damian watched, fascinated. There were four parts to the cane and they folded like a tent pole.

I was going to go down for the funeral, Roger went on.

Damian wiped the sweat from his forehead. He'd wanted his uncle to show up at the last minute, miraculously appearing from behind a curtain, except that there hadn't been a curtain. He'd expected him to come, even though Lisa had never met him. His mother had expected him to come. And they'd been disappointed – sharply disappointed – when he hadn't.

Well, Damian said slowly, a lot of people came. I didn't realize how many people knew Lisa. My father came.

I know him. Your dad.

You do?

Well, I did. I knew him years ago.

They sat together without speaking. The chestnut tree had darkened in the muted evening light. The grass was furred with stripes where the shadows fell across it.

When your mother phoned, she said you wanted to scatter Lisa's ashes here, said Roger. In the river –

Yes.

You'll probably have to do it in the dead of night so they don't slap you with a fine. That's what they're like. Very early in the morning – that's the best time.

Inside the house they heard a clatter of pans.

She doesn't know where I keep things, Roger mused. Can you hear her? She's talking to herself. My mother did that – your grandmother – she was always talking to herself.

She used to do that when she visited, said Damian. Granny. And she clucked.

A grey cat slunk through the grass under the chestnut tree, paused, leapt at a moth. It fluttered out of reach, and the cat, thwarted, began licking the fur under its leg.

Elvis came up the steps. He'd unhooked the guitar strap, and now he held the guitar by its neck so it banged lightly against each of the steps.

Hello, Elvis, said Roger. You met Damian.

Yes. He put his hand up, fist clenched. I met Damian. He has a boat on top of the car.

Does he?

Yes. A yellow boat.

Elvis's fist was still up in the air, and he turned it this way and that.

This is Damian, he went on. Damian Benjamin MacKenzie, May 31, 1987, Halifax, Nova Scotia.

THERE'S TOO MUCH, Ingrid sighed. She looked around Roger's bedroom at the piles of clothes on the rug.

Let's stop then. Roger was sitting on the bed, holding a bunch of silk ties. You've been here three days; you can't do everything at once, you know.

But who's going to go through this stuff? It's not something you can do with Elvis.

I never open that closet.

But we've got to *deal* with it. Look at all these suits of Dad's. I think they've been here for sixty years. And up here, his sweaters – let's at least go through the sweaters.

All right, he said, putting the ties in a bundle on the bed beside him. Sweaters it is.

She took a stack of sweaters out of the cedar closet and put them on the dresser.

Three navy sweaters, all V-neck. Would you wear any of these?

She handed him one so he could feel it.

Nice, he said. Feels like cashmere. He pulled the sweater over his head. God, it's hot for this kind of thing. Maybe I'll sleep on the couch downstairs tonight.

It fits you.

No, too small. Remember how Dad seemed to shrink toward the end?

Cashmere. She scrutinized the label. You're right – though you could hang on to these until you shrink.

Or give some of them to Damian, he said.

Damian wouldn't wear any of this stuff. You know, he comes home after staying with his friend Adam for three or four days and he's wearing Adam's clothes. They're baggy – they hang on him. He's heedless, but if it came to his own grandfather's clothing, he'd be picky. He wouldn't wear a thing here.

How's he doing, Ingrid? Roger asked.

She folded the sweaters and stacked them neatly again.

Oh, I don't know. In the early spring he went up to Adam's uncle's cabin, off in the woods. He wanted to be by himself, he said, and that he'd only go for a couple of days, if that. But he was gone for five days, and the place didn't have a phone –

And you worried.

He was very withdrawn when he came back. He wouldn't say a word to me. I'd been frantic about him, but when I tried to talk to him about it he just brushed me off. Since then he seems to have got himself back on track, more or less.

But not the same.

No, not the same. He's just so unpredictable.

He blames himself.

I've told him over and over that it was an accident. That it was no one's fault.

But does he believe you?

I don't know. I really don't. I think that Damian –

What?

Oh, I worry about him. I'm worried he might do something.

Do something?

That he might *do* something to himself.

You worry too much.

But if he says anything – if he opens up to you – will you talk to him?

If there's anything I can do, I'll do it.

All of this – oh, Roger, it's been so awful.

She put the sweaters back on the shelf in the cedar closet and went out of Roger's bedroom. Before going down the stairs, she put a hand against the wall.

Uhhh, she groaned, thinking of Lisa. Had Lisa been in pain? Had she known she was dying?

She must have known.

Ingrid stopped near the bottom of the stairs and tried to breathe steadily. Here she was, in her parents' house. Roger's house. She'd been a child in this house, once, a long time ago. She reached up to touch the skeleton of a snake that someone had hung from the light fixture with fishing line. What was it doing there? She couldn't reach it, but it quivered as if she had touched it after all.

Ingrid, said Roger at the top of the stairs.

Don't fall, she said.

She was speaking in a dream, but she wanted to shake herself out of the dream, so she walked down the hall to the kitchen. If she stood by the screened door in the kitchen, she might not hear him coming, the cane making its hesitant sounds against the treads of the stairs as he came down.

Ingrid had been at home in Halifax. The kids had gone up to the cottage at Cribbon's, but she hadn't gone with them. If she'd gone with them –

She remembered picking up the phone and hearing Damian crying.

What? – Damian? What's wrong?

She'd been staring out the window at a red van.

Damian, tell me what's wrong.

It took so long for Damian to tell her. All the time she was watching the red van in the driveway next door. Her neighbour Yvonne got out, bent down, and picked up her terrier, taking it into the house.

He couldn't stop crying. All Ingrid could make out was that there'd been an accident. Lisa. Accident. Lisa.

What *happened* to Lisa? she cried. What happened?

She was dead. Lisa was dead. Damian said this, finally, clearly, but Ingrid knew it was coming. She heard herself gasping. She found herself saying, in a voice she knew but didn't know, that she'd be there as soon as she could.

And then she slumped to the floor with the phone in her hand.

One minute she'd been staring out at that summery street, with a purple Hula Hoop on someone's lawn, purple on green. And then –

It was as though someone had thrown an axe, thrown it right into her chest, breaking the bones. She cried out. She had the feeling that the horrible sound wasn't coming from her mouth, and she wished it would stop.

Oh, *God*. Oh, God, oh, God.

She got up and staggered around the living room, bumping into chairs, crashing into things. Who was spinning her around and around? She threw down the phone, breaking something. She lurched around the room with her arms wrapped around herself. Was she up? Down? She didn't know. At one point she was on her knees, the full weight of the axe deep in her chest. There was no pulling it out.

She tried to think clearly. She put one hand on the couch to steady herself.

It could not have happened. It simply could not have happened. Lisa could not have drowned.

She returned to herself, floating down into her body. Here she was at the threshold of the pantry in the house where she'd grown up. When Roger came into the kitchen, she was standing with her back to him, twisting her hands together.

I don't know where Damian's got to, she said.

You asked him to take the books to the second-hand store at the mall.

Oh yes, I did. Let's go somewhere, she suggested. Let's go for a walk.

What about sitting on the lawn chairs? said Roger reasonably. Under the tree. It's hot – we could have a gin and tonic, if you like.

I'd like to go for a walk.

Well, we could. It's about thirty degrees out there.

They went down the porch steps at the front, along the flagstone path, and crossed the road to the sidewalk that ran next to the Niagara Gorge. It was laboriously slow. He took her arm near the elbow, and when they walked, close together, he was half a step behind her.

I have my cane, he said. If you get tired of this.

No, she said, no.

Up until a few years ago I had some peripheral vision, he said, as if she'd asked a question. But I couldn't see anything in the centre except a tight circle of sparkling colours. Now the circle has grown so much it fills the whole field of vision. They told me it would happen.

What if you fall?

I don't know. If I fall, I fall.

Ingrid thought of her mother coming home to find their father. Their father, who'd fallen on the kitchen floor. He'd fallen headlong as he came in from gardening. Her mother had come home to find him there, his shoes sticking out the back door. She'd told Ingrid that she stood by the hedge that ran along the driveway, letting the bags drop from her arms when she saw those shoes. She didn't remember getting from the driveway to the kitchen. And there was the cat stepping delicately over his arm: the cat, mewing for all it was worth. She forgot about the groceries, so things were all over the driveway when the ambulance came. The box of butterscotch ice cream had come open, and there was a little puddle of melted ice cream, cans of mandarin oranges and tuna had gone rolling under the car, and a crow was pecking at the roast. It was pecking at the roast, and she kept saying how much it upset her to see a crow pecking at a good three-pound sirloin tip roast. Just like a vulture.

You must think of them, Ingrid said.

Who?

Mum and Dad – living in that house, I mean. You must miss them more than I do.

Sometimes, Roger said, but they're a long way off. It's as if they both got into a little boat and started rowing away. I can hardly see them now.

Ingrid thought of Lisa in a rowboat. But she didn't want to think of her in a rowboat.

They go away from us, he said gently. It's what they do.

But they didn't go immediately, Ingrid thought. For a while they were too present to be dead.

Damian had got it wrong. Lisa couldn't possibly be dead.

Ingrid had to be calm, quite calm, because then she could go there and see for herself. She would drive; she would be fine. And she would take things. Food and water. She went to the basement, got the old cooler, and put bottles of water into it. Then she added bottles of cranberry juice and soda water, and she even put in a freezer pack, since it would keep things cold. Forks and knives and spoons and plastic glasses and napkins printed with clowns and balloons, from a long-ago birthday party. Sandwiches, she thought. She stood in the kitchen wondering about sandwiches and then got a loaf of bread out of the refrigerator.

She started sobbing again, standing in the kitchen with the loaf of bread in one hand. There was no need for bread or water or cranberry juice. She hung on to the counter. Perhaps she was on the floor, sprawled on its blue-and-white tiles, or maybe she got up from the floor, still holding on to the loaf of bread for dear life. She could have been screaming.

Greg, she cried, as if he were standing in the kitchen in front of her.

Greg would have to be told, she thought. Her husband who was not her husband any more. She didn't even know where he was living just then: whether he was still in his houseboat in Vancouver. She'd have to be the one to tell him. She'd have to say, Greg, your daughter is dead.

Maybe she said this out loud. Greg, *Greg* –

She put the loaf of bread in the cooler. She didn't make sandwiches; she just stuffed the bread in, squeezing it so it would fit. Bread – she had bread. She tried to think what else she needed, because it was a two-hour drive. But she had no idea. What did a person need on a trip like this? What should she take?

Nothing was where it was supposed to be. The car keys. Where were they? Things spilled out of the string drawer: tickets, paper clips, a bathing cap. Ingrid's mother's yellow bathing cap covered with plastic petals! String, tape, a glove. She couldn't see. Where were her keys? She didn't know, she didn't know. Then she saw the car keys where they were supposed to be, on the hook by the door. She yanked at them and the little shelf fell down, a jangle of keys springing off hooks. *Welcome*, said the shelf, upside down, the keys flung this way and that across the floor.

But she needed a nightgown, a toothbrush. She ran upstairs, two at a time. Why was she hurrying? Lisa was dead. She found herself in the bathroom taking the toothbrush out of its holder – could that be her own face in the mirror? She held on to the sink, groaning. Whose face was it?

No, she cried, banging at the mirror so the door of the cabinet flew open and her face disappeared.

Were these her own hands, putting a nightgown into an overnight bag? Yes, they must be. Underwear. The drawer fell on the floor when she pulled it open. Underwear, socks – a pile of things on the floor. She tried to zip up the overnight bag, but the zipper caught on the underwear. Why did she need an overnight bag, anyway? She left it on the bed and went downstairs. If she didn't hurry, her daughter would grow cold. Her own daughter, not someone else's.

She took everything out to the car. The cooler, her sunglasses, the car keys. That was right, wasn't it? Yes. That was right. Then she saw she'd forgotten her purse. Why did she need her purse? Her daughter was dead, for God's sake. But she still had to have her purse, and she went back for it, tossing it on the passenger seat. She sat in the hot car with her sunglasses on, tears streaming down her face.

Collect yourself, she said. Collect yourself.

She wiped her eyes and took deep breaths. If she wasn't calm, she wouldn't be able to drive. She wouldn't be able to do it, and she had to. But when she leaned forward to turn the keys in the ignition, she felt the axe in her chest. She felt the sharp blade.

Her hand was on the key in the ignition. Had she started the car? Was it running? Had she locked the door of the house? Oh, for God's sake. Did she care about the house and whether it was locked? No. She left. Or she tried to leave, but someone had let the terrier out of the house next door and she almost ran over it. She braked just in time, one of those screeching halts that left tire tracks on the street. The dog ran back over the lawn yapping and yapping. The dog was safe. Her daughter was dead. Oh, how was it possible? She hated the little dog, because it was alive and Lisa was dead.

Roger was speaking to her. His hand was on her arm; she was clutching it with her other hand. Tears were running down her face and she didn't try to brush them away. She glanced at him to see whether he knew anything was wrong.

No, nothing, except the slickness of sweat on his forehead. They were walking along a street, she thought. Yes, that's what they were doing. A car went past and a plastic bag lifted up languidly in the heat, ballooned into the air, and sank back down. What was he asking her?

Those two were close, weren't they? Damian and Lisa.

Peas in a pod, she said. Same hair, same smooth skin. God, when I look at Damian, I see her. His eyes aren't the same colour, but it doesn't matter. I see her hazel eyes looking into mine. For a while, I could hardly stand it.

Roger stopped, placing his hands on the low stone wall that ran parallel to the sidewalk. I'm sorry, Ingrid. I'm so sorry.

He wasn't looking at her; he was looking off to the side, as if there was someone else he was talking to just beyond her shoulder. She didn't know what to say. She faced the gorge and then realized she'd started crying again.

A few more blocks and we'll be at the Whirlpool Bridge, he said. What would you like to do?

I don't know.

What can you see from here? he asked soothingly, as if she were a child.

The gorge, you mean?

Yes.

On the other side of this wall – just weeds and shrubs. Chicory. Sumac. Something with a leaf shaped like a mitten.

Sassafras.

And in the gorge there's a shelf of stone all along the New York side, with trees at the top and trees down below. You wouldn't think trees would grow there. The river's a long way down – it's dark green, but there's a tint to the green.

It's rock flour in the water. The rock's been ground

down as fine as flour, and that's what gives it the green colour. It's from the shale and sandstone that comes –

How do you know all this?

I wanted to know, so I found out. Anyway, I can't see it. It's there – it's only a river – but I can't see it for shit.

They walked back a different way. Each time she lifted her foot to step forward, guiding him, she thought they could have been bounding, very slowly, across River Road onto Morrison.

What's the hardest thing that's ever happened to you? she asked.

Marnie leaving, he said. Finding out that Elvis was not going to be like other kids. And my eyes. But when Marnie left I dropped into a black hole. That was the worst.

You went a little crazy.

I don't remember much. I remember crying. But other than that, it was as if I blacked out for days.

Marnie, mused Ingrid.

You never liked her.

I liked her. There was a lot I liked about her – she was tough as nails. But I thought she was taking you for a ride.

You visited us when you were big as a house. You must have been about six months pregnant with Damian, and Marnie had just found out she was pregnant.

We had that argument.

Yes.

Ingrid remembered how she'd thrown a white plate with a blue flower on it. The plate had crashed against the refrigerator and broken right across the iris, across its graceful leaves. The plate had belonged to her mother, and she'd regretted it afterward. She regretted calling Marnie a lowlife, someone who just wanted to use Roger.

She hadn't known then how much he loved Marnie until he slapped Ingrid across the face, something no one had ever done, and she'd told him she'd never speak to him again. Her own brother. Words had come out of her mouth that she didn't mean, and then she couldn't take them back. She could hear herself saying them. She'd said she'd never darken his door again. And she could see the plate spinning across the room, knowing it would hit the refrigerator. Even in that moment she'd wanted it to fly back to her before it broke into pieces.

I said all those things, she said.

I hated you then. But we don't have to go over all that.

No, I'd rather not.

It's done. She's gone – that's the thing.

Ingrid didn't have enough gas to get from Halifax to Antigonish. She stopped somewhere after Truro, just before New Glasgow, at a gas station on top of a hill. One moment she was on the ramp, with the gas station in the distance, a castle in a fairy tale, and the next moment she was driving around, driving around, in a circle, first to the Self Serve, where there were too many cars, and then around again, where she tried to squeeze into a spot at a pump between a pickup and an old Pontiac. She couldn't do it; she couldn't reverse the car into the spot. People were getting in and out of their cars, slamming doors, and a radio was turned on full blast. Everything gleamed in the heat. She couldn't reverse into the spot. The radio was going full blast. It gleamed. *Baby, if you go –*

She drove around to the Full Serve. Windows gleamed, fenders gleamed. *Baby.*

When she stopped the car and got out, it was like stepping into an oven. A young man appeared; he'd already taken the filter gun out and he was just about to put the nozzle in the tank of her car. He said something to her; his mouth opened and closed. Everything wavered in the heat.

He spoke again.

Fillerup?

She nodded.

Regular, Premium?

What was he saying? He said it again.

Regular, she said. Regular. And some oil, maybe. I don't know.

He shoved the nozzle in the gas tank and went around to lift the hood and check the oil.

Her eyes were streaming and she took off the sunglasses to wipe them. She looked away from him, to the other side of the hill, where a dead elm stood. It was an old woman holding her arms up to the sky.

My daughter died today, she told him.

He had just raised the hood, and now he looked around it. She could see the greasy rag he used.

My daughter, she repeated. She died today.

He looked at her as if she was crazy, but then he must have seen that she was crying.

Would you like a paper towel? he asked.

He got her some paper towel. When he handed it to her, all bunched up, she saw his hand was grimy. The length of greasy rag was in his other hand and he wiped his thumb with it. He was young, younger than Damian. His face was tanned; he had a wispy little beard. But there were no lines in his face at all.

I'm sorry about your daughter. There was a furrow between his brows.

He went back to check the oil, then he put down the hood carefully, dropping it with a practised hand an inch above the catch.

I could get you something, he said, glancing at the coffee shop. Do you want something?

No. Thank you –

She didn't know what to do with the paper towel so she handed it back to him and he took it, in that grimy hand of his. He tossed it in the bin beside the pumps. It made an arc and dropped down, perfectly, exactly where he'd planned it would go. The phone had dropped on the floor and something had broken. *Damian, what's wrong?* A terrier went yapping across a lawn. The dog was alive. This boy was alive.

No problem, he said.

He stood there, hands at his sides, until she realized he was waiting. She got out her wallet and gave him four twenty-dollar bills.

I'm really sorry, he said, as he took them. He gave two of the bills back to her. I'll get your change. Your oil's fine.

My what?

Your oil. I checked it.

Good. Thank you.

She got in the car and started it, putting the air conditioner on high. There was someone in a silver SUV behind her, waiting, and she drove away from the pump. She kept going, and in the rear-view mirror she saw the boy come out with money in his hand. She didn't want it.

He waved to stop her, but she turned onto the blazing road and went down the hill past the dead elm to the ramp that led back to the highway before pulling the car onto the shoulder and getting out. She didn't know what she was doing; she'd hardly pulled the car off the road. It was half on the road, half on the shoulder. She left the door open so that anyone could have slammed into the car, taken the door off. A person was supposed to be in control. She was in control. Everything gleamed in the heat.

She walked in a straight, sure line through the weedy, dry grass by the side of the road, where the clover was all bedraggled, up the slope of the hill. There was a bald eagle at the top of the elm, but she only noticed it because it glided away. Her mother would have said it was a sign, if her mother had been alive, but she wasn't. It was a sign. She went to the dead tree and threw her arms around it.

Yes, she was crazy. She was half crazy. She wanted to hold something. She would have held that boy at the gas station. The man getting out of the silver SUV to put Premium in the tank. She would have held anyone.

She held the tree. She felt the coarse elm bark under her hands. There were tiny scratch marks later on her hands and her arms, and she didn't know how they got there. There might have been blood. Was there any blood? If only it had been her, not Lisa. She held on to the elm tree. She held on and held on. That tree was not living; it was dead, but she held on.

Down below, near the road, a boy passed on an ATV. He stopped. He looked up at her and adjusted his yellow helmet. She thought of a hornet, because of his yellow helmet, but he wasn't real. Some things were real and some things weren't. The eagle had been real. The tree was real. The boy with the yellow helmet was not real.

She kept holding the tree, and the boy went away after a while.

Elvis gets upset, Roger was saying to Ingrid.

He's just scared that everything will change, she said.

It's going to have to change.

You could have someone come in, said Ingrid. You could have a girl come in.

No, said Roger, not a girl.

Why not?

A few weeks ago he was on his way home from the workshop and he noticed a girl. He followed her home and stood across the street from her house for hours, until the girl's mother called the cops. If I had a girl come in, it would just be trouble.

Well, someone older then.

Maybe.

You'll be all right, Ingrid said. One way or another.

The blind leading the blind, said Roger.

They turned the corner from Morrison onto Ontario Street.

We used to go bicycling here, she said.

There weren't as many cars then.

And we'd go past those two kids. Remember that? The Petroski kids.

They had that disease – progeria, I think it was.

They looked as though they were ninety years old, she said. Remember how their mother put blankets over them when they were sitting on the front porch? They had Hudson's Bay blankets over them and a look in their eyes as if they were prisoners of war. We were probably about the same age, but they had that look in their eyes. I wonder what became of them.

She was silent for a moment. Well, I guess we know what became of them, don't we?

Yes.

Tears came to her eyes when she thought of this. The Petroski kids had never been children. They'd never had bicycles. They'd never gripped a bicycle's handlebars while going crazily around a corner, as she had, with the slender pink and blue plastic streamers whipping in the wind as she rode past the Petroski house, laughing, because Roger could ride his bicycle without hands and make faces at the same time.

No hands, she said. That's how you rode.

That's right. I did, didn't I?

Here they were, thought Ingrid, making their slow passage, step by step. Nothing she could say was going to change the fact that he was blind and he had to take care of Elvis, and nothing he could say to her would change the fact that Lisa was dead. It was just how life went, and people got through it. But *how*? Ingrid wondered. *How* did they?

I thought I could do anything back then, he said.

It had been like the Valley of the Shadow, going past the Petroski house, she thought. When they'd turned the corner at the far side of the house, everything was different.

It was too hot to sleep that night. Elvis had gone out to the carriage house to sleep on the futon there, and Roger was on the couch in the living room. Damian was in the guest room, the one at the front of the house. Ingrid was in the bedroom she'd had as a child; she lay awake, hands folded over her chest, thinking she could hear Damian breathing as he slept down the hall. The books of her childhood were on the shelves: *Katie and the Sad Noise, Paddle-to-the-Sea, Swallows and Amazons, Stig of the Dump, Anne of Green Gables*. In the shadows, she could still make out the dancer in the reproduction of a Degas painting. The dancer resembled a white bird.

It had been so sheltered, that world of childhood, where a dancer pirouetted inside a painting. There had never been any worry about money, and there never would be. The land their parents had sold off had been turned into blocks of condominiums near Niagara-on-the-Lake. The Greenborough Estates, for God's sake, had made their parents wealthy. But money hadn't saved her father from the slow deterioration of his eyesight and then, later, having a heart attack as he came inside after gardening. It hadn't saved her mother from getting melanoma.

It didn't save Ingrid from going into Emergency, leaving the bright afternoon and walking into the dimness of the hospital. It didn't save her from seeing the look on Damian's face, from holding him and trying to comfort him. It didn't save her from being taken, along with Damian, down to the hospital morgue. They could have been in a bank, with someone leading them to the safety deposit boxes, except that the smell of formaldehyde was all around them. A long metal drawer was pulled out of the wall, and there was her daughter, in a white zippered bag. Like a garment bag. They unzipped her.

Lisa, whispered Ingrid. Her whole body was trembling.

It was Lisa and it was not Lisa. The features were all the same features, but the skin wasn't right. It had been a matter of hours; that was all. Only a matter of hours. That very morning this daughter of hers had woken up alive and now she was dead.

Lisa's hair was still damp, though it had been quite a while since they'd brought her in. Her hair had dried in ropes, the way wet hair dries when it isn't combed. There was sand on her neck. Oh, there was sand on her neck. Why should it have been sand on her neck that brought tears coursing down Ingrid's face? Just a delicate tracing of sand, that was all. This was her daughter. Her daughter was dead. Ingrid kept thinking this, but it didn't make it real.

She had stood beside her mother at her father's wake. Roger on one side, Ingrid on the other. Her mother was like a bird, and it was only the two of them on either side that kept her from gliding away. It was like that with Lisa too. Her body was hard and closed, but Lisa herself was light and feathery. She would vanish, fly up out of that narrow, bright room, if only Ingrid would release her.

No, she couldn't release her.

She closed her eyes. Strangely enough, in that moment, she thought of Roger, in the Bomb Barrel, going over Niagara Falls. She had the sensation of being at the brink and realizing there was nothing to hold her back. Terrifying. How had Roger gone over the Falls? Twice. Not counting that other time he'd tried, or the time he hung upside down at the brink of the Falls for a film. She didn't know how he'd done it, hanging upside down like a fruit bat, with the water rushing away beneath him.

And here was Ingrid with the firm, waxed hospital floor beneath her, though everything had given way. Her life had given way.

WE'RE OKAY, THE TWO OF US, Roger said. We get by.

We get by, echoed Elvis.

They were eating a late dinner of tortellini and salad on the porch because Ingrid and Roger had spent the day in Niagara-on-the-Lake, tootling around, as Roger put it. Ingrid and Damian had been in town a week, and she'd shown him the Flower Clock, the Spanish Aero Car, Fort George. They could have gone to Crystal Beach that day, where Damian could use the kayak, but he offered to cut the lawn for his uncle just to spend time by himself.

Sometimes Damian couldn't be around his mother and uncle, listening to them talk about how Nancy Ann Jakubowski had lost her leg to diabetes and whether Jerry Sparks had ever come home from the Buddhist monastery on an island off eastern Thailand. When they realized how they'd been leaving Damian out of the conversation, they'd tried to draw him into it. But the people they were talking about had all been born at least thirty years before Damian, and he didn't want to know what a knockout Nancy Ann had been before she gained weight.

It had been a relief when they left Damian alone. He'd cut the grass absently in the heat of the day, and when he was finished he'd flung himself down on the lawn with a glass of lemonade, filled with ice, and watched a line of ants crawl over his arm. Now dusk had fallen and it was cooler. No one wanted to turn on the porch light as they sat there, though they could hardly see the food on their plates. Elvis was already in his pyjamas. He was sitting quietly, picking up the tortellini one by one and squishing them between his fingers before he ate them.

There'll come a time when I'm just no good for you, Elvis, said Roger. We'll need to go to a nursing home. Well, I'll have to go to a nursing home, at least, because I won't be able to take care of anyone, much less myself. I'm an old wreck as it is.

You do pretty well, said Ingrid.

Oh, something happens at least once a day. Last week Elvis was late getting to the workshop because he lost his Thermos, and you got panicky, didn't you, Elvis?

Elvis was peering at a pocket of tortellini between his thumb and forefinger.

He got a bit panicky, said Roger.

Elvis put down the piece of tortellini and got up. He went down the steps.

Elvis? said Ingrid.

Friday, November 22, 1963, 1:10 p.m.

JFK, murmured Roger.

Friday, November 22, 1963, Elvis repeated. The date of the assassination of President John F. Kennedy. Three months after the death of his son, Patrick Bouvier Kennedy, who lived thirty-nine hours –

Elvis, said Roger.

Both John F. Kennedy and Abraham Lincoln were shot in the head. They both had seven letters in their last names. Lincoln was shot at Ford's Theatre, and Kennedy was shot in a Lincoln limousine, made by the Ford company.

Ingrid went down the steps and put her hand on Elvis's arm.

Both of them were shot in the head, he said loudly.

Elvis, there's ice cream for dessert, said Ingrid. Chocolate swirl.

Shot in the head on a Friday.

Elvis turned on his heel and left them.

He's gone to the carriage house, said Roger.

I'll go, said Damian.

It was dark in the carriage house, and when Damian went inside he bumped into a cabinet, making something crash inside it.

Who's that? cried Elvis. Who's that?

It's okay, said Damian. It's just me.

I've got a big gun, said Elvis. There was a shuffling sound, a banging. I've got a Winchester 30.30 here.

Elvis, it's Damian.

I've got a big gun.

No, listen – it's me. It's Damian Benjamin MacKenzie. May 31, 1987.

Elvis turned on the light. He stood like a large shambling bear, holding a gun. His hand was on the trigger and he was pointing the gun at Damian.

Elvis – don't. Is there a safety on that thing?

But Elvis was looking down the barrel of the gun. What's a safety? he asked.

Christ, don't *do* that.

Why?

It could go off and you could lose your head. And if you point it at me, I could lose my head.

There aren't bullets, said Elvis, still looking down the barrel. Roger told me that there weren't any bullets in it. Did you know that a Winchester 30.30 shoots bullets at two thousand feet per second?

Why does that make me feel even more nervous?

Elvis turned the gun over and stroked the polished wood of the handle. Roger said that it's a Trapper Carbine. He said that it's a Trapper Carbine and that it's an antique and what did my mother need with a gun anyway. That's what he said.

I'd really appreciate it if you put that Winchester Trapper Carbine down.

Elvis dropped his arms down, but he still held the gun loosely.

Thank you, said Damian, bending and putting his hands on his thighs. His heart was doing acrobatics. Maybe you could put it away. In a locked gun rack or something.

I wasn't going to shoot you.

Elvis's sandy hair had been brushed up like a crest on top of his head, and he had the sleepy look of a small boy. He had large eyes, with eyelashes and eyebrows that were so pale they could hardly be seen. There were entire galaxies of freckles all over his body; his face and neck, especially, were covered with ginger-coloured speckles.

His blue pyjamas had small sheep and ducks printed on them. They were a little too small and he'd left the top un-buttoned. For some reason, Elvis's chest surprised Damian, just as it had the first time he'd met him. His chest was as

51

pale and hairless as his face, except for a few sparse curls of sandy-coloured hair; nevertheless, it was a man's chest.

I wasn't going to shoot you, he said again.

Well, good, because it scared the bejesus out of me.

For the first time, Damian looked around. He'd never seen a place like this before, filled with things from top to bottom. The glassy yellow eyes of a snowy owl were fixed on him; the bird had been stuffed and put in a huge mahogany case, lined with black velvet, on top of a cabinet. There was a small brass plate in front: *Nyctea scandiaca*. The creature's feet were downy with soft feathers, making it look as though it was wearing delicate boots, but its wings were outstretched in an ominous way. It wasn't an owl – it was a dead thing – but Damian couldn't help thinking it was real. Such yellow eyes.

Where did all of this come from? asked Damian.

It's Roger's stuff.

There was a three-legged table on top of a marble-topped sideboard, and on top of the spindly table was a birdcage, spray-painted with gold. Books were stacked in piles, with old, yellowed newspapers beneath them: there were Bibles and dictionaries, musty with age, and a full set of the *Encyclopedia Britannica*. A cabinet held treasures behind glass: a rock on which nested tiny ivory birds in ivory nests, and beside the birds, a miniature scene of Santa's workshop made to look as though it was a cave of ice, where thimble-sized elves were busy swinging hammers and using saws, and a Santa Claus waved his arms as if he were conducting a symphony. *Santa's Animated Workshop – $78.00*. Next to it was a pair of horns from a two-headed ram, according to the label, and a Ghanaian gold weight of a dancing woman. The gold weight held open the table of contents of a book written by Siamese twins (*The Left Page Being the Work of Simon and the Right Page Being the Work of Albert, Dated This Year of Our Lord, 1789*). Overlooking Simon and Albert was a pink music box, with the lid raised and a pink ballerina tilted precariously against a mirrored backing.

In an umbrella stand were five walking sticks, and Damian pulled one out, idly; it was an ebony and brass stick with a carved ivory handle that unscrewed and revealed a unicorn hidden inside. He put it back again, making a clatter. Lisa would have loved this place, he thought. She'd have felt at home.

An oil painting was half hidden behind a sewing machine, and though it was dusty, the colours glowed. Crimson bloomed out of darkness, soft and thick as algae on the surface of the canvas. Near the bottom of the painting was a soft, subtle strip of golden red that became, at the lower edge, the golden yellow of autumn trees. There were small black lines in the corner that resembled a signature. "Imgit," it seemed to say. Damian bent down to look at the oil painting, pulling it out so he could see it.

Roger lets me stay here all summer if I want, said Elvis. He says I can be in charge of things. I have a bathroom too. I've got a shower curtain with a picture of Elvis Presley on it. And I've got this Winchester 30.30. It was my mother's, but Roger said I could take care of it because my mother went to California. She took his motorcycle. He misses it because it was a vintage Harley-Davidson and you can't buy them cheap. He misses that Harley-Davidson, even if he can't ride it. But I have the Winchester 30.30. My mother went to California. She went all the way to the Baja Peninsula in Mexico, which is about as far away as you can get, Roger said. Now she lives in San Diego.

Elvis went around a bookshelf and Damian followed, watching as Elvis knelt down and shoved the gun under a futon on a frame. The duvet was covered with yellow happy faces, and imprinted on the pillow was Shania Twain, smiling broadly.

That Winchester Trapper Carbine, it can shoot two thousand feet per second, Elvis said, getting up. *Bouuff.* Like that. Bruce said he saw pictures of a bullet going through a pineapple. He said it looked like a head being blown apart. Bits going every which way.

Elvis stood with his head cocked thoughtfully to one side.

Who's Bruce? asked Damian.

He's at the workshop.

That's where you work?

Bruce says he gets paid the big bucks so he can call himself the Big Cheese.

That must make you the mouse.

The mouse, laughed Elvis. The *mouse*.

He laughed until he grasped his crotch. I have to go, he said.

That's okay – you go.

Elvis vanished into the bathroom, closed the door and locked it. When he came out, he stood looking at Damian, who had flopped down on the bed.

I don't want to go to a nursing home with Roger, said Elvis.

I don't think he really meant –

You never come out. I don't want to go there.

You could come out.

You go in a nursing home and you never come out. That's what happened to Bruce's grandmother. She went in a nursing home and she never came out. She died in her bed, Bruce told me. Right in her bed.

Lisa shouldn't have been in a coffin that looked like a bed, thought Damian. The casket that his parents had rented for the visitation and funeral service was made of poplar, and it opened like a Dutch door so they could only see the upper half of her body. The casket had a honey-coloured sheen. It had a crepe interior and a large white pillow, edged with lace. It didn't matter that they were not putting it in the ground, it still cost a fortune, not to mention the cost of the urns that would hold ashes after the cremation, and a keepsake box.

People could kneel by the casket, if they wished, and offer up a prayer. Or they could stand in silence, thinking about how tragic it was –

How are you doing? Ingrid murmured to Damian.

All right.

The open casket bothered him; he couldn't look at it.

The first group of people was clustered tentatively around the guest book at the threshold. Ingrid drew herself up. So did Greg. Damian, between them, tried to do the same. He knew his mother wanted them to do everything well for Lisa's sake.

Ingrid put her hand gently against Damian's back.

Then it began. Here was Mrs. Sullivan, who had arranged for Lisa's summer job as a cashier at the grocery store. And girls from high school: Breanna, and someone whose name Damian forgot, though it ended with "issy" or "esca." Fresca, thought Damian, but that wasn't right. She'd had a crush on him, and he'd always tried to avoid her. Both girls had tears streaming down their faces and it had smudged their eyeliner. Some women hugged him, but the men just pressed his hand, which was usually better than being hugged by people he didn't know.

Thank you for coming, said his mother or his father.

Damian was mostly silent.

His mother murmured to Greg that her own brother wasn't there. Her own brother.

Then Trevor, dressed in a dark suit that was a little too big for him, so that the cuffs of the jacket came too far down his wrists. His tie was knotted neatly, but it was striped garishly in red, blue, and green.

I'm Trevor, he said, speaking to Ingrid. I'm – he paused, swallowing.

Trevor, Ingrid murmured, to give him time. Thank you for coming.

I'm – I was a friend of Lisa's. I have something for you. I'll – maybe I'll come back later and –

Thank you for coming, Trevor, said Greg, taking over from Ingrid and passing Trevor along to Damian.

There were tears in Trevor's eyes, but he wasn't crying.

God, Damian, he said.

Yeah. Damian hated Trevor, hated him standing there.

I'm sorry, said Trevor.

Damian studied his shoes, polished by his father that morning, and when he looked up there was an old woman with a walker standing in Trevor's place.

Oh, she said faintly and gripped Damian's hand in her claw.

And then it was over; it had gone on for two hours. His feet were tired. Greg had gone to speak to the bird-thin funeral director in the hall.

Damian stood with his mother, gazing at the young

woman who was not Lisa, but a wax copy of Lisa, lying before them in her dark green dress with sprigs of cherries printed on it. It was true that everything had been done to make her look perfect. She was wearing coral-coloured lipstick and there was a rosy blush to her cheeks, though she'd never bothered with makeup. It wasn't Lisa. Lisa was long gone.

Look at this, said Elvis. Roger says this is his pride and joy.

Queen of the Mist, read the black letters on the barrel lid. And in smaller, stamped letters: *Property of Annie Edson Taylor.* Elvis took out the large cork in the lid, inspected it, poked the cork back down snugly in its hole, and took the lid off the barrel. Inside was a mattress, stained and yellowed with age. Elvis put his head in the barrel.

Oooooo, he called into it. Then he climbed inside.

What are you doing? cried Damian.

Now Elvis was stuck, with his chest and head inside, legs outside. Pride and joy, he shouted, and the words reverberated.

Pride and joy.

He kicked his legs, and the barrel fell over with a crash.

Elvis, are you okay? Damian dragged him out of the barrel. Are you okay?

Yes.

You're sure?

My head isn't okay, but the rest of me is okay, said Elvis. Do you have brain damage?

Not that I know of, said Damian, supporting Elvis as he got up. But I could have had some brain damage if you'd shot me.

Brain damage, Elvis laughed. You're right about that. You're right about that.

There was a fine, powdery dust on his hair and eyebrows. He was laughing, and he put his large, pale hands over his mouth. When he looked sideways at Damian, his eyes were wide.

Let's go to the casino, he said when he could breathe again.

No, I don't think so.

I want to.

No, Elvis.

He opened his mouth so Damian could see his tongue and throat, dark red. A strangled cry came out. He looked so strange with his mouth open, his molars showing, his face all twisted up in agony. Then he fled, vanishing out the door and into the night.

Elvis!

Damian stood for a moment at the doorway of the carriage house and then stepped out on the back lawn, not knowing which way Elvis had gone. If anything happened, it was Damian's doing. He shut the door and went across the lawn to the big house. He opened the kitchen door quietly, but Elvis wasn't in the kitchen and he wasn't in the hall. Damian could hear the low voices of his mother and Roger through the screened door as they sat on the porch, but he wasn't about to tell them that Elvis had run away. He hesitated. The ghostly coil of the snake's skeleton turned gently as it hung from the light fixture. Moonlight came through the window halfway up the stairs, slanting down the steps and across his sandalled feet, turning them into softly tinted fish.

Damian walked through the foyer of the funeral parlour, made to look like someone's home, past the photos of Lisa on the gilt-framed bulletin board on an easel: the photo of Lisa with her paddle raised in the air as she sat in her kayak; the photo of Lisa waving, with her best friend Alicia, just before the school trip to Atlanta; the photo of Lisa with Damian; the photo of Lisa at Christmas in front of the tree, with her hair in braids; the photo of Lisa as a little girl, wearing a yellow-and-white-striped dress that she held out on either side as if she were going to curtsy; the photo of Lisa as a baby in Ingrid's arms.

He returned to the viewing salon for Lisa Felicity MacKenzie, where a few people were still gathered in a corner, whispering respectfully. His mother was sitting in front of Lisa's casket; she had taken off her high heels and closed her eyes. Damian was about to turn away when Trevor approached and said something quietly to her. She opened her eyes and made an effort to greet him.

Hello, she said. You are – ?

Trevor.

Oh yes, Trevor. I remember now. You went to a dance with Lisa.

I have something for her – for Lisa, he said, uncrumpling a piece of paper. I wrote it. Would you mind if I read it?

Damian could see he was going to read it to her whether she wanted him to or not.

It's something you've written? she asked.

Yes. It's a poem.

Lisa would have liked that.

Trevor looked at Ingrid bashfully. I don't know if it's all that good.

Don't worry, said Ingrid.

For one ridiculous moment, Damian felt the urge to laugh.

Trevor composed himself. For Lisa.

Why don't you sit down? said Ingrid.

All right. He sat beside her. For Lisa, he began again. Lisa, you were my heaven and earth, though you were here just ten years and seven –

The paper trembled in his hands.

It was too short a time, he went on. Sun and moon can't – Sun and moon can't rhyme, now you're gone.

That's it, he said. That's my poem.

Ingrid put a hand on his sleeve. Damian could see that she wanted Trevor to be quiet, but he took it for encouragement.

I'm really going to miss her, he said.

Ingrid put her hand quickly to her mouth and got up from her chair. She went to kneel next to the casket. It wasn't her custom to kneel, or even to pray, Damian thought, but now she clutched the edge of the casket with both hands.

Trevor hovered nearby, folding the paper and slipping it into the casket.

I need to be alone with her now, Ingrid said, her voice quietly firm.

Thank you for listening to it.

It was – courageous of you, she told him.

Trevor brushed his hand over his eyes. He left the room and walked through the foyer without seeing Damian.

There were two beefy security guards at the entrance to the casino when Damian got there. One was chewing gum. He blew it out of his mouth in a transparent pinkish bubble, smacked it so the bubble collapsed, and drew it back into his mouth.

She really gets off on it when I do that, the other man was saying. You wouldn't think a feather would do it, but it does.

Damian asked if they'd seen Elvis.

Nope.

In the lobby, the lights were duplicated in mirrors, fractured and reflected, making them seem larger. A wide stream of water ran down a glass wall and cascaded into an illuminated pool fringed with palms. When Damian reached the top of the escalator and stepped off, he felt the luxuriously soft carpet under his sandals. A woman spun around on her stool with one leg in the air, so her shoe dropped from her foot, and Damian noticed that each of her toenails was painted a different colour.

My Lord, Mike, she said to the man next to her. I'm *all* jazzed up.

She picked up a little bucket and fed the machine some quarters. Damian heard the clinking sounds as the coins went into it.

Sir, said a girl. Her waistcoat had a satiny sheen. Her shiny mouth transfixed him, as if it were perfectly glued on. Sir, can I help you?

Did you see a man – a large man wearing pyjamas?

No, she said blankly. No one like that.

Damian looked around wildly at the people by the slot machines. A woman was laughing. A man was swinging his wife's purse just out of her reach, grinning as he did so. There was someone with slicked hair and a wide smile on his face as he bent to fill up his container with coins.

Damian went down the wide marble staircase into the lobby, past the potted plants and security guards, out into the summer night. When he looked up at the moon, it seemed smaller and more transparent than it had been before, as if it had been cut from gauze. There was a smell of diesel in the air, and a girl calling for someone named Justin.

Justin, where the fuck are you? *Justin?*

Through the sidelight by the funeral home's front door, Damian could see Trevor sitting in his truck in the parking lot, sobbing. The sight of him weeping like that – his head down, shoulders shaking – made Damian furious, so his throat burned. He went outside. As he walked toward the truck, Trevor raised his head. The window was half open, and Damian could see how pale he was. Damian didn't reach for the door handle; he banged the hood instead. He banged it over and over, spoiling for a fight.

What are you doing? yelled Trevor.

Get out of the truck, cried Damian.

Why?

You know why. You know what you did to Lisa.

Damian –

Christ, said Damian. Get out of the truck.

I don't know what you think, Damian. Trevor didn't move from the driver's seat. I swear to God it wasn't what you think.

Get the fuck out of there.

Trevor got out and closed the door. He loosened his tie, which looked like something a clown might wear. He took it off, balled it up, and put it in his pocket. He took off his jacket too and tossed it in the half-opened window. His shirt was very white in the twilight.

I loved her, Damian.

No, you took advantage of her.

I did not. I would have done anything for her.

She told me that the two of you – anyway, she was too young. I told her she was too young.

Damian, you can't blame me for what happened.

Damian gave the hood another bang.

It was an accident, said Trevor. What happened to Lisa was an accident. He wiped a white sleeve across his face. Shit, he went on. I can't stop crying. Okay, if you're going to hit me, watch out for my left shoulder. I've got a rotator cuff thing going on – it's from hockey.

I could beat you to a pulp, said Damian, bending over the hood and stretching his arms out flat on it. But I have to go back in there. His voice was muffled. Fucking shit.

Fucking shit, agreed Trevor.

No, you're the fucking shit.

I thought you were.

Damian stepped back from the truck, laughing. You're the fucking shit. Got that? You're the fucking shit. He drew himself up and stopped laughing abruptly. I have to go.

See you, said Trevor. Fucking shit.

Damian went inside. He walked down the hall, past the funeral director, who nodded solemnly at him, but he stopped at the threshold of the viewing salon where his mother was now sitting on the floor with her head in his father's lap. Her feet, without shoes, were twisted underneath her, and they seemed all the more vulnerable because they weren't naked, but clad in stockings, which were reinforced over the toes. There was a little hole by her baby toe, ringed with nail polish so it wouldn't run. Her face was turned away from Damian, but he could see she was crying helplessly. There was no sound. His father was touching her, soothing her.

It was possible that he'd never seen his parents together like this – his father had left when Damian was young. He thought briefly of the morning his father had gone away: that grey day with the wet snow falling. The colour of the taxi in that whiteness. It didn't matter how many times he'd seen him after that, there was always the finality of that morning. His father loved him, but that didn't make up for it.

Now he could see that his father loved his mother too, but it was all wrong. His mother was sprawled on the floor, in her black dress and jacket, and her stocking-clad feet, with one arm clutching her ex-husband's leg, as if she were trying to hold on to wreckage from a boat. The two of them had been brought back together, but not for long, and Damian knew this as well as anyone. He watched as his father lifted his hand to make the same gesture over and over, putting his hand down slowly, tenderly, on his mother's head to stroke her hair. She'd had it done that morning at the hairdresser's, but it was all disarranged across his father's lap, shimmering under the light.

It was a private moment between his parents, one that Damian should not have witnessed. Beside them was the casket, and in it was their daughter, cold as winter. Cold as January after a storm, when there was a glaze of ice over each stone on the beach. Cold as the white, frothy tide coming in and going out, restlessly.

Damian had kissed Lisa's forehead earlier and he knew. Over to one side, beneath a chair, were two black patent leather shoes. One was upright, and the other had fallen over. It was his mother's shoes that made Damian lean against the wall and cry.

Damian went up Clifton Hill, under the bright lights of Ripley's Believe It or Not! He passed Rock Stars of the Ages Wax Museum, and Don't Pay More Souvenirs, where T-shirts were ghosts in the window. Tits Up For Jesus. Cry When You Bite My Onion. Great Balls of Fire – Got 'Em, Flaunt 'Em. Just beyond the souvenir shop was a 3-D creature with antennae and large lime-green eyes, glaring above the sign for Alien Terrors: A Close Encounter with Creatures from Mars.

He saw Elvis, then, just past Alien Terrors. There he was, all alone. He looked like someone who'd just got out of bed for a glass of milk, except that he was standing on the sidewalk in bare feet, in the greenish glow from the sign. When a car went by, the driver honked at him, but Elvis didn't move. His pyjama top rippled out in the wind.

Hey, *retard*! someone yelled.

No harm had come to him. The sheep and ducks emblazoned on his pyjamas had protected him, as if they were magical symbols to ward off evil.

Elvis, said Damian softly.

Elvis looked around at him and turned back to the tattoo parlour window across the street from where he stood. The window was filled with light, and a young woman stood inside. She was slender, with glossy dark hair, and one brown shoulder showing where her wide-necked T-shirt had slipped a little. Her hair was caught up on top of her head with what might have been a large clothespin.

She had silvery bangles on her wrists, and the bangles moved as she worked on something, but whatever she was doing displeased her, because she frowned and tightened her mouth. She was drawing. Then she stopped, stepping back. She moved the pencil back and forth between her lips as she looked at the drawing.

Around her, on the walls, were hundreds of small pictures arranged in rows. Kittens, cats, puppies, dogs, guitars, mushrooms, hearts and arrows, motorcycles. Roses budding and roses blooming and roses in tiny wreaths. Smiling lips, pursed lips, open lips with the tip of a tongue showing. Angels. Devils. I love you. A cross, a flaming cross, three small crosses. Waves. A little boat. Noah and the ark. A wall of lions, tigers, zebras, Panda bears.

She flung the pencil on the table, but it jumped and rolled to the floor. Taking off her apron, she put it on the back of a chair and slung a drawstring bag over her shoulder. It was as though she were on a stage, Damian thought, and now she was going to speak to the audience. She looked out the window, though the glass must have been a square of darkness to her, and it seemed to Damian that he could predict how she would walk through the beaded curtain and part it exactly as she did, with one hand, going to the invisible back door where she would flick off the lights, as if she knew people were watching. Damian and Elvis both stood staring into the darkness, until Damian realized they were waiting for something. They were waiting for her to come back onstage.

Damian put his hand on Elvis's arm. Let's go, he said.

When Elvis didn't move, he took his hand. His skin was soft and pliant, unexpectedly pliant. And it was larger than Damian's own hand. If Elvis wanted to, he could crush it. It made him think of how Elvis had held the gun, as if he'd meant it.

Okay, said Elvis, allowing himself to be led away. Okay.

It was on the back streets that Damian noticed the moonlight again. It fell on parked cars, on street signs, on a Dumpster, on a small plaster boy fishing on someone's front lawn, flickering in and out of the pachysandra that grew thickly around the base of a group of birches.

They wouldn't let me in, said Elvis.

Who? asked Damian.

They asked me how old I was. Then they asked me if I had any money. You're supposed to have money if you go to the casino. I looked inside, though.

Damian imagined Elvis at the casino, looking in at the potted plants and marble floor, his breath making plumes on the glass.

You wouldn't have liked it, Elvis.

They told me it was past my bedtime. The men said it was past my bedtime and they said things about my pyjamas. Elvis turned to Damian, his eyes glistening. They laughed about my pyjamas.

EVERY NIGHT BEFORE ELVIS went to sleep he kissed Shania Twain, who smiled on his pillowcase. Once he'd said goodnight to Shania, he pulled a photograph out from under the pillow. There was a white crease across it, but the woman in it, though faded, could still be seen. Her long red hair fell over her shoulders. She wore a man's black leather jacket, and she was leaning against a motorcycle. In her arms was a baby, snugly wrapped in a blanket. There was a doll-sized knitted cap on its head. The woman wasn't looking down at the baby; she was looking directly at the camera, or she seemed to be looking directly at the camera, but she wore sunglasses so it was hard to tell. Elvis kissed the photograph twice. He kissed the woman on her sunglasses and he kissed the baby on its knitted cap. Then he slid it back under the pillow. On the back of the photograph, in a small, rounded script, were the words:

Elvis Graceland Hockridge
November 2, 1987
Toronto, Ontario

TO HELL WITH IT, Jasmine thought, tossing the pencil. She took off her apron and picked up her bag. When she looked out the window all she could see was her own reflection, a girl who was a bit on the skinny side, except for her hips, which she'd never liked. Hair in need of washing, twisted up on top of her head and held with a clip. Her grandmother's bangles on her wrist. But she looked like a nine-year-old, with or without bangles. Jasmine, who had been Sandra Blakeney, from Lanigan, Saskatchewan, on her way to Somewhere Else, preferably New York City, in the United States of America, before she went on to France, Italy, and Spain, was stranded for the moment in a tattoo parlour in Niagara Falls, Ontario, until she could make enough money to go Somewhere Else.

As for the drawing, she could tell herself it was fine, but it wasn't; she couldn't do foreshortening worth beans. The dragon was all right, but she couldn't do the motorcycle. A drawing for a tattoo, the guy had said. His name was Jordan, he told Tarah, and what he wanted was a dragon sitting on a Kawasaki motorcycle, with the bike shown from the front, not the side.

Jasmine had said she'd try to help Tarah out, because the drawing had to be done by the following morning. But it wasn't working. Why couldn't Jordan get a flash of a Panda bear? Why did it have to be a dragon on a Kawasaki?

In grade three, Jasmine's teacher had said that her trees looked like sponges. The teacher had been a jolly woman with red hair and large hands; she'd said the trees looked like sponges, and then she'd smiled. She didn't have to say anything about the sky or the clouds. After the teacher went up the row, Sandra-not-yet-Jasmine looked at her trees. She liked them. She didn't care what Mrs. Jewett said.

She'd gone home after school and yanked out all the hair from the head of her hand-me-down doll. It had been her sister Shirl's doll.

What kind of a girl *are* you? asked her mother when she found Sandra and the doll and the yanked-out hair.

What kind of a girl was she?

One who'd left Lanigan before it was really spring, on a bus that went down the highway past fields that were not yet green, not even close, because it was always cold in Lanigan, and the cold went deep into the sky and the fields and the trees and the driveways and the cars and the houses and the people in the houses. Of course, that wasn't entirely fair, because the heat of summer went deep into everything too, later on, but it was early spring when she left, and the world was grey-green. It was as flat as if someone had taken an iron to it and pressed it down.

One who'd saved a fortune cookie (from the Full Moon Chinese Restaurant in Saskatoon, while waiting for the bus that went via Winnipeg to Toronto) that read, in small green lettering: **Good fortune and great happiness will come your way very soon.**

One who had phoned home to tell her parents she'd left for a year and to wish her luck: a wish that went unwished. Her mother told her there'd be hell to pay and to come right home, what was she thinking, going off like that at the age of eighteen to live on the streets like some hussy, like some tramp?

One who was scared to leave Canada, in the end, and had got off the bus at the last possible place before crossing the border between Ontario and New York State.

One who found a place to rent after a bad night in the bus terminal, walking from one basement apartment to another before she found Tarah, who saved her life, because she needed someone to share The Dump on Stanley Street.

One who got a job in the Lundy's Lane Historical Museum by giving the impression she was bright and perky. Of course, it helped that she was majoring in Canadian history at – at the University of Toronto.

One who'd been in Niagara Falls, Ontario, for five weeks and two days.

One who couldn't draw motorcycles.

That was what kind of girl she was, if anyone wanted to know, but no one did.

She switched off the lights and went out the side door into the alley, making sure the door was locked behind her. She glanced down the alley to Clifton Street as she unlocked her bicycle, and it was then that she noticed the man in pyjamas. He was on the other side of the street. He was staring at her. No, he wasn't staring at her; he was staring into the window of the Ornamental Hand. One side of his face was green because of the light from Alien Terrors. His feet were bare, and this was the strangest part of it, because why would a person go outside without shoes? He was a nutcase, that's what he was. A car went by, and his pyjama top swelled out as it passed. She had a sudden, eerie thought that he must have been watching her.

A blond-haired man took his hand and spoke to him; she saw how they turned slowly, like people in hospitals when they'd come to the end of a long hall. It could have been an old-fashioned, complicated dance they were doing, with one leading the other. The blond man was tall and lanky, with a braid down his back, and the other was solidly built, with tufts of hair standing up on his head. The street-light turned their hair to silver, but neither of them was old. There was something about the way the tall one took his time, as if this was the kind of thing people did all the time, at midnight, on Clifton Hill, in Niagara Falls, Ontario; they could have been moving in a dream.

Once, on such a night, her father had woken her.

Wake up, Sandy, he'd said, tapping her on the shoulder.

She woke, frightened to see him standing over her. She'd been only seven. He whispered to her to come with him and she'd climbed down the ladder from her bunkbed. He got Shirl up too, but it was harder to wake her, because Shirl was sixteen and didn't see why they had to go outside. It was *dumb*. But she came anyway. They'd gone to the back door and he'd suggested they put on their rubber boots. Sandra rubbed her eyes, feeling weary, but then he took them outside, into the wide, dark prairie night, and she woke up. The night had been soft as the black velvet collar on her mother's red dress, the one that hung in the closet upstairs, all zipped up in a plastic case because she didn't want moths to get into it.

They'd made a procession: her father, then Queenie,

the dog, then Shirl, then Sandra. Shirl's boots made a *shouk*, *shouk* sound as she walked. It had been a wet spring, and moist leaves touched the skin of their arms. The three of them went through the damp grass, between the aspen saplings, down to the creek bed, and over the little bridge – where the thin line of water flowed out of the shadows and back into them – through the sparking of fireflies, and up the slight rise to a windbreak of poplar. When Sandra turned, she could see the comforting light at the back door of the house. It was close, yet she was in an exotic place that smelled of wet earth and wolf willow. Shirl slapped at the bugs, but their father had motioned for them to be quiet.

There was a plaintive cry of young birds, and it turned out to be owlets calling to the mother owl. She flew over them, large as a giant's gloved hand, making no noise. It had been strange to sense her flying over them, as if she could fly down and clutch their wrists with her talons. But she didn't; she flew back to her young.

Her father was not a man who usually noticed such things, Jasmine thought now. He tried to be practical, yet somehow he managed to let money slip through his fingers like water, as her mother put it. She said he would bring them all to grief one day. But that June night he stood watching for the owl attentively, holding up his face with a look of anticipation. Then Queenie barked, abruptly, and that was the end of the owl watching.

She held on to this memory of her father when her parents gave up the place outside Lanigan and bought a dry-cleaning business in town. Her mother had gone back into hairstyling; now she couldn't imagine life before the Hair Lair. But her father seemed to grow smaller. He grew fretful.

She thought about him as she walked her bicycle behind the odd pair, the tall man and the solid, stocky one, keeping her distance, following them to a parking lot at the back of the casino, where they seemed to vanish into the shadows. Perhaps they'd been carried off into the night sky, she thought. But they hadn't been carried off into the night sky.

She caught herself, wondering what she'd been thinking, then got on her bicycle and pedalled up Clifton Hill. She rode to Stanley Street, put her bicycle against the house by the back door, and sat on the picnic table, where the moonlight fell through the old willow, through its tangled branches and many-fingered leaves. It fell on the laundry that had been left on the neighbour's clothesline, turning each blouse and tea towel and washcloth into spirits of the air.

Damian wasn't the slightest bit drowsy. He lay on his bed thinking about the girl in the window of the Ornamental Hand. She'd been drawing. He turned on his left side. He hadn't drawn anything in a long time. He turned on his right side.

After a while he got up and unrolled one of the sheets of paper he'd brought with him, paper that his mother had urged him to bring along. Sitting on the bedroom floor, he clipped the paper to his drawing board and sharpened a few pencils with a bone-handled knife. He put the drawing board against his drawn-up knees, shutting his eyes to recall the exact shadows caused by the way the light fell, the bright tulips of the apron, the sarong under it, the shapely brown hands, gleams of hair.

The last time he'd drawn anything he'd been at Adam's uncle's hunting cabin. The day he'd arrived was the third of April, but it had snowed thickly, so the whiteness had clung to every branch of the birches just outside. He'd had a vivid dream that first night, and he'd wrapped himself in a musty-smelling orange-and-brown afghan and wandered into the kitchen. The fire in the woodstove had gone out, and, starting it again, he found himself fully awake. Bits and pieces of his dream came back. Lisa, standing on a stool, dressed in a blue satin gown that made her look years older. His mother pinning up the hem of the dress. A dance. Trevor coming to pick her up. He could see Lisa so clearly it was as if she were standing in front of him.

He'd found a pencil in a drawer in the kitchen of the cabin. He took one of the newspapers off the stack by the woodstove, opened it, and drew across the photograph of the high-school basketball team. Lisa, in a strapless dress with a small rhinestone brooch at the front. Standing on a stool, yes, that was it. In the dream there hadn't been enough time to pin the dress and hem it – the lack of time had been the problem, he realized. In the dream, both his mother and sister had been upset because of it. His drawing became more frenzied: he drew Lisa's arms, her neck, the sparkling brooch, her neat, small ears, her hair twisted up into a knot at the back of her head.

He wasn't drawing Lisa now. He had all the paper he could ask for, and good, freshly sharpened drawing pencils. If he half closed his eyes, he could see the girl again. He was motionless for a few moments before he opened his eyes and began drawing swiftly. After that he didn't stop, and it was a full half-hour before he set down the drawing board against the wall and stepped back. The eyes were too close-set, and the lips – the lips were too full. It wasn't even a ghost of what he'd seen. He gave a snort of disgust. He'd have to see her again to get it right, he thought, sprawling across his bed. It was almost afternoon when he went downstairs, rubbing sleep from his eyes.

He heard voices outside the kitchen, and then Roger came in, setting a trowel in the bucket by the kitchen door, taking off his gardening gloves and putting them, one at a time, on the edge of the bucket. He stood up, turning more or less in Damian's direction.

You slept in, he said.

How'd you know I was here?

My extraordinary powers of perception. What happened with Elvis last night? He shuffled to the sink.

We went out.

Out?

Well, he took off and I went after him.

I wondered if that might happen.

Damian watched how his uncle fumbled with the cabinet door and ran his hand along the shelf before he found a glass.

He likes you, Damian. But he'll do all kinds of things to test you.

I can see that.

Roger ran some water into the glass and drank it.

You have to be careful if you come into his life. Know what I mean?

I think so.

The thing is that the two of us – we're at a turning point. He doesn't like that. Nobody likes that.

A big man stood in the doorway of the Ornamental Hand and took a last, long drag on his rolled cigarette before stepping aside as Damian entered.

You want a tattoo? asked the man. He had small, beady eyes and a face that unfolded in pockets of skin from the pouches under his eyes to his jowls. Cleanest house in town. No dirty needles around here. Ever had a tattoo?

No, said Damian. He did, in fact, have a tattoo of two small oak leaves at the back of his neck.

What you've got is a machine working at sixty revolutions per second, injecting ink under the skin. See this — beautiful, huh? Puss 'n Boots. Hey, Tarah, get your ass out here. Tarah does the tattoos.

A hand parted the beaded curtain neatly, as if it were dividing air. It was such a delicate hand. A hand that could part the waters of the Red Sea. But, no, it was a different hand, belonging to a girl with short hair that was dyed magenta. She had black sleeves laced to her black bodice. She was tiny, and for all her tattoos and triple-pierced lip, she looked like a wren with a broken wing.

What? she said flatly.

We got everything under the rainbow, said the man. You ask Tarah.

D'you want something? she asked Damian.

Why else would he be here?

Fuck off, Gordie.

Bitch. He went outside and rolled himself another cigarette.

Tarah flicked something off her wrist. Her nails were painted dark blue.

I came by here last night, said Damian. There was a girl – a woman – working in here.

Girlwoman, Tarah mimicked. She ran her hand through the ends of her magenta hair and laughed. She softened, her fingers doing a little staccato dance on the glass counter. Are you some kind of asshole?

No.

Serial killer?

No.

How do I know that? She glanced through the window at Gordie. There's a real *fuck* for you, she said. Gordie.

She turned back to Damian. Her name's Jasmine – we live in the same house. She's at the Lundy's Lane Museum. Ferry Street. That's where she works, and don't fucking tell her I said so.

Thanks. Thanks a lot.

There was a wreath of hair in an ornately framed shadow box over the desk where Jasmine worked in the Lundy's Lane Historical Museum.

VICTORIAN HAIR WREATH
circa 1860-1865
Hamilton, Ontario
Human hair and horsehair, wire, wool, glass,
steel, and wood beads
Gift of the MacLeod Family

Jasmine had never coveted anything the way she coveted that wreath of hair. It reminded her of her grandmother's hair – long, silky, and white – which she had brushed and brushed as a child. Once, she had fallen asleep in her grandmother's lap, her fingers still entwined in the white hair, and her grandmother hadn't woken her.

The wreath was shaped like a crescent moon, with hair of different shades – blond, honey-brown, dark brown, red, black, grey, and white – which had been stitched into loops that formed flowers, sprigs, and leaves. The wreath was made into a crescent, with its ends pointing up, so it could hold the luck inside. Whoever had made it had done it by gimping, which involved looping the hair over a knitting needle, binding it along a wire rod, and making another loop – a technique that Jasmine was trying to learn from a library book on hair decoration.

When Tarah had dyed her hair dark blue, she'd let Jasmine cut some of it off. Jasmine had grouped the blue hair together in strands of twenty before making loops, and she was starting to get the hang of it. She hid the hair and knitting needle in a plastic bag in a drawer of the front desk of the museum. Maybe she could ask Tarah's boyfriend, Matt, for some of his hair, since it was sandy brown, a nice contrast with Tarah's. If it worked, she was going to give them the wreath, crescent-shaped, and open at the top, so they could hold their luck.

You can't keep people's hair, her mother had told her.

It was the first day that Sandra-not-yet-Jasmine had been hired to clean up the Hair Lair. She was swishing the soft broom across the floor, catching swirls of red, strawlike heaps of blond, wisps of grey.

Why not?

It's not hygienic, for one thing, said her mother. It's not right. It'd be like taking people's toes or fingers.

Look at it. It's wonderful. All those colours –

It's *hair*, for heaven's sake, Sandra. Put it in the garbage out back.

She put some of it in the garbage and saved the rest of it. She shampooed it, carefully, and dried it on paper towels in her bedroom. By the time she left Saskatchewan, she'd saved fifty-seven different shades of hair, each tied in a loop, and deposited into one of six zippered plastic bags. Black, brown, red, blond, grey, white. She'd carried them on her way Somewhere Else.

At twenty after four each day, Jasmine began locking up the museum. It took her ten minutes to make sure – even though she *was* sure – that the windows were locked and the doors bolted, before she put on the alarm system. It was like tucking a child into bed, she thought, as she went down the steps of the museum.

Tarah arrived home an hour later than Jasmine, slinging a few grocery bags on the kitchen table.

You did your hair again. Jasmine picked up the change on the table.

I did it before work today – it's called Magenta Madness. Tarah turned in a circle, arms out gracefully. What do you think?

Nice. I like it.

And Jordan didn't come in – you know, Mr. Kawasaki. After both of us killed ourselves trying to give him the tattoo of his dreams. Honest to God.

A jerk. Jasmine started washing the romaine lettuce in the sink.

Yeah. Tarah took orange and yellow peppers out of a bag and stopped to study her fingernails. I'll have to change my nail polish. You know, there was this guy today – have you ever come across a tall guy with blond hair? She held the fridge door open with her knee, a jug of milk in one hand and carton of eggs in the other. He was asking about you.

I don't know anyone like that. Jasmine patted the romaine leaves with a piece of paper towel.

He was *beautiful*. Tarah slammed the fridge door with her foot. That light's off in the fridge again. I mean on a scale of one to ten –

Jasmine grinned at her, opening the fridge to check the light. You're actually rating him? That light – yesterday I sort of wiggled it and it worked as long as I didn't slam the door. So, okay, this guy, what did you tell him?

Nothing.

Nothing?

Are you kidding? He could have been anyone.

The Lundy's Lane Museum was closed by the time Damian got there, so he returned the next day, early, and sat on the steps until it opened. No, he thought. Sitting there he'd look like a fool. He got up and went across the street to Tony's Watch Repair, where he paced in front of the window. Watches covered with a grainy dust. Fake Rolex and Cartier watches. Girlwoman. There she was. He could see her reflection in the glass through the letters of Tony's Watch Repair as she climbed the steps to the entrance of the museum and opened the red door.

Jasmine. Her name was Jasmine.

He crossed the street slowly, went up the steps, and stopped. A bit of time; he had to give it a bit of time. The door opened to a world of dimness inside, and he stepped over the threshold into the dark, waiting for his eyes to adjust. There was a desk in front of him, but no one was there and he flipped through a photocopied guidebook to the museum, a coil-bound brochure with plastic covers. *Welcome to Lundy's Lane Historical Museum.* There was a bell on the desk with a silver knob on top that could be pushed down – *dinggg!* – but he didn't ring it. He put three dollars in the woven basket with its hand-lettered card: *Adults $3.00, Children & Seniors $1.50.*

Taking the photocopied guidebook, he went around the desk into a shadowy corner where a happily grinning mannequin knelt beside a birchbark canoe. The mannequin, identified by a sign hanging from the wall (*Mature Ojibwa Male*) held a paddle clumsily in his hands, but for some reason he wasn't in the canoe. He was outside it, kneeling, about to start paddling air. Near his bent knees was an animal skull, where the water might be expected to flow. *Wolf Skull,* stated the card next to it.

Hello.

Damian jumped. I – I didn't see anyone at the desk, so I just came in here. I put three dollars in the basket.

I saw that, she said. Enjoy your visit – there's more upstairs.

She disappeared.

Shit, he whispered, looking dutifully at the javelin heads, arrayed on a board, the pieces of pipe, the bone pendant, the beaded Ojibwa fire bag. He studied the costumes of the British soldiers, the gold braid and buttons of the officers. *Captain Robert Henry Dee's Commissariat Uniform, circa 1824.* He examined the British boots. There were several pairs, and he looked at each one carefully. Why did the boot holes, the laces, the polished toes, make him feel anxious?

He steadied himself. He gazed with absorption at Laura Secord's cake plate, at the hand-drawn map of the journey she made to warn the British troops. Her cup and saucer. There was an account of her journey in a book that was propped open inside a glass case. *On the evening of the summer solstice in 1813, a young woman who had been forced to billet American troops in her farmhouse overheard the men planning their attack on the British forces.*

Come back, he thought, but she didn't come back.

Very early the next morning, Laura Secord began a treacherous journey, through the thick forests and marshes between Niagara Falls and present-day Thorold. She feared

He went around the corner, past more uniforms, which hung stiffly behind glass. The men who'd worn them were dead as doornails. In another case were shells, fossils, and arrowheads from Barnett's Niagara Falls Museum. There was no one on the second floor, and his sandals made a flapping noise as he walked from the telephone operator's exhibit to the model of the Honeymoon Bridge. There was a cradle, a sled, Victorian toys carved out of wood.

He went downstairs again and put the guidebook on top of the pile on the desk. Several of the guidebooks slid to the floor, and he picked them up. His hands weren't doing what he wanted. What would he say to her? He wandered over to the glass cases, away from the guidebooks.

for her life. Since the land was disputed, enemies abounded

All done? asked Jasmine, coming up behind him. Did you like it?

I liked, uhh, Laura Secord's cake plate.

Well, come back whenever you want to look at it. That cake plate.

He liked looking into her eyes – colour of ferns, colour of forests – and her dark, sleek hair, and her pretty shoulders. He was gawking at her, and she was smiling because he was gawking at her.

He went outside into the slam of light.

His sister's eyes had been a clear hazel, and they'd been fringed with long dark lashes. For months he hadn't been able to see her face as it had been while she was living. Lisa's dead face, with her mouth open, her skin losing its colour. What he remembered now was her animated face across the kitchen table as they played a game. Colonel Mustard with the knife in the ballroom. She opened the little brown envelope, sliding the three cards out one by one on the red-and-white-checked vinyl covering on the table, slowly, making him wait.

Yes. Colonel Mustard, she told him triumphantly. The ballroom. The knife. See!

Lisa laughing, glowing. Her lips were full; her face smooth as peach skin. I have X-ray vision, she said.

Then, just as quickly, her dead face.

He couldn't stop the pain, that rough animal, from picking him up in its sharp teeth. That cold April night in the cabin, he'd drawn Lisa, over and over, and then, in the early hours of the morning, he'd crumpled up the sheets of newspaper and thrown them into the woodstove. He'd gone outside, the orange-and-brown afghan still around his shoulders, with Adam's uncle's gun, a Marlin .22 lever action rifle, walking fast along the dirt road in the hard, grey light – shooting at crows – and missing them. If he hadn't fallen asleep that day at Cribbon's –

It was unbearable; it was all he could do to block it out. He turned around and went back to the museum.

That was quick, said Jasmine.

He had just gone out the door and now he was back.

Jasmine – will you go out with me? he asked. Just for a walk or something?

Now?

No, not now. You're working now.

Jasmine wasn't sure she trusted anyone who looked the way he did. His skin was tawny, and his eyes were dark, maybe grey or blue, and deeply set. His hair was the kind of honey-coloured blond that should have been washed and brushed and braided much more carefully than it had been. People might have turned around just to look at him, but he didn't seem to care. Then she blushed, remembering what Tarah had said. A tall guy with blond hair. *Beautiful.*

You know my name, said Jasmine.

She'd seen him before, she realized. It startled her. He'd been on the street with the man in pyjamas.

Well, I asked someone, he said. Someone with spiky hair – purple hair.

Tarah.

Jasmine straightened the pile of guidebooks on the desk.

This is not – this isn't something I do, he admitted. Usually.

Okay, she said.

Okay?

You asked me out. I said okay.

Good, okay.

But maybe I should know your name.

Damian.

Hello, Damian.

She was smiling.

What about tomorrow night? he said hurriedly. Or the night after that if –

Tomorrow is fine. When?

I could come by at seven or so.

You'll need to know where I live.

She drew a map on a scrap piece of paper. She drew the Niagara River first and a curving line for the Falls. Then she drew a hill. That's Clifton Hill, she told him. And this is Stanley Street here – I live on Stanley Street. She drew a box with a hat. In this house. Where will you be coming from?

He pointed to the river. My uncle's place is here. River and Bampfield.

Well, if you go up Clifton Hill from the river, turn left onto Stanley Street. Here's the phone number.

He took the piece of paper. He turned it one way and then the other.

She laughed. I can't really draw.

DAMIAN WAS NERVOUS. God, he was nervous. World's Most Nervous Man.

He parked the car in the driveway and studied the house. Yes, it was the right address.

Hi, he said to the windshield. Hi.

Shit.

He got out of the car and turned to check the kayak. It was Lisa's old kayak, and he'd meant to use it on Lake Erie, but so far he hadn't. He should have taken it off the rack on the car.

It had rained earlier, but now there was less humidity in the air and the sun was coming through the clouds. Dead irises were flattened this way and that on the small patch of lawn in front of Jasmine's house, like purple-brown cavalry fallen on the long grass. The fibreglass awning hung dangerously over the front door as if it might detach itself at any moment, and bits of peeling paint fell from the door like snow when he knocked.

Jasmine opened it, bangles jangling on her wrist.

Damian – come in, she said. Just give me a minute. She left the door ajar.

Instead of going into the hall, he sat down on the all-weather carpeting of the front step. Maybe he smelled too much of scented soap. He sniffed, as surreptitiously as he could, under his arms. No, it was all right.

Across the street, at the Impala Motel, was a statue of a white horse, a creature that might have been made out of soft ice cream. It reared up elegantly on its hooves, its mane a series of swirls and its tail a curving, perfect S. It looked as though it belonged on a merry-go-round. Above it, near the gas station, was a billboard for a soft drink that showed shining teeth and monstrous lips and tongue. A child in the outdoor pool at the Impala Motel was shouting. I can *too* do a jackknife. I can *too*.

When Jasmine stepped outside she had a length of material around her shoulders. Her arms were tanned; her hair was silky. Damian liked her hair, her brown skin, her pale green dress, and her scarf with its tasselled ends. He liked everything about her. And he liked the statue of the horse and the S of its tail, and the sound of children's feet slapping around the motel pool.

We could walk to Mount Carmel, she suggested. It's the old monastery – we could go along Stanley Street.

All right.

He'd walk anywhere. He'd walk to Buffalo.

You look sort of like Leif Ericsson, she said. Has anyone ever told you that? You have the hair.

No one's ever told me that, he laughed. I'll have to get a helmet at Wal-Mart or something.

He was aware of the cars rushing past and warm air brushing his skin. He wanted to say something witty, but nothing came to him as they walked along the street to Mount Carmel. The large, red-roofed stone buildings of the monastery faced perfectly kept lawns, where old oak trees stood like sentinels. Shafts of evening light turned the grass to gold.

You're not from around here, are you? She'd taken off the scarf and was playing with its tasselled ends.

No. What about you?

I'm from Saskatchewan. Lanigan, Saskatchewan. I took a bus from Saskatoon, thinking I'd go to New York City.

She tipped her head back and looked up at the fanned-out branches of an elm tree.

I chickened out at the last minute, and then I was angry with myself for not going on to the States. She turned to him. Sometimes I feel stuck here, but working at the museum suits me for now.

I liked it there. It was quiet.

It's quiet, all right. Let's see, your favourite thing is the cake plate –

The cake plate. He smiled. What's yours?

The wreath made out of hair just above the desk – did you see it?

No.

I've been reading about how the Victorians made decorations out of hair. When people died, they'd cut locks of hair as keepsakes. They'd boil the hair and then make it into flowers and birds and trees –

Keepsakes?

They'd make pictures of willows and bridges over streams, to go in lockets.

Out of hair?

Yes. Do you think it's weird?

No, it's not weird.

I found out how to do it – now I make things for people. I even have a card. She fished in the pocket of her dress. Here.

So if I wanted my Leif Ericsson hair cut off and made into a wreath or something, you'd do it.

You hold on to that card. Just in case.

He put the card in his pocket. A keepsake.

On the April morning when he found himself outside the cabin, he walked for hours. It grew warmer, and the snow – heavy and clotted – that had fallen the day before began to melt. The sun glinted in the puddles as he descended the dirt road on the flank of Brown's Mountain, which wasn't really a mountain at all. He didn't think about how long it would take him to get back to the cabin, climbing uphill on a muddy road. When he came to the spring, which was nothing more than a pipe with a spigot at the side of the road along with a handmade sign, saying, "MacLean's Spring," he remembered the path he and Adam had once taken to the river. He nosed the barrel of the gun among the brown tangle of raspberry canes, searching for an opening; he was sure the path was close by. Then he saw it, and laughed out loud – a sound that was harsh to his ears.

A snowshoe hare bounded onto the wet path, where it froze. Damian could see how its white fur was turning brown, so that its back was mottled. He raised the rifle, cocking the hammer with his thumb – the afghan dropping from his shoulders – and lined up the hare in the sights, firing before he'd given himself time to think.

Jolted by the impact, the hare dropped to the ground.

Tell me about you, said Jasmine.

What?

Tell me about you.

There's not much to tell, he said. I live in Halifax. For the last while I've been painting houses, on and off.

And before that?

Art college.

You went to art college? she said. My family wouldn't have sent me there if their lives depended on it. Not that we could afford it.

I dropped out last fall, he said.

They walked across the parking lot and over the lawn toward a cluster of trees. There was a grotto there, and a statue, with arms spread generously.

Well, anyway, it must seem like collecting bottle caps to you, she said. Victorian hair decoration.

No, it's not like that at all. It's –

Jasmine smiled. What?

I don't know. He shook his head.

This is St. Thérèse of Lisieux. She stopped in front of the statue. The one they call Little Flower.

The light came through the trees and fell on the statue's head, with its slightly yellowish face, which was bowed meekly, gracefully.

You're Catholic? he asked.

Oh, I was brought up Catholic. I read tarot cards now. I could read yours – I could tell you things about yourself.

No. Thanks, but no.

Just before St. Thérèse died, she sat straight up in bed, said Jasmine. Up to that time she'd been in so much pain that she couldn't move. But at the end, when she sat up, she wasn't quite in the world and she wasn't quite gone. They said she talked about what she saw. Her face was all lit up.

Damian went close to the hare, pushing at its body with the toe of his boot. He'd shot it through the chest: where the bullet had gone in there wasn't much blood, but there was much more of it where the bullet had exited. The fur was thick with blood. The head was completely intact, turned on its side, so that one liquid dark eye seemed to gaze directly, balefully, at him. Its mouth was slightly open, and some of the whiskers around it were very long. Its ear was velvety soft, and thin enough that it would have become pink if light had passed through it.

Fuck.

He didn't know what to do with the dead hare, so he left it where he'd killed it, without making any attempt to bury it, and kept going along the path. He heard a raven making a noisy croaking, and it made him want to put his hands over his ears, except that he was holding the rifle.

Damian? said Jasmine.

It was hard to tell whether her eyes were green or hazel. There was a ring of amber, or topaz, around the black of her pupils.

Do you think there's such a thing as grace? Damian asked.

What do you mean? She was baffled.

Let's go. What do you think – do you want to go?

All right.

They walked down through the ravine and crossed the road to Table Rock Plaza, where he bought her ice cream.

That's Goat Island, she said, pointing to it as they came out of the plaza. I know that much.

A hermit used to live there. It was sometime in the nineteenth century.

Strange place to live.

You could get to Goat Island from the American side, even back then. There used to be a pier between it and the point, close to the Falls, where there was a tower – Terrapin Tower – and one section that jutted right out over the edge. No one in his right mind would go out there, but this guy –

The old goat?

He laughed. Young – a young goat. The guy was fearless. Sometimes he'd lie down on the pier, on the part without railings that jutted out, and he'd hang right over the Falls.

And then he fell in.

No, he committed suicide later. Or at least that's what they think. But maybe you're right, maybe he just fell in.

It'd be hard to tell, she said, suppressing a smile. I mean, hard to tell between an accident and suicide, don't you think?

I guess so.

You've been reading up on the Falls.

My uncle knows everything there is to know about them. It's a family obsession. Look, your ice cream –

Oh, it's dripping.

It'll get on your dress. Here, I'll do it.

No, they're *my* drips. She wheeled away. You just want my ice cream because you've finished yours.

You're not even going to give me the cone?

No, not even the cone. She eyed him as she ate the last of it.

Was it good?

Oh, very good, she smirked.

They pressed against the railing, looking at the river.

What did you mean about grace? she said.

Oh, I don't know.

Well, what's grace anyway, when you think about it?

It was cool by the river and she drew her tasselled scarf over her shoulders.

He let himself become hypnotized by the rush of water. A faint, subtle scent emanated from her. A flowery scent, with a tang of lemon.

You think hard about things, don't you? she said.

It depends.

Sometimes I get preoccupied, she said. I'll be thinking about something and I'll just go off somewhere. Does that happen to you?

Yes.

She shivered.

Cold? he asked.

No, I like it here.

Did you mind leaving home? he asked.

No, she said.

Frothing water curled and dipped and rushed before it spilled over the edge. Mist touched their faces and arms.

Well, yes, she said. I *did* mind leaving. But it's complicated. My family's complicated.

All families are complicated.

I guess I'm most like my father, not so much like my

mother or my sister. But the one I loved most was my grandmother.

You have a sister?

My sister, Shirl. She's older than I am, and she got pregnant, and you know, maybe my mother was right, maybe it was a disaster. But when Shirl got married to Gary, I thought *that* was a disaster. I was just a kid at the time, but I thought it was a disaster.

You don't have any brothers?

They told me Gary was my brother when Shirl married him. Jasmine snorted. Gary wasn't my brother. Gary was an asshole.

You're not exactly impressed with him.

Gary Petryshyn. Anyway, I want to know about your family, she said. You must have brothers or sisters – well, unless you're an only child.

He grinned. I'm a spoiled brat.

No, you're not.

Oh, my parents split up and all that shit. It doesn't make for good conversation.

Well, then, tell me what kind of art you do.

I did a lot of different stuff.

Painting? Drawing?

Drawing.

She threw up her hands.

What? he said.

You don't give me a lot to go on.

Well, okay, he said. I used to draw everything. You name it: stones, feathers, dead flies. And if you asked me what I'd like to do, well, I guess I'd do studies of people, each one large enough to cover a wall.

If that's what you'd like to do, why did you stop?

I stopped because – I just stopped. I don't know.

He played his hands along the railing as if it were a piano.

Your turn, he said. Tell me about your grandmother.

You want to hear about my grandmother?

You said you loved her.

I did. Her farm was next door to ours. I liked my grandparents' place better than ours. My grandmother had two gardens: a kitchen garden and a rose garden. It's not easy to grow roses in Saskatchewan, because of the winters, but she did it. She grew Morden roses. When I had the measles, she took care of me – she had cool hands. But she died two and a half years ago, and I miss her – and I miss that house, that garden. There was a cottonwood tree near the porch that I thought of as my own. I thought of the whole place as my own.

So it was like leaving a part of yourself behind – when you went away.

I guess so.

You'll have to go back there.

No, not for a long time. She drew the scarf more tightly around her shoulders. Have you ever left part of yourself behind?

I've never really thought about it.

A couple passed them. The woman's back was humped over with osteoporosis, and she walked slowly with the help of a cane. The man kept pace with her, nodding at something she was saying.

Are you staying here for a while? asked Jasmine.

A few weeks, maybe more – it's up to my mother. We're visiting my uncle.

What's she like? Your mother.

Oh, she's strong. Strong-willed.

It's good to be like that.

My mother could get through anything. I couldn't, but she could.

The river was real and unreal at the same time, he thought. The water was flecked with silver as it flowed to the brink, tumbling into the gorge below. Jasmine had propped her elbows on the railing, and he could feel the fine hairs of her arm against his skin.

La Cascada, she said. That's what it is in Spanish.

You speak Spanish? Damian asked.

No, someone told me that. I just know one or two things. I know the word *cariño*. It means dear.

Cariño.

Except that you'd have to say *cariña*, she said. I mean, if you were saying it to me.

He leaned over. They were so close he could feel her breath. He could see the green of her eyes. He wanted to kiss her, but he didn't, even though she expected him to. Even though he wanted to. She didn't kiss him, either, but she stayed where she was, close to him, watching with those eyes of hers, green or hazel, or a colour between green and hazel. She didn't move away.

INGRID HAD TRIED TO SLEEP. Then she dozed off and had a nightmare and woke, gasping. She looked at the clock on the bedside table, which informed her, in sharp red numerals, that it was twelve-thirty. Getting up, she took an old *New Yorker* magazine from the table and went down the hall to the bathroom, thinking that this was what she'd be like when she was old. She wouldn't be able to sleep. She'd sit on the toilet long after she needed to, flipping through a *New Yorker* to look at the cartoons. A June issue. Eleven years old. Lisa had been alive eleven years ago in June. Enough. She rolled up the magazine and put it under her arm, flushed the toilet, and went downstairs.

It had been a nightmare about Greg.

She opened the screened door quietly and stepped outside, padding in bare feet around the porch, but, of course, Damian had not yet come home, had not parked the car in the driveway. She returned to the front of the house and sat down heavily in a chair. It was a curse not to be able to sleep. Out of the indigo shadows came the headlights of one car, another, flashing on the lawn as they drove along River Road.

When Greg told her he was going to leave, they'd been in the kitchen in the house in Halifax. They were doing dishes; or he was doing dishes and she had the red-and-white-checkered tea towel in her hand, ready to do the drying. He'd go to Vancouver; his friend Lance had asked him to work at his new plastic surgery clinic. Vancouver was the other side of the continent – the other side of the planet, she heard herself saying. Then she must have asked what would happen to the kids, because he told her he'd support the kids; he'd support Ingrid. But she'd never worried about money, and it wasn't something she worried about now. There were larger, more terrible things in the world, like the way the kitchen walls had fallen away. A gale-force wind was blowing through.

They'd be civilized about it, he told her.

Civilized, she thought.

She asked him whether there was anyone else.

No, there was no one.

If there'd been someone else it would have been easier, in a way, she imagined.

He put things in the drying rack, making a precise tower of bowls, saucepans, and pot lids. She worked more slowly than he did; she dried things methodically and put them away. This was a game of Prisoner's Dilemma, she thought. As the game went, Prisoner A and Prisoner B had the option of remaining silent after arrest and receiving a six-month jail term. But there were options. Prisoner A could escape punishment by betraying Prisoner B, who would then serve a ten-year jail sentence. Or it could be reversed: Prisoner B could betray Prisoner A and go free. But if they both betrayed each other, neither would be off the hook. They would each serve a five-year term.

Silence, betrayal.

Greg would escape the marriage. She'd be the one left behind, while he went scot-free.

She was calm, but she was also furious. Why didn't she scream? Why didn't she sink down to the floor, banging at the tiles with the flat of her palms? No, she stood staring at the checkers in the tea towel, after putting the salad bowl in the cupboard. Red, white. Red, white. It was a pattern.

If he hadn't suggested this, she knew she would have done it herself. He'd just beaten her to it.

It was time, he said, and they both knew it. They'd spent their marriage being angry with each other.

She turned off the radio, midway through a terse warning of snow squalls during the night. He was right. She could start a new life and so could he. It made sense to her, she answered, given that she was the one at home, while he worked constantly. But she hadn't absorbed the fact that he really meant to go to the opposite end of the country.

It's no one's fault, he said.

But they were both at fault, she thought. Prisoner A, Prisoner B.

La vita nuova, she said.

What?

La vita nuova. The new life.

That's Dante, he said.

But she hadn't been thinking of Dante. She thought of Dante years later, because Greg had mentioned it that night in the kitchen, and it was only then that she read about Dante and Beatrice. When she'd read all the poems Dante had written about Beatrice, she got angrier than she'd ever been. What did Dante know? He didn't know Beatrice, that was for damn sure.

She thwacked the rolled magazine on her arm, killing a mosquito. What she hadn't counted on was Damian, and how upset he'd been. Running out into the snow after his father. Damian, who loved people so intensely it was dangerous. She unrolled the magazine and looked at the cover. She could make out a picture of people on a beach lined up as neatly as bowling pins, and a couple of sharks getting ready to knock them over with a beach ball. That very night, Damian had said he was going out with someone, and then he'd gone and had a shower. When he came downstairs he was wearing a white shirt and blue jeans, and his good looks startled her.

You look nice, she told him. The keys are right there on the table. Maybe you could put some gas in the car.

Sure. Thanks a lot.

Catch you later, said Roger, who was sitting at the table.

She watched Damian through the window. He still hadn't taken the kayak off the roof of the car. He swung open the door. He looked happy – that's what it was. Handsome as a bridegroom.

Behold, she murmured. He cometh, leaping upon the mountains, skipping upon the hills.

Damian drove away.

Thinking of this, she got up, went inside, and turned on the light in the kitchen. Ah, she thought with a pang – 1:42 a.m. He wasn't home yet. He'd come home, she thought. Of course he would. He'd come home before too long. He was responsible in his own way.

She remembered Damian getting in the car with Lisa, just before they drove to the cottage for the weekend. Ingrid bent down to speak to him, telling him to drive safely, which she always did. And Lisa had leaned over so she could see her mother.

Bye, Mum, she said. Hazel eyes, wide smile. Dark blonde hair caught back in a ponytail.

I love you both, said Ingrid.

She'd thumped lightly on the roof before they backed out of the driveway. But if she had gone to the cottage with them. If she hadn't had a Saturday lunch date with Kristie, who'd just been diagnosed with multiple sclerosis. If she'd been there, she might have been able to stop Lisa from driving Damian's ATV onto the beach. And if she hadn't stopped her, she would have chased her. She might have been able to save her.

It was no one's fault.

It was no one's fault, but if only –

She went to the cupboard where Roger kept his hard liquor. She opened it, took out the gin, and put it on the table. She sat down and stared at the blue liquor – Bombay Sapphire – the blue of swimming pools under an August sky. What had Roger told her? This gin was the world's best, flavoured with almond, angelica, cassia, coriander, cubeb – how did she remember all these things?

It was no one's fault that Damian was with a girl right now.

She put the beautiful bottle of gin, with its ornately framed picture of Queen Victoria, back in the liquor cabinet.

For God's sake, she said, latching the cabinet.

She was not going to do anything so stupid. She was not going to be jealous of her own son's happiness. No. Instead, she opened the fridge and took out the milk. She'd have hot milk with marshmallows on top, that's what she'd do.

But Greg came back into it as she stirred the milk on the stove.

He stood beside her, explaining why the casket should be open during the visitation. Ingrid didn't want an open casket, but Greg did. They'd been in the kitchen of the house in Halifax, talking about an open versus a closed casket. They could have been discussing the details of Lisa's wedding, but they weren't.

Are you doing all right? asked Greg. Talking about this stuff?

She was stirring the milk, but she saw him, plain as day. I'm all right. No, I'm not.

His face was older, but the same, except for more wrinkles around his eyes. He had a little less hair, especially where it had receded around his temples. It was flecked with white, as if a little snow had fallen on it and he hadn't shaken it off. The only thing that was different was that he had a new habit of putting his fingers up to his temples when he was trying to concentrate.

How familiar, yet how strange it all was, that he should be back in the house they'd bought as a young couple. They went into the living room and sat on the couch to gather themselves, to make funeral arrangements. The couch, she couldn't help thinking, had been one over which they'd deliberated. Should it contain a pullout bed, or shouldn't it? They'd settled on a subdued but practical oyster-coloured cotton duck fabric, with olive-green piping around the cushions. Twenty years later, they sat on it without caring about the coffee stain on the arm, the frayed hem of its oyster-coloured skirt. The couch was floating around in the ocean and they were adrift on it.

She looked down at her hands, dazedly, fingering her thumbs as if she were just learning she had hands.

Oh, *Greg*.

He put his arm around her, the way a brother might have done.

I know, he said.

But then he was up from the couch and out of the living room. He'd gone back to the kitchen to get the forms from the funeral home. She heard him moving around, lifting keys, putting something down on the counter. Silence. Then she heard the sound of a pig being slaughtered. No, not a pig. She ran to her ex-husband, sobbing by the back door.

Stop. Greg, *stop*. She held him as he sobbed crazily.

She was so young, he cried, his face contorted. God. I didn't see her enough – a couple of times a year wasn't enough. I thought there was all the time in the world, you know? And now she's gone, just like that. He snapped his fingers.

You'll get me started again.

I know. He moved away from her, clumsily, and wiped his face on his arm the way a child would do. Here – what was I doing? I was getting the forms.

He wiped his face again.

Why don't I make tea? he said. Would you like tea? The kettle's warm – it won't take long.

All right. I guess so.

She washed out the teapot and got out the box of tea with a picture of a tiger lying on the side. He made the tea, his hands shaking. It didn't really matter if she had tea or yak milk. She'd have been happy with a glass of cold water, but he wanted to make tea.

We'll have an open casket, she said. If that's what you want.

She put a cluster of small marshmallows on top of the frothy milk in her mug – green, pink, yellow – though she would have preferred a large white one. She sat at the kitchen table, dunking the marshmallows with her index finger, but they were cheerfully unsinkable. Green – who was Damian with? Pink – where on earth could he be? Yellow – had he been in a car crash, perhaps?

Greg was sitting across from her. She knew he was thinking of Damian.

You want to know how he's been, said Ingrid. How he's weathering it.

Greg waited.

You know how he used to draw all the time? You couldn't get him to stop. But now – nothing. He used to be passionate about it. Once he wanted to draw my hands: not both hands at the same time, which would have been easier. No, he wanted the left hand on one sheet of paper, the right hand on the other. Very flattering. The hands of a giantess.

Anyway, she said. The last thing he drew – that I know of – the last thing was Lisa, sitting on a deck chair at the cottage. It must have been the day they arrived there.

She drank her warm milk.

It's 3:40 and he's not home yet. Why do I worry, you ask? He's a man now, after all. I should go back to bed and forget about it.

She got up and took the mug to the sink. She put some water in the saucepan in which she'd heated the milk.

There are things I can't solve for Damian, she said. And I can't release him – I can't release him from guilt.

But by the time she'd turned around, Greg had disappeared.

Ingrid wandered from the kitchen into the living room, as if pacing would help her. She turned on the light. The room was elegant – rigidly elegant – without a breath of air moving in it. Under the pressing burden of heat, the furniture appeared heavier and darker. Ingrid sat down in her father's desk chair and fingered the frames of the photographs piled up there. Once they'd hung in the upstairs hall.

Here was the one of her mother and father, newly married, posing for the photographer. Her father's head was inclined toward her mother's as if she'd been telling him something and he'd been listening intently. An attractive couple, people said. Her father, tall and slim as a beanpole, was, nevertheless, handsome in his suit, and her mother, who was nearly the same height, seemed petite beside him. Her dress had a train that had been artfully arranged on the grass. Her mother's arm tucked into her father's. And behind them, part of the facade of an Anglican church was showing, and in the background, far off, the branches of a great elm that must have been cut down since then.

She put the photo to one side, careful not to scratch the walnut of the desk. And here was the hinged photo of Roger and Ingrid together. Roger had been a boy of about seven or eight, yet they'd already made him into a young man: he wore a crisply ironed white shirt, a jacket, and a tie. His hair, youthfully blond, was neatly parted and combed, and his wide smile reminded her of Damian. He was on the left of the hinged photograph and Ingrid was on the right. She was younger, chubbier, and full of glee. She had a white satin ribbon in her wispy hair. She'd been named for Ingrid Bergman, whom her mother adored, but it didn't seem to be the right name for such an exuberantly happy creature. Could she really have been this child?

A photo of Roger standing beside his bicycle, looking roguish, and another of him in grey flannels and a blazer with a crest, taken the first year he'd been sent to Ridley College. He'd been well brought up, Ingrid thought, just as she had been. Silver spoons in their mouths. There'd been no need for him to do *stunts* for a living, as her father had said to him, in an aggrieved tone, without raising his voice. He could have gone on to Harvard or Cornell. *If* he'd applied himself.

Roger with Lesley, the lovely Lesley with her arched brows. How their mother had wanted him to marry Lesley! She could hear her mother saying how bright Lesley was, and what a fine tax lawyer she would be. But Roger had waited too long and Lesley had married someone named Richard from Montreal. Anyway, Roger had dropped out of graduate school by that time. He'd been on scholarships, studying physics at the University of Toronto, something Ingrid would never have dreamt of doing.

There was no trace of Marnie among the photographs. Of course not. These were her parents' photographs. Marnie was bold and strong as a thoroughbred horse, and she would have made Lesley look wan. Ingrid had admired this about Marnie. She was the kind of person who'd worn black for her wedding, while Roger had worn a green jacket and joke bow tie that blinked on and off.

She paused. Another photo in an oval frame: Ingrid and Greg on their wedding day.

Greg had come back to the house with Ingrid after the funeral. She'd been planning on driving him to the hotel, but they talked quietly in the living room, and then, exhausted, they'd fallen asleep on the couch. In the middle of the night she turned sleepily, her body nestled close to his. He shifted, half waking, and put his arm around her. She pulled him closer. He was awake now, and his mouth found hers; they kissed each other hungrily, his hand sliding along her thigh, until she broke away from him. Her foot caught in one of the cushions as she got off the couch and stumbled, yelping as she fell.

Don't come near me. She was sitting on the floor, knees drawn up.

I'm not –

You shouldn't be here now. You don't have a right to be here. She got up, leaning against the armrest of the couch so she could rub her foot.

Ingrid. Listen –

Was there someone else? You said there wasn't another woman, but *was* there?

No. I told you.

There was Erika.

That came later. I was with Erika; you were with Joel. Let's not talk about this.

You left us. You left your kids. She sat down heavily in the armchair, apart from him. And here you are again, back for the funeral of one of those kids. Ironic, don't you think?

We're tired, he said. We've been through hell.

One hell leads to another, she said.

Don't do this.

How could I have loved you? she said. I don't think I ever loved you.

Ingrid, it's not the time –

It might not be the time, but it does me good.

Does it?

No. No, of course not.

She went to the window and parted the curtains so he wouldn't see her crying. There was only blackness, rain slipping down the glass.

Nothing does any good, she cried. Why go on?

You have to. We have to. There's Damian.

Yes, there's Damian.

He needs you.

Sometimes I can't think about Damian. I just want to swallow a whole bottle of pills and go to sleep once and for all.

No, you don't.

He went to her, but she didn't want him.

It's despair, he said. That's what it is.

What do you know about despair? She twisted herself into the curtains so the sheer white material covered her head, her shoulders, her back.

I know about it, he said. She was my daughter too.

Ingrid was still wrapped in the curtains, so her head was swathed in white. She unwound herself.

I wish it had been me.

It's what I wish too – that it had been me – but you can't think that way.

I *do* think that way.

Just don't talk about doing yourself in, he told her. It's bad enough losing Lisa.

I don't want to live.

Yes, you do. You were always tough-minded. Of the two of us, you were the strongest.

Why are you being kind to me?

You know why.

No, why?

Because it's what we need. You need it, I need it, Damian needs it, or we'll never get through.

She stood still, looking at him.

I wasn't telling you the truth before, she said. About us, about – I did love you, you know.

I know. We loved each other, Ingrid.

She stacked the photos carefully in several piles and rose from the desk, going back to the kitchen where she scrubbed out the saucepan in which she'd heated the milk. Her scrubbing was fierce, more than the saucepan needed. She wasn't safe in the living room; she wasn't safe in the kitchen. She wasn't safe from herself anywhere in the house.

In the game of Prisoner's Dilemma, prisoners didn't have to stay silent, betray each other, or suffer punishment. They could co-operate. But what if, thought Ingrid, her thoughts apparently swimming from one side of her head to the other, what if Prisoner A was also Prisoner B?

What if the game was played against the self?

It was impossible to sleep; it was too hot. She went back into the living room and lay down on the chesterfield. She must have dozed for a while, because when she woke it was dawn.

She wondered, confusedly, whether Damian had come home. Maybe she hadn't heard him. She went down the hall and opened the screened door, where she saw Damian cutting across the front lawn, large as life. But when she stepped outside to look around the corner of the porch, there was no car parked in the driveway. He continued walking across the soft grass of the lawn, with an easy, confident way of carrying himself. It was as if he didn't have a care in the world.

Ingrid had spent the night worrying. Damian had been with some girl.

She watched as he crossed the street and stood by the stone wall next to the gorge. A man on a bicycle zipped by, and a plump woman jogged slowly along the sidewalk, but he didn't notice them. Finally he sauntered back to the house, stooping to pick something when he got to the porch steps. He sniffed it. When he came into the kitchen, Ingrid saw that what he'd picked wasn't grass; it was a bunch of clover, with rounded purple blossoms that nodded in his hand. He looked like someone who'd opened a door at the beginning of the world.

DAMIAN HAD FOUND HIMSELF in Jasmine's bedroom. She'd invited him in, first to the kitchen, where they'd talked, and then to the bedroom, where she lit a candle and loosened the tie-dyed curtains, drawing them across the window. There was a mattress on the floor, neatly covered with a thin quilt, and, beside it, a girlish lamp with a china ballerina holding her arms up to the lacy shade. Jasmine had invited him into her room, but the mattress on the floor hadn't invited him. The tie-dyed curtains and the china ballerina hadn't invited him.

She stood near the window, shyly, her hair falling around her face.

Scared? he asked.

She unbuttoned her pale green dress.

I've never done this. She didn't lift her head as she spoke. I mean, I have done this, but not as fast as –

We don't have to sleep together. Not if you're scared.

I know.

He kissed her bare shoulder, where the dress had slipped. She shifted a little and let the dress drop to her waist. She looked at him squarely, naked to her hips. Her breasts were not large, but they were full. Her ribs showed under the skin, and he was aware of the rapid way her chest rose and fell. She was frightened; he was frightened. She stepped out of her dress.

There, she said.

You're sure you're all right with this?

She nodded.

He took off his shirt, his jeans. Come here, he said gently, holding her close so he wouldn't be nervous.

She pulled him down to the mattress with her.

You're so smooth, he whispered. Your skin is smooth. You taste – he ran his tongue over the lobe of her ear – sweet. You taste like clover.

Clover? She laughed.

Haven't you ever eaten clover?

No.

It's sweet. You can taste the honey in it.

She blew out the candle. When they made love, he came, but she didn't, or at least he didn't think she had. They lay close together, entwined in each other. He didn't speak for a long time and neither did she. Words would make it smaller.

He drew a finger along her neck.

Are you okay? he asked.

Yes.

No, you're not.

What did we just do? she asked.

I don't know, he said. It was like lightning.

She kissed his arm, she kissed his shoulder and lay back, stretching her arms.

You taste of salt, she said.

He stroked his hand along her rib cage, along the pale

brown skin of her stomach. The hair between her legs was a triangle of blue-black. Her thighs were strong. And her knees – he circled his finger around the cap of one knee and then the other – her knees were perfect. He kissed the left one, the right one. He kissed her flat belly, her breasts, her neck.

You're beautiful.

You don't even know me.

I know enough to want you.

When he kissed her, she kissed him back. She put her tongue inside his mouth, her eyes half-closed.

He gave himself up to it.

She'd been sleeping when he woke, early. The sky was already light, and he could hear a robin outside the window. She was turned away from him, dark hair against soft skin, and he wanted to kiss the place where her hair sloped over her neck, but he'd wake her if he did. He got up and dressed, but he couldn't help himself, and knelt to kiss her neck.

You're going? she asked, turning, her eyes fluttering open and then closing.

Yes.

It can't be six o'clock yet.

It's just after five.

And you're going?

He combed his hand through her hair.

Don't go yet, she said, her eyes still closed.

You have to go to work later.

But you don't have to work. You could just stay here.

I'll come back tonight, he told her, tucking her hair behind her ear. He bent down and kissed her earlobe.

Mmmm, she murmured. Come here. You can't go just yet.

He took off his jeans quickly and lay down with her again. She wrapped herself around him.

I could stay like this all day, she said. With you inside me.

I couldn't last the whole day.

She laughed. I'd wear you out. Then she grew serious. What?

What if you don't show up tonight? Would that make it a one-night stand?

I'll show up, he said.

He'd show up.

When he got to his uncle's, he didn't go inside the house; he walked across the road to look at the Niagara Gorge. He'd left her. Why had he left her? Her body had been soft against the sheets. She'd been warm. When he kissed her, he felt her open up to him, as if their bodies already knew each other.

He could have made her coffee and taken it to her in bed.

His mind was racing. He stopped and leaned against the stone wall, looking down at the swift river far below. It was hot and hazy already, but the trees were thick with light, and overlaid against the darker clusters of leaves were pale green ones, tissue-fine. There was nothing on the road yet, except for a man on a bicycle. Damian could hear the roar of the Falls, even though they were a long way off and partly obscured by mist. A jogger went past, slowly, so he could hear the heavy sound of her breathing. Her hair was grey; she was overweight. She plodded by him.

He didn't want anyone to come into it: not this woman or the man on the bicycle. He wanted to be alone with the thought of Jasmine lying on the bed with her back to him, so he could see the curve of her spine, and, under the sheet, the swell of her hip.

Where's the car? asked Ingrid. She was in the kitchen when he got back, furiously washing out a mug. The water was running hard in the sink.

The car?

She turned off the tap and put down the wet mug on the counter with a bang.

You took the car last night, she said. If you *remember*. You wanted to see some girl, and you took the car and stayed out all night and I was sick to death worrying about you. You stayed out all night.

He didn't look at her. He'd forgotten all about the car. He must have walked right past it in the driveway when he left Jasmine's.

I have the keys, he said, taking them out of his pocket and staring at them. There was the pink elephant attached to the key ring. There was the white plastic Eiffel Tower that always caught on the zipper when Ingrid was trying to get the keys out of her purse.

Where the hell were you, Damian? she cried. I've been up all night, sitting on the porch until the bugs ate me alive. Then I came inside and – where were you? I almost called the police, but I didn't. But you know, you're as bad as Elvis, you're just as bad as Elvis. Someone has to watch out for you.

You don't have to watch out for me. I'll go back and get the car, he said, realizing he was very tired. I'm sorry, he added.

You're sorry. You're sorry, but there's no car. Damian, there's no car.

I know, he said. I'll get it.

Her face was pale and there were dark shadows under her eyes. He looked at the floor instead, but the nails of her bare feet were curiously yellow. The hem of her cotton bathrobe was frayed and a few threads hung down.

It's six-thirty in the morning, she said wearily. I can see that you didn't give a thought to any of this, did you? I'm going to bed, and when I get up I'd like to see the car back in the driveway.

I said I'd get it.

Yes, you get it. It's not my business if you're with some girl, but at least you could have some consideration.

I didn't know. I mean, I didn't know I'd be with her.

You've been here less than two weeks, so that means you've known her about five minutes.

It's not like that.

No?

No, it's not like that.

Well, I hope you have a few condoms in your wallet when you're with whoever she is. I hope you know what you're doing. That's all.

She went down the hall; he could hear her bare feet against the floor.

I'll be with her tonight, he said, with a harsh edge to his voice. Maybe I'll be with her the night after that.

Suit yourself, she said, quite calmly. I thought you had a reason for coming here, but I see I was wrong.

He heard her on the steps. He wanted to go to the bottom of the steps and shout after her not to wait up for him, never to wait up for him.

Fuck. He banged the screened door behind him when he went out. He didn't care if it woke his uncle.

It was only when he was walking beside the gorge ten minutes later, pitching pebbles over the stone wall, that he allowed himself to think of his mother, lying on the bed in her frayed cotton bathrobe, her eyes shut tightly, the way people do when they're trying not to cry.

He stayed with Jasmine that night, and the night after that. The third night, they smoked a joint and ate a large bag of chips at the kitchen table.

You never talk about your family, she said.

There's not much to say.

But –

But what?

I saw you one night. You were with a man in pyjamas.

You saw me?

Yes.

I was with Elvis. He's my cousin.

You were watching me, she said, drawing a little circle on the table with her index finger. The two of you. And then you tracked me down the next day. Why did you do that?

When I saw you, I don't know – I wanted to know who you were.

And now you know me?

I know you come from Saskatchewan. Lanigan, Saskatchewan. I know you have a sister called Shirl, and that once you had a dog named Queenie. You're smart and talented, and God, every time I look at you I get weak in the knees.

Weak in the knees?

Yes, he laughed. I can't stand up. I have to lie down.

He leaned back in his chair.

You're right, he went on.

About what?

I know a little about you; you know a little about me. We don't know a lot about each other. I'm just going on instinct here. Aren't you?

Yes.

She took him by the hand into her bedroom, lit the candle in the butter dish, and blew out the match.

Okay, just one thing, she said. I want to know whether you're going to go back home and leave me in the lurch.

He lay down beside her, breathing the acrid smell of the match. She put her leg over his.

I have to go home at some point, he said. But I don't plan on leaving you in the lurch.

She was quiet, looking at him.

Don't you trust me? he asked.

Yes.

I trust you. Everything about you. You're so –

I'm so – ?

She shifted herself on top of him. She sat astride his body, bending down and kissing him. He felt himself coming apart, as if she were taking him out of a skin he'd always been inside. She pulled him out of one skin and then another; he felt her lifting him out of each one. When she leaned back and rocked him, slowly at first and then faster, he came too soon, all in a rush.

Sorry, he said. I –

Shhh.

She lay next to him and he ran his hand over her belly. Her body was lovely in the half-light of the candle: her legs were long and slender. How dark they seemed against the white, rumpled sheets.

You were going to tell me about the daredevils, she said, kissing him again. She kissed his body, all over, tasting his skin. You were going to tell me about the woman who went across the Falls on a tightrope.

How can I tell you when you're doing that?

There, she said. I stopped. She leaned over and picked up the dish with the candle, holding it between them so the glow of the flame made their faces luminous.

She traced the side of his face with her finger. Your eyes are sort of grey, aren't they? They've got a dark rim and then they get lighter toward the pupil.

She put the candle down, in its blue and white dish, on the floor near the bed.

You're the best thing that's ever happened to me, he said.

You'd say anything. Do you say that to every woman?

No. Mostly I don't know what to say. I start to stutter.

You start to stutter.

He liked it when she laughed. Her teeth were very white.

I've been with two women, he said. That's it. One of them thought I was an economic risk. The other was put off by the stuttering. What about you?

She looked up at the ceiling. I had a boyfriend in high

school. His name was Jared – he liked dirt bike racing. And cream soda; he was the only guy I ever knew who liked cream soda. He could drink five or six at a sitting. Once he drank thirteen and then he threw up on my black capris. I had a lap full of pink vomit.

He must have really liked you. I hate to think what he'd do if someone gave him beer.

She hit him with the pillow, but he caught it, laughing, and kissed her. He kissed her eyes.

It feels like butterflies, she said.

She stroked his braid and sat up so she could undo it.

It's weird when you do that, he said, his eyes shut. Lisa used to –

Lisa? said Jasmine, dropping her hands.

Fuck, he murmured, without opening his eyes.

He'd done it. He'd let Lisa come into it and already he could feel the brief, sharp joy slipping away from him. Away it slipped, through the upturned fingers of a hand, under a four-wheeler, down to the ocean.

My sister, he said. Lisa.

Your sister? But you said you didn't have sisters. Or brothers.

You asked me, but I didn't go into it.

So you have a sister.

I had a sister, he said. He sat up and undid the rest of the braid.

What do you mean?

I had a sister, but she's dead. Her name was Lisa. She was seventeen when she died.

Oh, said Jasmine in a small voice. I'm sorry.

It was an accident – she drowned in just a few inches of water.

God, whispered Jasmine again. She lay down and pulled the sheet up to her neck. When?

Less than a year ago.

He sat very still, his face withdrawn into shadow. His eyes were wet with tears.

Jasmine, he said softly.

Yes?

He was looking down at her. A moment like this couldn't last and last, he thought. How could it last? It would slip away, like everything else.

Maria Spelterini, he said.

What?

Maria Spelterini was the first woman tightrope walker at the Falls. In 1875 or 1876 – something like that. She came out of nowhere, and disappeared after one summer. They criticized her because she didn't do stunts, so she started wearing peach buckets on her feet, or she'd go across in chains and shackles. But she was just as good as the rest of them, probably as good as Blondin when he was the same age.

How old was she?

Twenty-three. But everyone talks about Blondin. The Great Blondin. He was the first to go across the gorge. He could do anything on a tightrope: push a wheelbarrow, cook an omelette, carry his manager on his back. He went across blindfolded, but they all did that. Maria Spelterini put a paper bag over her head.

But how could you do it without being able to see? she asked.

I don't know.

Damian saw how she was turning it over in her mind. Maybe she was thinking about the whole world reduced to a tightrope strung between one side of the gorge and the other, and Maria Spelterini with a paper bag over her head, balancing on it, with only a shuddering cable under the arch of each foot, trusting a pole to keep steady while the wind gusted this way and that, knowing there was nothing under the tightrope but thin air, and, farther below, the swift, dark water.

SO YOU'RE JASMINE, said Ingrid.

Yes.

Well, I'm glad to meet you – finally. You're a very pretty girl.

Thank you.

Damian's mother was the same height as her son, Jasmine thought. They had the same bone structure, and though her hair was white, her skin was tanned in that same smooth way. Her eyes were penetrating. She must have been over fifty, Jasmine thought, but like Damian, she was striking.

Is that what's called a nose stud? asked Ingrid. In your nostril?

Yes.

I suppose you could get anything pierced, couldn't you? Your ears, your eyebrows, your nose. You could just go on and on, getting things pierced.

Anything at all.

Ingrid raised her eyes to the ceiling, as if considering it, before going back to slicing the havarti into neat pieces.

Jasmine didn't think Ingrid liked her. It had to do with

the way she was slicing the cheese. Then she reminded herself that Ingrid had lost a daughter, and that made her feel sorry for her. But she also thought that Ingrid was the kind of person who wouldn't want anyone feeling sorry for her.

Ingrid put the cheese, the slices fanned out, on a green plate on the table. And you and Damian have known each other now for –

A week and a half, interjected Damian.

A week and a half.

Jasmine moved her silver bangles up and down her arm.

Jasmine, help yourself to lemonade, said Ingrid briskly. Or there's white wine. Would you like some white wine? It's probably not the best Chablis around, but it'll do. Yes? I'll get you a goblet. There, no, not that one, Damian, I think we'll use the other ones. That's right. So, Damian said you're from Saskatchewan, Jasmine.

Yes, from Lanigan.

And does your family live right in Lanigan?

They moved in from out of town.

It must have been nice being out of town.

It was. But my parents sold the land when they ran out of money, and now they have a mini-home. A mobile home.

They went bankrupt? Ingrid handed Jasmine a goblet. There are crackers – yes, help yourself to some of that liver pâté that Roger wanted, and to the vegetables and crab dip, and then we should all go out on the porch, don't you think?

Jasmine sat down in a chair at the kitchen table. She felt weary. It was true: her parents had gone bankrupt. She recalled her mother and father in the kitchen during that time when they'd realized they would have to declare bankruptcy. Her mother had put her arms around her father.

We'll be fine, you know, Tom, her mother had said. We'll be fine.

Jasmine put the goblet of cool wine to her lips and closed her eyes as she sipped it. When she looked up, Damian was gazing at her fondly. But she was still nervous. A house like this made her nervous. Even the kitchen was big.

She'd asked Damian what dress to wear – the yellow or the blue – and he'd said the blue. She had flip-flops with daisies on them, and they slapped against the floor when she walked, so it was better to sit still, waiting for someone to ask her whether she had any navel piercings.

Oh, and here's Elvis, said Ingrid brightly. You're back early from the workshop, Elvis, aren't you? Well, come in and say hello to Jasmine. Jasmine is Damian's friend.

Elvis simply stood in the doorway looking at Jasmine.

The man in pyjamas, Jasmine thought. It unsettled her, even though she knew he'd be here. He no longer resembled the man in pyjamas. He wore a silky black shirt, unbuttoned to the fourth button, and the black contrasted with his soft, childish skin, and freckles scattered in a blizzard of soft brown specks all over his face and the V of his exposed chest.

When's your birthday? said Elvis.

My birthday? asked Jasmine, puzzled.

Full name, date of birth, place of birth. Elvis clutched a Mickey Mouse lunch box.

Sandra Blakeney, except I changed my name to Jasmine, after a little white flower, because I liked it better than Sandra. I decided that on the bus outside of Saskatoon.

You did? said Damian.

Yes. So, it's Jasmine – Jasmine Jane Blakeney, August 2, 1989. Saskatoon, Saskatchewan.

Ingrid dropped a knife with a clatter. August 2, she said. She picked up the knife. That's less than a week away. You'll be all of nineteen years old.

Yes, I know, it's kind of a shock to think of being nineteen.

You're just eighteen. You're so young – Elvis, stop staring, and come and wash out your lunch box. Yes, we'll have to have a birthday party, won't we, Damian? Now where's Roger? Here I got the pâté specially. Yes, we'll have to have a cake and some champagne. That's what we'll do. Elvis, stop staring, please. It's rude.

I'd like a party, agreed Jasmine.

You have a nice face, said Elvis suddenly. I like your face a lot.

Thank you.

Jasmine wished Elvis would stop staring. She wished that Ingrid would stop making her feel as if she were an animal in a zoo. Something large and lumbering, like a bear.

There you are, Roger! said Ingrid. I was wondering where on earth you were.

I was lost. Roger shuffled forward into the kitchen.

Lost? Ingrid motioned for the others to move out of the way.

On this street, yes – this street.

How did you do that?

I got turned around coming outside Wang's Variety because there was a truck right up on the sidewalk and I had to go around it. I could smell tar –

Oh, they're paving that little parking lot between Wang's and the triplex. I forgot to tell you.

Roger found a chair and sat down abruptly. He wiped his forehead, and folded up the sections of his cane, but his hands were shaking. His hands didn't stop working when the cane was folded up. His fingers unfolded it and folded it again.

Jasmine watched him helplessly. Damian had warned her that his uncle was blind, but she had no idea what to do or what to say.

Damian, why don't you show Jasmine around the house? suggested Ingrid. Show her the butterfly cases on the wall upstairs.

Jasmine followed Damian, but the voices floated along with her as she ascended the stairs.

I couldn't get situated, Roger was saying. I just couldn't get my bearings.

Here they are. Damian stopped at the end of the hall and gestured at the cases on the wall. My grandfather's collection.

Will your uncle be all right? Jasmine said. He didn't look very well.

No, he didn't.

It must be frightening for him sometimes.

Damian took her hand. Look, he said.

The butterflies and moths were pinned, row on row, in three framed shadow boxes covered with glass. The labels were printed carefully with the Latin name first and the common name in brackets.

You really *are* showing me the butterflies.

I get to be alone with you this way. See, this is the Mother-of-Pearl Morpho.

Morpho laertes, Jasmine said. The white is almost shiny – like silk. And the markings – see? They're so delicate.

He kissed her neck.

No, don't. I'm looking at them.

Should I leave you alone?

Here's the Madagascar Moon Moth.

Mmmm.

Jasmine could hear Ingrid's voice grow louder downstairs.

Roger said something in a low voice.

Your mother doesn't like me, said Jasmine.

She likes you, said Damian. What she doesn't like is the fact that I'm being, as she says, irresponsible. I said it was none of her business. But we cleared the air, and then she said she wanted to meet you.

Jasmine heard a door bang downstairs. I can tell when someone doesn't like me.

Damian put his arms around her. He held her tightly and they faced the butterflies and moths on the wall.

You could draw them, she said.

I could, but I'd rather draw you.

They'd spent the day in her bedroom as he drew her from different angles. It had taken hours. He hadn't wanted her to move, but it had been hard to keep the same pose. There was something about him, she realized, something that drove him in a way that was completely single-minded. What was it? It was as if he'd forgotten about her and yet he hadn't forgotten about her. It was just that he'd gone so deep into her, he didn't see her anymore. And then, when he was finished, he wasn't happy with what he'd done.

There's the Luna Moth, he murmured into her hair. I've seen one of those.

It's pretty.

They're nocturnal, so it's rare to see one. I saw one hanging on the screened door at home. It didn't move. And then I realized it was dead.

Actias luna, she said.

Come here. He took her down the hall.

What?

My bedroom. Well, it's the guest room, but right now it's mine.

It's a little weird to be in your bedroom, she said.

Why?

I don't know. Your mother's downstairs with your uncle. Jasmine went to the window and stood pensively.

He joined her. You can see the Niagara Gorge –

Elvis came into the room and put his guitar down on Damian's bed.

Hi, Elvis, said Jasmine.

That's where the old Schoellkopf Power Station used to be, there, across the river, Damian said, pointing. You can't see a whole lot, though, because of the trees.

I'd be looking out this window all the time, she said.

Looking out the window all the time. Elvis laughed, bouncing a couple of times on Damian's bed.

Jasmine touched the box on the top of his bureau. What's this?

Oh, said Damian. Nothing much.

It's all taped up, she said. Pandora's box.

It's nothing.

Elvis got up from the bed and took the box. He shook it, listening, putting it up to one ear and then the other.

Don't, Elvis, said Damian.

Why not?

Because it's not yours. Leave it alone. His voice was sharp.

Not yours. Elvis put down the box and lay on the bed again, his sneakers sticking out like clown feet. He gazed at

Jasmine. You have a nice face, he repeated. I like your face.

Well, thank you, Elvis.

I want to kiss your face all over. Is it okay if I kiss your face all over?

No, Elvis, that is not okay, said Damian.

But she has a nice face, said Elvis mournfully.

Yes, she has a very nice face. I think it's time to go, Elvis. Time to go.

Elvis picked up his guitar and went slowly to the door, which Damian shut behind him. He locked it and turned to Jasmine.

What? he said.

I don't know. It was the way you were with him.

I just put a stop to it.

He didn't mean any harm.

But I don't want him saying those things to you, said Damian, going close to her. He can't kiss your face all over. You don't want him doing that, do you?

No, but it's almost as if you're jealous.

Jealous of Elvis?

Well, if it's not jealousy, it's something else.

I want to put a wall around us.

A wall?

To keep things out. Maybe I'm selfish. He pressed against her. You're so –

Don't say I'm beautiful, she said. She felt the weight of his body against her as she leaned against the wall.

Why not? You are. God, you are.

He found the hem of her sundress and pulled it up, sliding his hands up her thighs.

Don't. She flung herself away from him, and stood by the door, straightening her dress, smoothing it.

Jasmine –

What *is* in that box, anyway? she said angrily. That box you won't let anyone touch?

It's – never mind.

The screened door banged as Ingrid went out.

He'd made her angry. Well, to hell with it. Roger finished the wine in his glass and ate a little pâté straight off the blunt knife. He fumbled around for a couple of crackers. He'd scared himself. His heart was still racing.

He'd lost his way. It was like being in Antarctica in a snowstorm. But he was always in a storm. The snow whirled around him, day and night.

Abruptly, he recalled kissing the waitress from Giorgio's. He'd put his hands up to her face. Mandy, from Amanda, she'd told him. She was twenty-two and he was fifty-six. Her lips were like plump cushions; he could have gone to sleep on them.

Christ, she'd said to him. I thought blind guys knew how to kiss.

As soon as she spoke he realized he didn't want to kiss her. He'd got it wrong. He was fifty-six and he'd got it wrong again.

Now Damian had met someone. The way it went was that one of them would give something and the other would give something and after that they'd start taking from each other. He and Marnie had taken from each other until nothing was left. But he'd get fucked up if he kept thinking these things. Anyway, the way he'd been with Marnie wasn't the way Damian would be with Jasmine.

Roger went slowly to the sink, leaned against it, and

took two plastic tumblers out of the cabinet. He ran water in one and then the other, checking the levels with his finger and pouring a little out of them until they were three-quarters full. This was the test, he thought, the thing he hadn't been able to do. He could carry one glass of water, but not two. With a glass in each hand, he moved in the direction of the kitchen table. It was only a few paces from him, but it might have been half a mile away. Cautiously he went, trying to balance the glasses, shifting from his left foot to his right foot.

On the fifth step he bumped into a chair, his own chair, the one he hadn't pushed back close to the table. He tripped and the glasses flew out of his hands. He cried out as he crashed to the floor.

Tears came to his eyes as he lay there. He couldn't do anything for himself. He'd got lost that very day on his own street.

When he'd been suspended upside down over Niagara Falls, he'd been, as he said later in the bar, scared shitless. The cameraman got him a beer, but he hardly touched it. It was on the table in front of him, a blurry glass, hardly a glass at all. The cameraman asked him what had possessed him to do it then, if he'd been scared shitless. It wasn't so much the hanging over the Falls that frightened him, Roger had said, trying to recall everything exactly. It was when the crane was lowering him down to the brink that he'd wanted to get out of it, but he'd been in a straitjacket, and there was no getting out of it. He'd heard people yelling, despite the thundering noise of the water.

He'd had better vision then. He could see that the water was a rush of green before it went over the edge, then a rush of white as it fell, roaring, to the river. And as they lowered him down, the Falls came closer and closer. The cable gave one shudder, then another. It would break, he'd thought. It would break and he'd fall into those depths.

He hung upside down. He hung from the cable, looking into his own death. That's what he was doing, he'd thought, looking into the whiteness of his own death. He'd felt himself grow calm. It wasn't such a bad thing. He'd circled this way and that as he dangled at the end of the cable, but he felt his heart grow calm.

Roger? Are you all right, Roger? It's Jasmine. Do you want me to help you?

Roger was lying on the kitchen floor in a puddle of water. Jasmine picked up two plastic glasses and put them on the table.

Yes, he said, if you could help me up – there. Thank you.

She saw how his hands gripped the chair as if he thought it might tip over.

We haven't really met, he said, settling himself on the chair. I'm Roger and you're Jasmine.

Pleased to meet you.

Likewise. If I had a hat, I would doff it.

Doff it?

Yes, he laughed – a quick, strangled sound. That's what men do. No, it's what they used to do when they had hats. They'd doff them.

She laughed.

You think I'm crazy, he said.

No, not at all.

If Ingrid were here she'd say I'm crazy. But she's not here. Do you want to smoke a joint? he went on. I really think I'd like to smoke a joint.

Jasmine imagined Damian, upstairs in his room, listening.

We'll go outside to smoke it, though. That way the forces of good and evil won't be able to discover us. What do you think we should worry about most? The forces of good or the forces of evil?

I don't know. She didn't know what to say to calm him.

The forces of good always worried me most, he confided.

He made his way down the hall and she saw how his clothes were all wet. He'd been lost on his street and then he'd fallen down in his own kitchen. A wave of tenderness came over her as she held the screened door open for him. He fumbled his way to a chair on the porch and lowered himself into it, rummaging in his pocket before he found a plastic bag of rolled joints and a small red lighter.

I'll get you to help me, he said, handing her the bag and the lighter.

She lit a spliff, inhaled, and passed it to him. He drew the smoke in and passed it back.

It's good stuff, he said. Pure.

Mmmm.

They sat quietly for a long time, listening to passing cars.

This is one of the rare moments, he said. One of the lustrous moments. There are thousands of them, but this is one of them.

She turned her head toward him.

Strung together like pearls, he continued. Sometimes bad shit happens, but the string of pearls hangs in the air. Don't you think?

Jasmine lay back in the chair, feeling lazy, though something in the back of her mind kept bothering her. She pushed it away, concentrating on a string of pearls hovering just above her head. Roger had put the pearls there.

You went over the Falls once, she said, dreamily.

Twice. I didn't want to go over the Falls ass over teakettle and find myself going down headfirst. So I designed a barrel with a steel frame, about eight feet in diameter, with a six-ply –

Ass over teakettle, she said, laughing. God, that's funny. She took the end of the spliff from him again. But you didn't, she said. Go ass over teakettle.

No, the barrel went over just fine. We called it the Bomb Barrel – Ed Kusack and I. Ed was the one who helped me build it.

You must have been scared, though? Weren't you scared?

I was scared. Did we finish that one already? Let's light another.

Okay.

That's more like it, he said, when she lit another and passed it to him.

You went over the Falls twice, she said, so you must have got over being scared.

Jasmine felt light-headed now; she had the feeling her body could drift up to the top of the chestnut tree. What had she said to him? She'd forgotten what she'd said. Scared. She'd asked him if he'd been scared. She wished Damian would come downstairs, even though she was still annoyed with him. But her body was drifting away, over the roof of the neighbour's house.

I tried three times, you know, not just twice, Roger was saying. I tried three times and it worked twice. I got stuck once. The damn thing wouldn't go over; they'd lowered the water level. They saw me, and they lowered the water level, so I ran aground near the brink. It took the Parks Department two hours to haul me in, and they gave me a fine right then and there. But, you know, it doesn't always work.

What doesn't always work?

Lowering the water level, said Roger. That guy from Tennessee, for instance – Jesse somebody – was stuck just above the Falls. He was trying to go over, and they lowered the water level. So there he was, near Goat Island, getting out of his boat and dragging it over the shallow places. He went over, finally.

Jasmine was trying to follow him. Certain words snagged her. Tennessee. Goat Island. Dragging.

Sharp, yes, that was his name, said Roger, suddenly. Jesse Sharp. They never found him. Never found his body, I mean.

They sat without speaking.

But why couldn't they find it? she asked.

The Falls have a way of taking things and never giving them back.

Oh.

God, it's humid, said Roger. What time is it?

I don't know.

You're stoned, aren't you? said Roger. Well, that's because the stuff was pure. He put his hand on her arm for a moment. You've got to be alive and kicking when Ingrid comes back, kiddo, he said. Or she'll think I've corrupted you.

It's nice here, she said, but the small, nagging thing surfaced again. Tell me about Damian.

Damian?

Yes.

I may be his uncle, but it's not as if I know him well. Why?

She shook her head from side to side. I don't know. He gets – I don't know – kind of obsessed. It's like he wants to put me – put us – somewhere where no one else can come into it.

Maybe it has to do with losing his sister. He could be afraid.

Of what?

He could be afraid of losing you.

Maybe.

People can seem a little weird when they lose someone they care about. I was a little crazy myself, once.

She sat up to clear her head, but realized that things were clearer if she slid back down in the chair.

Are you okay? he asked.

Yes.

You're sure?

Mmmm.

Seems to me that you've got a wide-open heart, he said. And if you've got a heart like that, you just have to go easy.

I'll go easy, she said sleepily.

DAMIAN STOOD VERY STILL in the bedroom after Jasmine had gone downstairs. He could hear her talking to Roger, their voices muted. Then he realized that they'd gone out to the porch. He'd hear their conversation if he left the window up, but he didn't want to, and he closed it as noiselessly as he could. The room was stifling. He gripped the frame of the window.

It was a question of balancing. When he closed his eyes tightly he saw bright yellow spots blooming here and there in the darkness. But the bottom might fall out of things; he'd learned that the hard way.

Maybe it was just exhaustion. He moved to the bed and sat on it, rubbing his face hard with the palms of his hands. It didn't help; he couldn't stop crying.

Fuck, he whispered. Fuck.

The day he'd shot the hare, he'd left its long body slung across the muck of the path and kept going. The snow became thicker underfoot, and when he stepped between two spruce trees to avoid a slushy drift, he saw a small pond, iced over, though the ice had softened and turned the colour of pale jade. The limbs of a birch, frozen in it, were caught in such a way that he thought of a hand. A dead hand. No, not a dead hand. A birch limb.

He drew the afghan around his shoulders, like an oversized scarf. He didn't know why he'd brought it with him, because it was heavy and smelled vaguely of mould. He shouldered the gun, Adam's uncle's gun, which wasn't his to take. But Adam had shown him, on an earlier trip, one May weekend, that the key to the gun rack was just above it, on a ledge, and Damian found himself wanting to handle the Marlin. There was a Remington-Lee there too, and Adam had taken it and given Damian the Marlin. Then they'd drunk a lot of beer outside and shot up some of the beer cans. Damian liked the popping sound as the bullets struck the cans, though they didn't hit them often.

And afterward, when Adam had said that Damian wasn't a bad shot, Damian laughed. They were lying on the dead brown leaves that had fallen the autumn before, looking up at the bright canopy of green. Everything was alight up there. They lay without talking, and then one of them said a few words and the other answered, and they slipped back into silence. There was nothing to disturb them.

But there was no going back into that time. It was a time before.

Damian knew he should go downstairs to Jasmine and say he was sorry. But somehow he knew this was not what he would say to her. He would tell her something else, blurting out things he didn't mean to say. He'd say that his mother had given away Lisa's clothes, all of them, from her summer dresses to her good cloth coat and brown leather jacket. Even the blue dress she'd worn to the dance with Trevor. He'd watched his mother doing this, sorting things methodically in Lisa's bedroom. But Damian had managed to save the blue high-heeled shoes, taking them out of Lisa's bedroom with the intention of putting them on his own bookshelf.

He'd balanced them on his palms, one on each hand, without knowing what to do with them. Each shoe had a thin shaft of heel, supporting a cushion for the foot, then a slope, gently curved, down to the delicately shaped place for the toes, with two straps across, finely engineered as miniature suspension bridges, with the rosette linking the straps. He'd turned around in his room looking for a place to put them, still holding the shoes on the palms of his hands. Then he noticed where the toes – Lisa's toes – had pressed down on the insole. It was the merest imprint, a ghost of her.

He would tell Jasmine about the shoes. She'd look at him strangely, with no idea what he was talking about.

When Jasmine was near him, he wanted her to be closer. She was miraculous to him. He wanted her to lie down with him so he could feel the ridges of her pelvic bones and the supple skin of her stomach between those bones. He wanted her. Even when he drew her, when he was some distance from her and concentrating on observing her precisely, it was a way of going inside her, of having her, a way of leaving himself behind.

Before he arrived at the hill above the river he knew what he was going to do, as if he had already seen both the hill and the river in a long-ago dream. He knew he would sit down in the snow at the top of the steep incline. So when he got there, and brushed the snow from a stump, seating himself, he was simply confirming what was inevitable. He drew the afghan close, wrapping it around his body, since his skin was clammy with the cold. He put the gun across his knees.

From his vantage point on the stump he could pay attention to the late-morning sunlight jittering across the water below. The riverbanks were edged with a crust of ice, and the water was the colour of ink. The river widened out and then narrowed so the water churned through a gap; here the rocks above the water's edge were decorated with a frieze of ice. Warriors, maybe, running with spears in their hands.

His teeth chattered and his eyes began to fill up. It was too fierce a thing; it came over him and there was nothing he could do but let it come. He could feel himself begin to heave, and he retched a stream of yellow vomit into the snow next to him. He sat still until the nausea passed, then dug a handful of clean snow and put it in his mouth to rinse it. He spat, dried his eyes on his sleeve, and took up the gun, cocking the hammer and placing it in the best position between his legs. Now he saw that he'd have to extend his arm to get at the trigger. He'd have to drop one shoulder to extend his arm fully, though it was entirely possible to do it. The trigger would have to be pushed rather than pulled. He hadn't thought any of it through, and now it came to him as if it was part of a slowed-down film. One action, then another. Each action was separate; it was not linked to the next. The wiping of his nose, for instance, had nothing to do with him leaning forward to rest the gun against the trunk of a birch tree.

He got up and paced around in a circle, and then went

back to the stump and sat down, wrapping himself in the afghan in such a way that it would leave his arms free. Then he took up the rifle and realized the bulky afghan was in the way. He flung it into the snow and put the rifle between his legs, sliding the end of the gun's barrel into his mouth, immediately wanting to retch again because of the taste of the metal. But he willed himself not to. As he raised his fingers to the trigger, it seemed to him that the gesture resembled that of a cellist getting ready to play.

All his senses were alert and keen. He thought of the snowshoe hare and its twitching nose. Everything dazzled his eyes. The water in the narrowed gap of the river could have been plunging horses: down they went, and down again, into the pitch-black water. The sound was soothing, blending with the wind. And the woods too, though he hadn't noticed until this moment, were laid bare in the first warmth of spring, with the birches vulnerable and white in the midst of the spruce.

Within days, weeks, everything would be furred with the softness of new growth. The leaves would unfurl from new buds, pink as kittens' noses, and open fully, allowing the light to pierce them and reveal a tracery of veins. Hundreds and thousands of leaves would come to life. And the river, unspooling in its long, winding bed, would move above stones and around them, pushing against one bend, another, dropping over the side of an old beaver lodge, so it could keep rushing in full spate.

And spring would turn to summer, and the days would pour from one to another, warm as honey.

Nearby, a slate-coloured junco landed on a rotting log, measuring him with its dark eye before it flew to the other end of the log, surveying him from a greater distance, as if inquiring what he was doing there. Its head and back were sooty, almost blue, but its breast was white. Its beak was the colour of butter. It stayed for a moment at the far end of the log, then flew away.

It would take a while before anyone found him. He'd be nothing more than a corpse.

Damian took the gun from his mouth and shoved it away so it fell into the snow; he didn't want anything more to do with it.

He stood, picked up the afghan, and shook it, putting it around his shoulders as he'd done before. He retrieved the rifle – making sure the safety was on – and brushed it off, walking back along the path the way he'd come. When he came to the dead hare, he bent over it. He took up the creature by its ears, so it hung loosely from his hand. Later, when he got back to the cabin, he leaned the rifle inside the door, found a rusty shovel in the corner of the mud room, and went back outside. The ground was still hard, and it was difficult to dig a hole for the body. He wound up taking it away from the cabin, since he knew the crows would find it. He covered it with snow and returned to the cabin, taking off his boots on the steps before going inside. He was breathing rapidly, he realized, as he washed his hands at the sink, and to calm himself he sat for a while on the couch.

He closed his eyes and thought of Lisa. How they'd once argued over Trevor. It was so long ago now, and it seemed idiotic to have let the argument go on, twisting into something else that had nothing to do with Trevor, about things that hadn't mattered.

He made himself get up and go to the stove, putting a little cooking oil in the old cast-iron frying pan and cracking four eggs into it. What mattered, even now, was the look on her face. He'd made her so angry she'd shouted at him. He scrambled the eggs and made himself some toast, eating straight out of the frying pan by the stove, breaking the toast in two and scooping up the egg with the pieces.

What do you know, Damian? Lisa had said. You've never loved anyone. You haven't, have you?

He put the frying pan in the sink and ran water in it. The water bubbled and hissed as it landed on the hot pan and spatula.

Lisa, he shouted. He banged the frying pan against the sink so the spatula jumped out of the pan and onto the floor. Get the fuck out of my head.

The room was hot and Damian got up from the bed and went to the window, which scraped as he opened it. He didn't care if it made noise, whether they heard it on the porch. He went into the bathroom and dropped his clothes on the floor, and stepped into the shower. The water washed over his head and chest, and he turned to let it pummel his neck and back. He soaped himself down, rinsed and stepped out onto the mat, reaching for the green towel, which was the one he'd been given, rather than the blue one, which he'd used earlier. The blue one belonged to his uncle, and it was positioned exactly where Roger knew to reach for it. There was a striped one on the hook at the back of the door; this was the one his mother used.

He put his clothes back on and went downstairs, but it was the last thing he wanted to do, so he went slowly. No doubt she was still angry with him. But it was strange that he heard no conversation, not a word between Jasmine and his uncle.

He opened the screened door onto the porch and found her curled up on a chair. She was sound asleep, and her mouth was half-open. Roger was sitting next to her, so still that he could have been asleep too.

Jasmine, said Damian.

She blinked, then sat up and brushed her hands through her hair.

I'll walk you home, he said. It's getting late.

Oh.

Are you coming?

It looks like it's time for me to go, she said, but she wasn't speaking to Damian, she was speaking to Roger.

She stayed where she was. She looked sleek as a cat, with her hair falling across her face.

Need a hand? Damian asked.

All right. She slipped her feet into her flip-flops, studying them.

I'll walk you home, he said again, after she got up. I don't think you're clear-headed enough to ride your bike.

All right. She put a hand out to the chair to steady herself. Good night, Roger.

Be good, said Roger. It's the witching hour.

She laughed.

It irritated Damian. It was as if they'd known each other for years. Yet Damian was the one who took her hand, who led her through the house and out the back door.

Jasmine tossed the hair from her face and slowly turned to get her bicycle. Damian didn't help her, though she probably could have used some help, judging by her unsteadiness. And yet he'd have done whatever she asked. He'd fallen for her, and this, too, made him angry.

INGRID BOUGHT A TICKET for the *Maid of the Mist*. She'd been on it as a child, and now she saw it exactly as it had been then, when she'd waited in line, together with Roger, with one tall parent on either side. She'd stood very straight, because there were two things she had been told she could improve: her posture and her manners. She was very proud of her black patent leather purse with a gold clasp, a purse that opened and shut with a *click*, and had a blue lining that she was sure was made of silk. All she had in the purse was a handkerchief with lace around the edges, a piece of Dubble Bubble gum that her parents didn't know about, a comb, and a tube, banded with gold, of Ruby Pleasure lipstick that her mother had thrown away and Ingrid had retrieved. She wore a grey dress, a hand-knitted white sweater, a black hair ribbon, and white gloves, each fastened with a single pearl, and she'd fanned out her white hands to look at the gloves as they waited. She had been deliciously happy because of her new dress, black ribbon, and white gloves, soon to be covered in a poncho, because they were going on a great adventure. But it was not a great adventure for Roger, who had been told to stop frowning.

How infuriating he was, thought Ingrid. Even now, so many years later. When he'd been lost on the street that very afternoon, she'd worried about him. He'd come in looking strained and exhausted, his forehead glistening and strands of grey hair falling about his face. His hands had worked frantically, folding and unfolding his cane. How could she calm him? She'd suggested getting a guide dog, but he didn't want a guide dog, because he knew what would happen – he'd give it a name like Bounder and start getting fond of it, and then it would just get hit by a car or something. So she'd changed the subject; she'd told him about meeting Jasmine.

That's the name of a flower, he said. Jasmine.

She has a nose stud, Ingrid said. A little green emerald. She probably has her nipples pierced too, for all I know.

So what you're saying is you think she's a slut.

No, I'm not saying that at all. She's a pretty little thing, Ingrid went on. You can see why – ·

You can see why someone like Damian would be all over her.

She's sleeping with him. He's sleeping with her.

Ingrid, said Roger. Get over it.

I'm going out.

And she'd gone, banging the door behind her.

So here she was, no longer a child, but an adult in line with thirty or forty others, and together they made the descent in the elevator. She imagined that the elevator would get stuck, and then she'd have to spend the night with Jason, who had a Buffalo Bills cap and a whining voice, his mother, with her pink shorts and bulging thighs, and his uninterested father. There was a man with sallow skin and green clip-on glasses, and his wife, two feet shorter, who wore a peacock-coloured sari patterned lightly with flowers; when Ingrid looked at it she felt as though she'd entered a jungle. An older woman with mauve-tinted hair dug her elbow into Ingrid.

Oh, she was sorry, she was awfully sorry. The woman clasped her hands in front of her and whispered to her friend that she felt claustrophobic, so claustrophobic in places like this.

When the elevator opened and disgorged them, it was as though they were moving down a tunnel to the gates of Hell. It was suffocatingly hot inside the terminal. Ingrid waited to be given her raincoat, which felt like plastic wrap when she put it on, and followed the peacock-coloured sari past the turnstile and up the ramp to the boat. It was cool on the deck, and even from this distance there was a fine spray from the Falls.

Though she'd been on the *Maid of the Mist* on that Saturday outing years before, Ingrid was surprised that the boat managed to move upstream at all. She could feel the river resisting them, as if at any moment the boat might be spun away and driven downstream. Yet the boat kept chugging deliberately toward the Falls, first to the American Falls, with the yellow ponchos making their way down to the lookout and back up, and then to the Horseshoe Falls. How dreadfully predictable it was.

There was so much spray as they approached the Falls that Ingrid had to draw the raincoat close and put up her hood. She felt the vibration of the diesel engines against the thunder of the water. Lisa would have loved it, thought Ingrid. Lisa would have wanted to go far too close – she'd have wanted to be dangerously close. How like Roger she was, thought Ingrid. No. How like Roger she *had been*.

Ah, this was familiar, wasn't it? Tunnel of rage, tunnel of sorrow. It was at this point that she would blame Damian, even though it was no one's fault. It was no one's fault, but why shouldn't she blame Damian, who had left the keys for the ATV where Lisa would find them? Who had been sleeping as his sister drowned? She wanted to throttle him, yes, she did. What allowed him the right to mess around with a pretty young thing named Jasmine, who had a nose stud, and possibly a belly button stud – a stud for this and a stud for that?

She wasn't being fair. No, she wasn't.

She gripped the rail of the boat. How she hated the woman with the mauve-tinted hair who was claustrophobic, and the podgy-looking woman next to her, with the gentle face. She hated Jason, with his Buffalo Bills cap, and Jason's mother with her grotesque thighs made even more grotesque by the nearly transparent blue raincoat, and Jason's father, who hated it all as much as she did. She hated the boat and she hated the captain, who was just now turning the boat downstream, away from the Falls that Lisa would have loved.

When the captain turned the boat it was as though someone had let out a breath; something was released. It did absolutely no good to get angry, Ingrid thought, but she was angry. She couldn't stop it. What would put an end to it? Some miracle would put an end to it. She looked back at the wall of rushing water.

Why did it make her think of the boating accident? A man had taken his neighbours' children out for a boat ride. They'd struck something and the shear pin had broken.

Without the shear pin, the boat had no power. She knew this as if it had happened to her.

One of the children had gone over the Falls. She imagined the boy's flight, his fall. His name had been Roger Woodward. She thought of him floating over the Falls like a gull's feather. She could see him whirling in the air so he was only a pale figure with legs and arms windmilling out from the orange square of his life jacket. She saw him falling. There was a long moment of nothingness, then the plunge into the water, the jerking down into a wild, swirling darkness, the bobbing up to the surface of the river. A boy, coughing, with his mouth full of water.

He had lived. Ingrid's mother had saved the newspaper story about him, with a photograph in which he was gripping a life preserver that had been thrown to him by a man on the deck of the *Maid of the Mist*.

His name is Roger, Ingrid's mother had said, as if it were the name of an angel. Roger Woodward. Isn't that something? Just like our Roger.

The child's legs were thin as needles. He had lived; it was impossible, but true. Ingrid imagined him looking up at that wall of whiteness from below. Perhaps he was still alive now, so many years later; perhaps he was dead. All his life he must have remembered that moment, Ingrid thought. He must have remembered being saved.

He'd had a sister, Ingrid recalled, as she filed behind the others down the ramp from the *Maid of the Mist*. The terminal was as hot as before, and even when she took off her plastic raincoat and put it in the bin, it didn't make her feel any cooler. He'd had a sister called Deanne. Roger Woodward's sister, Deanne, had been thrown out of the boat above the Falls. There hadn't been a picture of Deanne in the newspaper article, though; there was only one of Roger. The two children had lived, but the man who'd taken them out in the boat had died. Honeycutt – his name was Jim Honeycutt. The story had been all about Roger, though, because he'd gone over the Falls, while Deanne had been thrown out of the boat above the Falls, close to Table Rock, where a tourist had rescued her.

Ingrid moved into the elevator, and people followed, pressing against her. She hardly noticed. She was thinking about how Honeycutt's boat had struck a shoal that broke the shear pin, so the propeller didn't work. By that time the boat must have been rolling forward, carried by the rushing water toward the brink. There must have been time for Honeycutt to realize, as he tossed the remaining life jacket to Deanne, that all three of them would likely die. But it wasn't a big thing that had gone wrong: it was a small thing. The shear pin had broken.

Ingrid walked back to the house thinking about how Lisa's fascination with the Falls had begun. Maybe it had all begun with the book. Ingrid had bought *Paddle-to-the-Sea*, for Lisa's fifth birthday. She had bought it because the same book had been bought for her, years before. There was a bookplate sticker on the fly leaf that read, in large letters, that it was the property of Lisa Felicity MacKenzie. They'd sat on Lisa's bed looking at the pictures, and Lisa had sucked her thumb. Ingrid told her big girls didn't do that.

Lisa had liked all the pictures, but the one she liked best was the illustration of Niagara Falls, with a rainbow rigidly painted in the lower left corner, and a speck in the upper right corner that was the wooden canoe with its carved figure, going over the brink.

I grew up there, Ingrid had told her.

Lisa looked up at her with her large hazel eyes, her thumb back in her mouth. Her lips quivered as she sucked on it.

There? asked Lisa.

I didn't live inside the waterfalls, said Ingrid. Just close by.

She'd turned to the next page, which showed the canoe and figure being tossed by the green swirls of water in the Whirlpool. But Lisa wanted to turn back the page to the full picture of the Falls. She ran a child's hand over it.

I'll have to take you there, said Ingrid. I'll have to take you to meet your Uncle Roger.

She closed the book and put it on the bedside table. She kissed Lisa's head.

Kiss my tummy, Lisa said, pulling up her nightgown.

Ingrid kissed her tummy and she burst into giggles.

Strawberries, she said.

Yes, I've made strawberries on your tummy. Look at them all!

It had been the gift she'd given her daughter. It was a way of passing on her own history – this lore about the Falls – to Lisa.

She approached the white house, her old family home.

But why, she wondered, had Roger Woodward lived while Jim Honeycutt had died? In the newspaper article, the boy had said that Jim Honeycutt had cried out that he would hold him, after the boat had turned over and thrown them into the water. He'd tried to hold the boy, but the water had torn them apart. One lived and the other died. But what if the man had lived while the child had died?

Ingrid stood at the edge of the sidewalk, about to cross the street. She heard the man calling I'll hold you, as he was swept away.

Her eyes were bright with tears. How did all the fine things on the face of the earth vanish away?

I'll hold you.

A car honked. The driver was waiting for her to cross. She crossed the street because the driver had no way of knowing about all the fine things on the face of the earth.

The house had been turned upside down in her absence. The back door hadn't been latched and there were bugs whirling around the ceiling light in the kitchen. There were dishes in the sink, a scattering of crackers on the table, water on the floor. No one had put the pâté or cheese in the fridge. The wine was nearly gone. And someone had gone rifling through the drawer that held the tea towels, and the drawer had been left open.

She recognized the acrid scent of smoke in the air, but it wasn't cigarette smoke, no – it was dope. She followed it through the house and outside onto the porch, where she found Roger.

Hi, he said.

Where is everyone?

Damian just took Jasmine home.

You've been smoking up. I suppose you were smoking up with Damian and Jasmine.

Not Damian, no.

With Jasmine?

Yes.

Elvis is wandering around out there in the back, singing to himself. And –

Have a seat, Ingrid.

No, she said, her voice rising. This house has gone to hell in a handbasket.

Roger leaned back in his chair.

Everything's gone to hell in this house, she went on. It's our parents' house, and look at it. Just *look* at it.

I can't, he laughed.

What?

I can't look at it, which is just as well. Ingrid, this is what you do. You come into a place and you're fine for a while and then the shit hits the fan. Why do you always have to make the shit hit the fan?

I don't make the shit hit the fan.

I thought it might be a good thing for both of you to come here. Spend a month, two months. Whatever you needed. But I don't know. It's always the same – you drive everyone away from you. You have such high expectations of people, and then they can't meet them. I never did. It's no wonder that kid of yours kept that girl a secret for as long as he could. She's a really great girl. She's perceptive and she's kind. I wouldn't be surprised if he's in love with her. But you've got to stand back and let him –

In love with her?

I said I wouldn't be surprised, but you have to let him find out.

I don't drive everyone away, said Ingrid. And I do stand back. I just don't slough off my responsibilities the way you do.

We could go on and on here, he said. I'd rather not. I'd rather not ruin a nice evening.

You mean you don't want to argue when you're stoned.

Well, you're right about that. You're right about so many things, Ingrid. He got up and snapped open his cane. All except one thing.

She wasn't about to ask what that one thing might be. She waited while he put the cane in front of him, tapping forward. She didn't help him by shifting one of the chairs out of the way as he walked to the door. He'd bump into it. He did, but then he went around it. When he got to the door, he stood groping for the handle until he found it.

This isn't our parents' house any more, he said with his back to her. And it's not your house. It's my house.

Ingrid lay on her bed, her arms by her sides, her legs splayed. It was too hot to pull up the sheet.

Had she driven people away from her? Yes, of course she had. She could have made a list: her mother, her father, Bryce Morrison, who kept hanging around her locker in grade ten, Randy Kelly, Steve Phalen, with that springy rust-coloured hair of his, her cousin Melanie Vickers, Ralph LeBlanc, except Ralph didn't count because he was an arsonist, Dick Schluter, her girlfriend Donna Paugh, who had that tiny mole on her forehead like the eye of a Cyclops, Gerry van Ryswyk, who used to write her letters in green ink, quoting Dylan Thomas, for God's sake, Roger and Marnie, and Greg, her husband who was now her ex-husband. Damian. And Jasmine. She couldn't bear to think of Lisa, and whether she'd driven her daughter away.

No, she said.

She didn't want to drive people away. Maybe people only felt close to her when she was a wreck. She remembered sitting next to Greg at the end of the visitation. Ingrid had been on the carpet, without her shoes, and she'd simply put her head in Greg's lap. She'd been sobbing; she couldn't stop sobbing. Greg had stroked her head over and over. He put his hand gently on her head and stroked it.

Oh, she groaned softly. She would have given a great deal to feel a gentle hand on her head, so she wouldn't feel desperately alone.

But she was alone. They were all alone, the living and the dead. They were being carried forward in the rush of water. Roger Woodward, Deanne Woodward, Jim Honeycutt, the overturned boat. All of them were being carried forward: the young Mr. Hockridge, newly married, and inclining his head to the young Mrs. Hockridge, the child who had been Ingrid with her patent leather purse, and the child who had been Roger, frowning, and the photograph of the two of them, a brother and a sister – a happy, expectant sister – held together by a hinge.

JASMINE GOT HER BICYCLE, which was leaning against the side of the house at the back, and, together with Damian, walked along the street in silence. A couple of cats yowled horribly. A man turned on the light on his front porch and came out with a bag of garbage that he tossed in a can. He listened to the cats for a few moments before going back inside.

What time is it? Jasmine asked. It can't be all that late.

She'd been watching clouds from the porch as she talked to Roger. The clouds had been soft and purple, as if they were long couches made out of velvet. She'd wanted to stretch out on one of them. Now dusk had fallen and lights had been turned on inside the houses they passed.

I don't know the time, said Damian.

You know, it's strange – your mother didn't come back.

She'll be back.

Are you all right, Damian?

You're the one who's stoned.

A hardness had come between them. If he wouldn't talk to her, she wouldn't talk to him.

As they walked across the intersection at Victoria and Clifton, Jasmine noticed a bright red box at the corner. It looked like a mailbox, but it wasn't.

Just a second, she said.

The Love Machine.

Oh God, snorted Damian, walking on ahead.

TEST YOUR RATING, commanded the machine.

She propped the bicycle against the window of a fabric store, dropped a couple of quarters into the slot, and put her palm down on the glass surface. The hand below, matched with hers, began to light up.

The Girdle of Venus, the Heart, the Head, the Inner Life.

You are $\mathcal{S}$*exy*, said the illuminated hand. *You are* $\mathcal{S}$*ensitive*. *You are* **Curious**. *You are not always* $\mathcal{F}$*orgiving*. *Your Girdle of Venus shows* Vulnerability. *You are* **LOYAL**. There were several glowing exclamation marks. *!!!!!!*

You are **Impetuous**, it went on to say, but then the lights flashed and something buzzed and everything went dark. The magical hand beneath the glass faded away.

She caught up to Damian, who was waiting near a pawn shop on Clifton, looking at a saxophone in an opened case. He was irritated with her.

I asked your uncle about you, you know, she said.

You talked about me – the two of you?

Yes.

I'm sure my uncle knows me inside out.

He doesn't, really. But he did say that maybe you were afraid.

Afraid? Damian scoffed.

Yes.

What do you think?

I don't know, she said.

It was too much effort, and she wasn't thinking clearly.

He didn't understand her, because if he understood her, he would have seen her sister, Shirl, who'd come from Lethbridge with Gary and the new baby, Jessica. He would have seen her parents, leaving the house that August morning, with Shirl and the baby. Leaving Gary behind. Leaving twelve-year-old Sandra behind, with her friend Marci.

Marci had a red-and-orange bathing suit, and she'd snapped her straps and twirled on her bare feet in the wet grass. Sandra had a yellow two-piece bathing suit; it was new, and her mother had bought it for her in Saskatoon when they'd gone shopping together the Saturday before. The yellow showed off her tanned skin, her slender arms and legs. She'd worn it to bed under her nightgown.

She and Marci had laughed and shrieked all morning, running back and forth, back and forth through the sprinkler, under the hot sun, their hair wet as seals. Gary lay on the couch in the living room, because he was on disability from work and that gave him the right. Something had happened to his heart. He wasn't yet twenty-eight and he'd had a heart attack.

Sandra didn't like going inside the shadowy, cool house when he was there, but they'd had to go in for lunch, and he'd given them exactly what they asked for, with extra peanut butter and lots of grape jelly. He was a big man, with a stubble of chin hair and a handsome square jaw. Shirl had said once that he was the love of her life, but that had been a couple of years before they were married, when he'd had a motorcycle. She'd said that to her mother, slamming her purse down on the table so the lipstick fell out of it. Gary was the love of her life.

A pall hadn't come over the sky as Sandra and Marci had been eating their sandwiches and drinking two per-cent milk out of unbreakable glasses at the kitchen table. No, the day was bright as ever, the sun shining through the windows that Sandra's mother had cleaned the day before, and the driveway where it had always been, with one crabapple tree on either side, though the rose-pink blooms were long gone. Queenie was playing with something out by the garage, running around in circles. And then Marci's father had come by in his pickup truck, that old brown truck with the rust around the wheel wells, and Marci had gone, leaving her half-finished sandwich on the table. Her father had tossed her a striped towel, and she'd wrapped it around herself, and then, leaving wisps of dust where her feet had been, she'd climbed into the truck.

Sandra had dawdled over her own sandwich, looking at the blue mirror ball in her mother's garden. She'd taken her time, hummed a song, run her fingers through her wet hair. Gary came into the kitchen and stood against the door jamb.

You're a nice little kid, he said. I've been watching you all morning.

She moved her plastic glass in a circle on the Arborite of the kitchen table.

That sure is a pretty bathing suit you've got, he went on. His voice was sort of lazy and calm. She got up from the table, but there was only one way out of the kitchen, unless she went through the window, and why would she go through the window? She stood uncertainly by her chair, and then she took her plate and glass to the sink where she ran water over the plate, into the glass. A bird came to the feeder, and its wings made a quick shadow against the window. It terrified her – it was only a bird and it terrified her. She ran out of the kitchen, out of the house. She ran down the dusty driveway, glancing behind her. Queenie was following her, small ears flipping back, barking.

Maybe I overreacted about Elvis, she said, as they turned onto Stanley Street.

I shouldn't have treated him like that. Damian stopped under the street light. I know. It's just that – well, that was my sister.

Your sister? said Jasmine.

In the box – the box you asked about, in my room.

Your sister, repeated Jasmine uncomprehendingly.

What's left of her.

She made a small sound, as if breath were being pressed out of her. Oh, Damian.

He groaned. Don't.

He looked so strange under the harsh brightness of the street light. His eyes were caves. There was something desperate about him.

I don't want to talk about it. He shook his head. Not with you. Not with anyone.

It's tearing you apart, she said softly.

He took hold of her abruptly and kissed her. He held her shoulders firmly, clutching her.

His eyes were open, but they were in shadow. They

frightened her. When he stopped kissing her, she found herself gasping. He was still gripping her, his face inches from hers.

Sandra ran down the dusty driveway, glancing behind her. Queenie was following her, barking and barking.

No, Queenie, she gasped. No.

But Queenie came with her. They took a shortcut across the front lawn, the wide expanse of golden-green grass, beginning to be burned by the sun. She stumbled once, and the dry grass felt like little spikes against her skin. There was no one behind her, but still she ran. She went to the meadow, with its trickle of water flowing through. The wolf willow rose up to meet her with its fragrant scent. She scrambled down to the thin line of glittering water and followed the stream bed to her grandmother's house, cutting her feet on the stones as she went.

Her grandmother was at home, bundling sheets off the line into the wide laundry basket. Sandra ran to her, panting, and threw herself against her.

What is it, dear? Look at you. What is it?

She'd cut herself on something, and a thread of blood was running down her leg. The yellow bathing suit was covered in dust and bits of grass. Sandra stood with her head down since it was impossible to speak.

What's the matter, dear?

Jasmine stepped back and wiped her mouth with the back of her hand.

Once, my sister kissed me, Damian said. We were children. She kissed me, right on the lips. She told me to kiss her back, so I did.

That's the kind of thing kids do.

You're right, he said. That's what they do.

He reached over to her and she shivered at his touch. All he'd wanted to do was tuck a strand of hair behind her ear. He stroked her cheek.

I could come in or go home, whatever you want, he said.

I don't know what I want.

He put his lips to her ear. What if I don't stay long? he murmured.

All right. You can come in, she said, still unsure.

He came into the house with her, following her to the bedroom.

Maybe we could just open the door of the refrigerator and sit in front of it, she said, turning on the fan. It's so humid.

She gathered up the drawings he'd done of her that afternoon. Some of them were on the floor and one was still clipped to the drawing board. She rolled them all up and found a hair elastic to put around them. That afternoon he'd been so tender, drawing one picture of her, then another.

There, she said, handing the drawings to him.

He took them, silently, crushing the papers in his hand and letting them fall. He held her, hard, against him.

What are you going to do with them?

With what?

Those drawings.

They're no good.

What is it? she asked. Tell me.

But he wouldn't tell her anything. It made her tired to think of it, and she undressed and got into bed, still feeling a little stoned.

Nothing had happened when Sandra ran away from Gary. But something had happened the second time, four years later, when he came to the mud room when Sandra was doing the laundry. He hadn't moved out of her way when she tried to go past him. What would she do, she wondered, holding the laundry basket, full of a stack of neatly folded clothes? The laundry basket was between them, but he was looking at her. He wouldn't let her go past. She put the laundry basket on top of the dryer and kicked him in the groin, the way Lindsay Ruel had kicked Liam Andersen. And that was the end of that, or so she thought.

Damian yanked off his clothes and got into bed, pulling her against him, roughly, so he could kiss her. His tongue filled her mouth, and as he kissed her he shifted position, so he was on top of her.

Damian, she said, breaking free of his kiss.

But he didn't take his time, and even the way he held her body – his fingers pressing into the skin of her buttocks – was uncomfortable. He pushed himself into her.

Damian, *stop* – what are you doing?

He was gone; he was far away.

He didn't stop even when her head began to hit the wall each time he shoved against her. Both of them were sweating, and his body slapped against hers. She wanted it to be over, but he kept on.

He moaned as he came, and she drew away from him before he was quite finished.

Jasmine. His voice went up and down as if he'd lost control of it.

My God, she whispered.

I'm sorry, Jasmine. I'm so sorry.

I could hate you for that –

I'm sorry.

You're *sorry*.

And then – right then – Gary had his second heart attack. He'd made an awful groaning sound, tried to hold the edge of the washing machine, and toppled to the floor. He'd almost fallen on her. It was uncanny to see him lying there. He was such a large man, sprawled like a prostrate bull on the floor.

Sandra stepped around him and went into the kitchen – whether he was dead or dying, she didn't know. She put a slice of raisin bread in the toaster, waited for it to come up, buttered it, and ate it slowly. Then she cleared the crumbs off the table and went back to the mud room.

There was a pale cast to Gary's face as she peered down at it. Something about his mouth was different. She didn't touch him; she went back into the kitchen and phoned 911. In a level voice, she told a woman that her brother-in-law had fallen down and she couldn't tell if he was still breathing. Then she returned to Gary, bending down to touch his cold neck, and went into the bathroom and threw up.

She turned away from Damian and curled up on her side of the mattress, without saying a word.

He dressed. She heard the sound of paper in his hands – maybe he was picking up the drawings. But she didn't care about the drawings. She hated them.

He left. She heard the door.

Her eyes were stinging with tears. She'd allowed it to happen because she thought she was in love with him, but the truth was that she didn't even know him.

What had he done?

He'd fucked her.

DAMIAN WAS SITTING ON THE PORCH beside several unopened cans of paint. He hadn't started painting the steps as he said he was going to do, and here it was nearly noon. And if he wasn't going to paint the steps, the least he could do was phone his girlfriend, Ingrid told him. But he wouldn't. He was stubborn as an ox.

It's not a good idea – a party. She won't come.

The most he would do was to give Jasmine's phone number to his mother.

As she went back into the house, it occurred to Ingrid that maybe he was right; maybe it wasn't a good idea. Had he seen Jasmine at all in the past few days? She wasn't sure what he was doing with himself.

This is absolutely insane, she muttered. The mother phoning the girlfriend.

But she'd been hard on Jasmine the first time, when nothing had worked out.

Sorry, who's calling? Jasmine asked when Ingrid phoned.

Damian's mother, said Ingrid.

Oh, I didn't –

And it's your birthday, said Ingrid. Happy birthday. We've prepared a little celebration for you –

For me?

Yes, you'd said you wanted a party.

I did?

Yes.

Ingrid looked at everything she'd arrayed in the kitchen: the cut-glass bowl for punch, the Limoges dessert plates stacked on the counter, the goblets for champagne, because she'd even gone out and bought some Veuve Clicquot, the newly iced cake, on which the small pink roses, the ones she had so carefully made with the icing bag, were beginning to droop in the heat.

You can't make it? said Ingrid.

No – I'm sorry. I help out my friend sometimes – at a tattoo parlour – and I already told her I'd cover her shift.

Well, that changes things. I guess I should have reminded Damian, said Ingrid. I just assumed, and I went ahead and made a cake.

Thank you for making a cake.

It's got your name on it. It says "Happy Birthday Jasmine" in pink letters, though it's a white cake, not a chocolate cake. You'd said you'd be nineteen, Ingrid added. So I got candles in the shape of a one and a nine. It's really very nice.

She'd wanted to stop herself from chattering, but she couldn't. If Roger had been there, he'd have pointed it out.

Maybe I'll get a chance to come by later, said Jasmine.

Well, it's yours. The cake. You could take it home.

Did Damian – Oh, I'm sorry about this. All the confusion.

No, don't be sorry. It doesn't matter.

When she hung up the phone, Ingrid looked at the ridiculous pink and purple streamers, and, as if on cue, one of them came down. She'd taped them to the ceiling, twisting them before she fastened them with bits of tape she'd stuck like tags on her T-shirt sleeve. To fasten them, she'd had to stand on a chair to get onto the table, but she'd fallen off the chair while getting down. She'd hurt her shin; it would leave a bad bruise.

She opened the freezer and pulled out a bag of frozen peas. She'd stubbornly gone ahead with it all. A part of her was sure she could bring the family together by putting up streamers and making a cake for someone she didn't know. Why had it been so important to her? A girl turning nineteen wouldn't have wanted a birthday party like this. She wouldn't have wanted streamers, or candles shaped like numbers on her cake.

Ingrid sat with her leg propped up on the table, the bag of frozen peas like a saddlebag over her shin. After a few minutes she got up, tossed the peas back into the freezer, and took the Veuve Clicquot out of the fridge. She popped the cork and watched as it hit the ceiling. It might have made a mark, though she couldn't be certain.

Well, it's not my house, she said cheerfully. Her voice sounded loud. She was alone in the house except for Damian, who was outside, and Elvis, who wandered in and out like a lost soul.

She poured the champagne into one of the goblets and took a gulp. It was like drinking a thin, bubbly stream of pure gold. Was it the first time she had ever stood in this kitchen with a bottle of champagne in one hand and a goblet in the other? Yes, she thought it was.

So much had happened in this kitchen. She took another gulp, though she knew it wasn't the way to drink it. She should be sipping it. Oh, what the hell, she thought. She drained the glass, poured another, and drained that one too; she set the glass down in the sink. It was the strangest of coincidences that August 2 should be Jasmine's birthday and that it should also be Greg's birthday. It was his fifty-fifth birthday. Carrying the bottle by the neck, she stepped outside, drew the screened door shut behind her, and sat down on the steps. She and Greg had got married in this very backyard, in May, when the crabapple trees were in bloom.

There they were. It was broad daylight, but she saw them dancing under the trees, exactly as they had done at the wedding. A curve of moon. Voices, laughter. She saw the crabapple blossoms in her own hair. She saw the lacy shawl, fine as a spiderweb, over her smooth young shoulders, the one Greg had brought back from Antwerp. It had to be perfect, he'd told her. Perfect for her. But she wouldn't look at the ghosts: her own mother, and her father, gesturing as he conversed with her friend Marilyn – Marilyn, who had Stage Four breast cancer now – she walked through them all. There was J.J., playing the guitar, and just beyond him was Roger, without his white cane. Younger, wilder. Roger, with his arm around Marnie. Just about now, the bride would catch her satin-shod foot on the rotted stump of the plum tree because she hadn't seen it in the shadows – yes, just there – and the groom would catch her and laugh. He'd kiss her and everyone would clap.

There, all the ghosts were clapping.

Greg, she murmured, with a pang.

There's a cake, said Elvis. A nice cake. But it's getting all slidey. The flowers on top are slidey.

Ingrid, still sitting on the steps outside, thought Elvis was talking to her. She turned to talk to him through the screened door, but Damian spoke.

Why aren't you at the workshop?

Damian sounded annoyed.

It's a day off, Elvis explained. Bruce said we get August 1 and August 2 for holidays. We get weekends too, but holidays are extra.

Well, don't eat the cake. My mother made it for Jasmine.

A cake for Jasmine Jane Blakeney. August 2, 1989. Saskatoon, Saskatchewan.

Yes. Don't you have something you want to do?

I'm waiting for the party.

There's not going to *be* a party. Elvis, can't you go somewhere?

No.

Well, do what you like.

There was the sound of someone's bare feet going away down the hall. Damian, thought Ingrid. If she stayed where she was, Elvis would discover her and ask about the party. She put the champagne bottle down on the grass beside the steps, got up, and walked to the carriage house.

Ingrid woke to find Damian standing over her. She jumped. How had he found her here, asleep in the carriage house, lying on a bed with a hundred happy faces? He looked terrible. He stood rigidly, the way he had long ago, when he'd scared her one night after he'd had a nightmare.

What? She sat up quickly. Is it Roger? Has something happened?

Elvis has taken Lisa's ashes. He's taken the box and gone off and I have no idea where he is and –

Are you sure it was Elvis?

Who else could it be? Elvis was in the house, wanting to eat the cake, and I wouldn't let him. Who else could it possibly be?

Damian, she said, putting her hand gently on his arm.

I have to find him. He's got Lisa's ashes and I don't know what he'll do with them.

I'll come with you, she said.

No. No, I'll go. You look around the streets here. I don't know – he might not have gone far.

I'll do that – you take the car, she said. The keys are in my bedroom. Take them.

No, I don't want the car. He flung up his arms. God, how could Elvis do it? How could he?

It'll be all right, Damian.

But Damian tore away from her, leaving the door wide open behind him.

Ingrid gathered herself and went into Elvis's bathroom, where she was confronted by a full-length Elvis Presley on the shower curtain, with his guitar slung low across his hips.

Oh, for God's sake, she said.

What would Elvis do? she wondered. He was liable to do anything. She stared at herself in the mirror of the old medicine cabinet. And what would Elvis do with Lisa, the dust of Lisa? She splashed her face with water.

She went out of the carriage house, walking quickly through the wedding guests, though some of them had dispersed. A group had gone into the kitchen, where Marilyn was singing "Both Sides Now" in her clear, high voice. In a while, someone else would start playing the spoons. They would be up all night, and then, finally, she and Greg would leave. They'd get in the car and drive to Vermont under the sweet curve of moon, and the pale dawn, and at intervals Ingrid would hum "Both Sides Now."

She went around the house and down the slope of the front lawn. She crossed the street, but once she was on the sidewalk on the other side, it was clear Elvis wasn't anywhere to be seen. She leaned against the wall for a moment and looked down to the mysterious shadows deep in the gorge. Far below, the water swirled, making white calligraphy across the dark green of the river.

Crossing back over the road, she began to run along Bampfield. Elvis could be on any of the side streets; she had no idea where to begin, but she didn't slow down. She kept going.

Do you feel different, being married? Greg had asked Ingrid as he drove and she hummed.

No, not very different.

Things open up, he said. From this point on.

She'd been watching the mist as he said this. All over the state of New York the mist was rising. She'd seen it in the fields that dipped down to a creek they passed and might never pass again. It rose, gently, and there were large white pines standing at the place where the road twisted away in the distance, into the generous, expansive world.

She stopped running and bent over, as breathlessly as if she'd just finished a race. How upset Damian had been, she thought.

The tears slid down her cheeks; she wiped them quickly. More, there was always more. There was no end to it. Why had she made the cake? Why had she gone to the trouble of doing all of it for someone who was not her own daughter? Why couldn't she have made a cake that said "Happy Birthday Lisa"? Her own daughter, who would never be nineteen.

She sat down on the sidewalk, halfway up the street. A car passed at a snail's pace, as if the driver was wondering whether or not to stop. She didn't care. It shouldn't have been Lisa; it shouldn't have happened that way. Ingrid should have been the one who'd tipped the four-wheeler and fallen under it; Ingrid should have been the one who'd drowned.

How she'd failed. Everything had been turned to stone: father, mother, bride and groom, each of the wedding guests, the fields of New York State, the white pines, the road curving to the east, the faint moon. Her own daughter. Rigid, cold. She knew it; she could feel the hardness under her palms. She scraped her palms back and forth against the rough surface of the sidewalk.

God, she cried.

Gradually, very gradually, her crying subsided. She grew quiet and her breathing grew steady. She became aware of someone sitting next to her. Someone was beside her, and because of it she dared not open her eyes. It made her feel tranquil. But she didn't open her eyes. If she opened her eyes, the vision would disappear; the vision of a hand next to hers, a hand with tapered fingers, much like her own, and on the slim wrist, the bracelet Damian had made.

DAMIAN STOOD, ASHEN-FACED and sweating, in front of Wang's Variety. A man passed, glancing over his shoulder at Damian as he went into the store. The light was beginning to fade from the sky, but the air was leaden, filled with the smell of tar from the newly paved lot between the convenience store and a rambling house that' had been divided into three rental units.

He had no idea where to go. He had no idea where Elvis might have gone. The man who had passed him came out of Wang's with a large bag of potato chips. He put on a pair of sunglasses, swung into his red SUV, and thumped the door shut. A dog barked sharply. Someone revved a motorcycle, and a car passed with a chain from a trailer hitch dragging on the pavement, making a spray of red-gold sparks. A muscular arm hung out a car window. A mother walked with a baby in a stroller; she dangled a bottle of water between two fingers. She was lightly singing a song. *The wheels on the bus go round and round, round and round.*

Daddeee, Daddeee, called a jumping child.

The velvet heat lay thickly on the leaves of the oaks and mountain ash trees, and on the small mulberry trees,

Japanese maples, and juniper bushes by the front doors of the houses. *Round and round, all around the town.* Heat lay on the grass of each lawn, on the sidewalk, and on the puddles of oil in the street. It was an aureole around a man with a red baseball cap, who had dropped his keys as he was leaving an Italian restaurant. He bent to retrieve them, while a child jumped from one side of the sidewalk to the other. Damian started running.

Daddeee, called the child.

The night before Damian's father left, he came and sat on Damian's bed. The light from the hall fell across the pillow and his father closed the door a little, so it wouldn't bother him. His father's eyes gleamed, even in the half-light.

Tell me a story, said Damian, looking up at his father's glistening eyes.

I love you. His father cleared his throat after he spoke. You know that, don't you?

Yes, said Damian impatiently. Tell me a story. He didn't want his father to go to bed and leave him alone.

No. I can't.

You always do.

His father laughed a little, but it wasn't his usual laugh. He ran two fingers along his lips. Well, let me see, he said. Let me think for a minute.

Damian waited. It was a long silence. A minute's up now, he said.

I don't think I have a story tonight, Damian. I just don't think I do.

Damian ran up Clifton Hill, past the Guinness World Records Museum, with its huge, granite ball floating on water outside the entrance, like a planet. World's Tallest Man, the World's Largest Pencil, the World's Most Tattooed Lady. Bees covering someone's face. Shortest, fattest, oldest, biggest, smallest. A yellow funhouse, its red clock set to no time, numbers out of order, with a large plaster dog, dressed in lederhosen, on the roof. Rainforest Café, Ride Over the Falls, Travelodge, Arby's, Wendy's, the headlights of the cars streaming down the hill in the twilight. The smell of exhaust, the screech of a baby.

And then, accompanied by a pretty jingling of bells, came a group of people on bicycles. There was a police car leading the way, and a cluster of cyclists, with a pink van drawing up the rear. Down they went, down to the Falls, the pink-clad cyclists floating down the street, all with pink helmets – *The Coast to Coast Bicycle Adventure for Breast Cancer Research* – and dancing bells announcing them.

Elvis wasn't at the tattoo parlour; the lights were out and the door was locked. The sign looked cheap in the last light of day, with its badly painted hand. The Ornamental Hand. In the middle of the green hand was a loose knot of red: a glowing scarlet serpent. He watched as someone in the dim interior changed the sign from *Come In, We're Open,* to *Sorry, We're Closed.*

Damian crossed the street and stopped in the middle of the sidewalk, where he stood drawing breath in ragged gasps. People made arcs around him as they passed, but he didn't move. Jasmine had stood in a cone of light when he'd first seen her through the window. When she finished her drawing she had moved, gracefully, between the coloured strands of beaded curtain. Maybe he should have left her alone.

Try, Damian had said, when his father couldn't tell him a story.

Well, said his father. There's a story about – it's about a dragon and a little boy. The dragon is hideous. In fact, this dragon is so hideous he scares himself when he sees his own reflection. He's green and purple. Let's see, he has green fur on his stomach and purple fur on his back. His eyes are –

One is green and one is purple, said Damian.

Yes, one is green and one is purple. And he doesn't smell very good when he's afraid. He smells like a skunk when he's afraid. But when he's happy, he smells of delicious things. He smells like violets in the woods, or sometimes he smells of woodsmoke, or cedar, or grass when it's been freshly cut, or the salt smell of the ocean. And other things, lots of other things –

Chocolate chip cookies, said Damian.

Yes, chocolate chip cookies. He smells of that too. And, well, let's see, one day he meets a little boy who is eight years old. He meets that little boy out in the woods, in the snow. It's a very cold day in the middle of January, and the little boy is unhappy.

Why?

Well, because his father has to go away for a long, long time and this is something the little boy doesn't understand. So one day he goes outside in his snowsuit to kick snow around. He doesn't want to slide down the snowbank. No, he just wants to kick snow. And then, lo and behold, a hideous dragon appears on top of the woodpile. This dragon is so, so hideous that most people would have run away in fright, but not this little boy.

What's his name? asked Damian.

The little boy? His name is Sam, and his mother won't call him anything else but Samuel, or sometimes Samuel John, which he doesn't like.

I wouldn't like that either.

Well, Sam is just Sam. But there he is, face to face with the hideous dragon, and since he thinks the dragon has seen him crying he says, in a big, loud voice, What do you want?

The dragon doesn't answer.

So, Sam tries again. What do you want?

Damian would have punched Elvis if he'd had the chance. Didn't Elvis understand? He must have known that taking the box was wrong. He must have.

But, still, Damian would have hit him. He'd have kicked him. His foot caught a soda can on the sidewalk and sent it spinning; a teenaged girl, wearing a strapless top and a tiny pair of shorts, gave him a withering look as the can rolled in front of her and off the curb onto the street.

It was too hot to run any more. His arms didn't belong to him, his legs were not his own. His head was not on his neck, he was not holding himself up. He walked until he saw Jasmine and Tarah's rundown bungalow on Stanley Street. He hadn't seen Jasmine since the night he'd made such a mess of things, and it had been five nights and six days since then.

The house looked the same, with the awning over the front door, and the limp stalks of long-dead irises by the steps, and the uncut grass of the pocket-sized front lawn. Inside the house was her room, a room he could see in his mind, with its mattress on the floor and the miniature ballerina on the lamp stand. He could see Jasmine's body: the flat stomach with its three dark freckles. He'd kissed that stomach, the triangle of freckles.

What did it feel like, she'd asked him once, to be a man inside a woman? He couldn't describe it. He'd asked what it felt like for her. Like being filled up, she'd said. He'd held her close to him and kissed her hair, her ear, her neck. He'd kissed her wrists: first her left, then her right. He'd kissed her stomach again. Her knees, each ankle, and the soles of her feet. He recalled the curtains at the window; how they'd billowed, then slackened, making the soft sound of breath.

A slim girl came out the front door of the bungalow. She put her head down and then tossed back short magenta-coloured spikes of newly washed hair. Drops of water sparkled as she flung her head back, flying diamond-bright into the air. So Tarah hadn't been at the Ornamental Hand, after all. She was turned away from him; she didn't see him.

He almost shouted her name. But he kept walking, past the gleaming white horse and the motel swimming pool on one side of the street, and Tarah brushing her hair with a yellow-backed brush on the other side. If she saw him, she didn't call out. Cars streamed between them. He went as far as the monastery, with its wide lawns, and took off his sandals to walk through the grass, feeling the coolness under his bare feet, but the air was oppressive, even here. Dusk had fallen, but he could make out the trees looming above him as he crossed the lawn, wiping his face with the sleeve of his T-shirt.

The statue's face seemed uglier than he remembered. There were roses in a new mayonnaise jar at her feet, but the petals were edged with brown. Little Flower. The statue regarded him benignly, sweetly, despite her jaundiced face, and spread her arms, as if to gather up the world. Little Flower. Daisies, hawkweed, clover. Wild roses above the sea. Little wildflower, flower of the wind. Sweet Little Death, blown on the wind.

It defeated him. He threw himself down on the lawn near the statue.

He thought of Elvis tossing the box over the wire mesh of the observation platform at the Skylon Tower. The box fell lightly, almost gaily, to the earth below. He saw it falling from a helicopter, or tossed from a gaudy striped balloon that rose and slowly descended. There it was, opening in the darkening sky, with the ashes drifting out in a long tail of sparkling dust.

Or maybe Elvis had simply tossed it into the trash, the flaps of the box torn, the urn cracked in two, ashes spilled among the candy wrappers, cans, cigarette butts, tickets, crushed napkins, ends of hot dogs, ketchup, coffee cups.

You can't stop there, Damian had said, looking up at his father.

What?

You can't stop there. Tell me what the dragon wanted.

Oh, but I don't know what the dragon wanted. What do you think the dragon wanted?

He wanted dill pickles.

Yes, said Damian's father, standing up. Dill pickles.

You can't leave. Not in the middle.

His father looked down at Damian. I love you so much, he said. Do you have any idea how much I love you?

Damian looked up at him, his eyes large. If he was as quiet as a mouse his father might stay.

La vita nuova, murmured his father, but he was looking out the window. He wasn't speaking to Damian.

If Damian stayed where he was, he'd fall asleep. Evening was turning to night; the world had become almost completely dark. He got up.

Time had a shape, he thought drowsily. It began in one place and turned back on itself. Here he was going down through the ravine again, just as he had on the first day he'd come to Niagara Falls, descending the steps of the ravine through the shadowy trees. Just as he'd done with Jasmine. Now he'd returned, at the end of a long, sultry day. In the parking lot, cars were precisely slotted into place. Damian crossed the road to the brilliantly lit plaza at Table Rock. He walked along the path by the railing, without caring about the Falls shimmering with coloured lights for the tourists, and even though he felt the river rushing past, he didn't look. He was tired, and all he wanted to see was Elvis's large, solidly built body, in his bizarre clothes that didn't quite fit: his bell-bottoms, his unbuttoned shirt. He wanted to see Elvis's big hands holding a box.

Someone laughed in Damian's ear and danced in a circle in front of her boyfriend. She teetered on her platform sandals, and put her arms out, leaning forward, giving a little yelp before her boyfriend caught her.

They've started the fireworks, she said. See!

Damian raised his eyes to see a bloom of gold that flowered above and fell slowly to earth, accompanied by popping sounds. *Pfft, pfft,* up went another, and he couldn't help but watch. It was a globe of ruby lights, clinging to the sky. Down it came, after a moment or two. And then one, two, three, four, five, six, up went a series of rockets, each one exploding like gunshots. Red, white, blue, red, white, blue. The colours sprang into life and disappeared, shooting gloriously into the night.

Ahhh, sang the crowd. *Ahhh.* At each feast of light, people turned up their faces excitedly.

There was a rain of silvery threads above them, a rush of brilliance. And then, in front of him, he saw Elvis's white shirt, and it was so luminous that it might have been alight. But no, he was wrong. It was someone else's white shirt. Above them, an explosion of rose-coloured pinwheels caught in the air, hanging like decorations, before they descended and faded away, tinting everyone pink for a few moments, so their faces were flushed with colour. The man in the white shirt was stained blue, then green, gold, crimson, and blue. The Falls were tinted at the same time, a skirt pleated with soft hues. The last of the fireworks fell in a spangled chandelier of orange and red. *Pfft. Pfft.* It was the finale. *Pfft. Pfft. Pfft. Zzzzztttt.* The lights flickered down the sky and there was a flutter of cheers and clapping.

In the southeast there was a rumble and then a distant flash of sheet lightning. But Damian was so exhausted he could barely put one foot in front of the other. What did he care about fireworks?

When he got back to his uncle's house, he went to the door at the back. He was just about to open it, but he stopped short.

Jasmine was in the kitchen, sitting close to his uncle, and through the mesh he saw her reach for him. She took him in her arms, hugging him in the full glare of the overhead light in the kitchen. Roger's hand moved up her back to the nape of her neck, and she lifted her head as his hand caressed her. Then she shifted so she could hold his face in her hands. She was going to kiss him.

Damian backed away from the door and went down the steps.

He moved toward a lawn chair, dazedly, but there was already someone there. Even with the light spilling out of the kitchen window, it took him a moment to see that it was Elvis.

Where the hell have you been? Damian cried. Where's the box? Just where the hell is it, Elvis?

IT WAS EVENING by the time Jasmine got to Damian's uncle's house, unsure of whether to go in. Ingrid had made her a cake, and Jasmine thought she should take a piece of it home for the sake of politeness, but now that she'd arrived, her heart was thudding; the last person she wanted to see was Damian. She didn't want to see Ingrid either. No one really expected her to get a piece of cake just for the sake of formality.

But she knocked and waited. No one came, and finally she opened the door and stood uncertainly at the threshold. Should she turn on a light, or should she just go away, now, before anyone saw her? She flicked on the kitchen light, and a purple streamer floated languidly to the floor.

Oh, Roger, you scared me, she cried. You were sitting in the dark.

Is it dark?

Well, not quite. I knocked.

I heard something. It sounded like a June bug, except it's not June any more, is it?

That's flattering – a bug.

Come in, he laughed. Ingrid wanted to give you a party, as you can probably see.

Yes, she phoned me, but I couldn't get here earlier. I was taking a shift for Tarah, but I closed up before I was supposed to. There was no one around.

Well, you'll have to forgive me – I think I did something to the cake. I didn't know it was on the counter.

The cake was a sad-looking affair with its drunken roses, and one side had caved in completely. Roger must have put his hand in it.

I'm sorry I spoiled it.

That's okay, she said.

The cake made her want to cry.

I just got back, but no one's here, as far as I can tell, said Roger. Bernie took me home after the first set at the pub, because Ingrid told me to be here. But I don't know where she's gone. I don't know where Damian is either. He must have gone out with Elvis.

I didn't come to see Damian, she said briskly. I came to take a piece of cake home.

Why don't you sit down and have a bite of it?

No, she said.

What's wrong?

I don't know.

How about cutting me a piece of that cake – what's left of it.

Jasmine cut a piece of cake and put it on a china plate with sprigs of pale blue flowers, but it was only then that she realized it didn't matter what she put it on. He couldn't see it. She put a fork on the plate and took it to the table. He had a glass of Scotch and she could smell its smoky flavour.

The cake's right there, with a fork, she told him.

She watched him find the fork.

I think I'll just eat it with my hands, he said, breaking off a piece and stuffing it into his mouth.

I'm not a pretty sight, he confessed. I get crumbs all over.

She laughed.

Happy birthday, he said.

Thank you. As of today, I'm nineteen.

Nineteen, he mused. That's a surprising age.

Surprising?

Yes, you can see everything, all the shining things that are to come.

Shining things, she said.

Don't you believe in the shining things?

I don't know. You always talk like this, don't you?

Not always.

Do you think that people – well, like you – do you think people like you –

Blind people?

Yes, she said, reddening. I was going to ask you something, but it's going to sound stupid.

Ask away.

Are you able to sense things in a way that's, well, clearer?

Clearer than other people?

Yes.

No, he said. I'm as bewildered by the world as the next guy.

When you meet people, what's it like? You can't see them.

Voices just come out of the air, he said. They come out

of nowhere. Sometimes people talk as if I weren't there, because they don't know how to talk to me. They're usually afraid of me, and I think, why are they so afraid? I'm a human being, doing ordinary things, making the usual blunders. Getting slightly pissed right now on this Scotch. Would you like some of this very good, single malt Scotch?

No, thanks. I should go.

Keep me company.

Well, just while you eat the cake.

It's good cake, he said. But it doesn't go with Scotch. A person should either eat cake or drink Scotch, but not both. He ran a finger around the rim of the plate, feeling its edges.

This is one of the dessert plates, he said. My mother used to put these out for guests. It's Limoges.

It's pretty, she remarked. There's a gold border around the rim. We never had plates like that. We had unbreakable plates in our house. You could throw them on the floor and they wouldn't break, but these are as thin as robin eggs.

Robin eggs, he mused. You know – you have a musical voice. It's a singing voice.

Thank you.

It's sweet and full. And your laugh, it's sort of husky and deep. It's not what you'd expect.

I never really think about my voice, she said, sitting down in the chair next to him.

I like it, he said. Do you look anything like your voice? I mean –

She laughed, reaching out for his hand. She guided it to her face. His fingers moved rapidly across her mouth, her cheeks, back to her nose, her eyes, first one eyelid and then the other, and up to her forehead. He found her lips again, and traced the upper lip, the lower one.

She stiffened.

Ahh, he said, dropping his hand. You're so young. So sweet.

Damian had said she was beautiful, so beautiful. It stung her to think of it.

Oh, now, you're crying, he said. You shouldn't be crying.

I don't want to – it's just –

Did I do that? Did I make you cry?

No.

She wiped her face.

Damian doesn't give a shit about me. She put her head between her hands.

Of course he does.

No. He's fucked up.

He blames himself for what happened to his sister. I told you that.

What *did* happen to his sister?

She took his ATV and went down to the beach. I don't think she'd ridden it before. It rolled over into a stream and she was caught underneath it.

Oh, that's awful.

Damian was asleep somewhere else on the beach. He did everything he could when he found her, but she was already gone.

That's what happened?

Yes.

Does he think if he hadn't been asleep –

He must go over and over it, asking himself what might have been.

That must be awful for him. She pictured Damian on

the beach. But even so, it's no excuse. It's no excuse for being a prick.

Was he a prick?

Yes. He was.

Can you forgive him?

Why should I have to? Why does it have to be me, forgiving him?

Because, he said slowly, if you don't forgive him – okay, maybe not now – but if you don't, then whatever he did could get right inside you, and that wide-open heart of yours could become small and shrivelled, like a leathery, old apple. Mine did.

No, it didn't.

Oh, you believe I'm better than I am. But I'm not. It's not as if I've ever learned the wisdom of the sages. I've failed Ingrid – I didn't go to Lisa's funeral, for instance, and I'm all the family she's got. As for Damian, he could have used someone like me in his life. A man, laughed Roger softly. As if I could help him be a *man*.

She reached over from where she was sitting and put her arms around Roger.

You *are* a man, she said.

He held her, running his hand up her back and through her hair. She leaned back, away from him, but his hand kept moving through her hair. She could smell the Scotch on his breath.

Roger, she said very quietly.

There was a sound at the door that might have been a moth hitting the screen.

She took his face in her hands. She kissed him tenderly on the cheek.

You're a good man, she murmured. A kind and generous man.

They heard an angry voice, Damian's voice, yelling at
Elvis in the backyard.

Elvis, said Roger, starting for the door, his cane clatter-
ing to the floor. What's going on? He bent down to find his
cane, hands fumbling this way and that before he found it.

Here, she said, tucking her arm into his. They went to
the door and she opened it, awkwardly, since she was
leading him.

Damian was standing in front of Elvis, feet apart, as if
he were about to hit him. Where did you take it, Elvis? he
yelled. Where is it?

Damian, said Roger.

No, no, no, no, cried Elvis.

Wait, Roger said, going forward down the step, so that
Jasmine had to keep up with him. Damian, calm down.
You're scaring him.

Damian was shaking.

Calm down? He's taken Lisa's ashes and I've been
looking for him for hours.

Elvis, said Roger quietly.

But Elvis walked around in a circle, his hands over his
ears.

Elvis, said Roger. Listen to me.

Elvis took his hands from his ears but wouldn't stop
moving.

Did you take the box from Damian?

He didn't answer. He put up one hand, his fingers
clenched.

Where is it? said Roger.

He took it, said Damian. He had no right.

Lincoln's secretary was named Kennedy and Kennedy's secretary was named Lincoln, said Elvis rapidly. Kennedy drove a Lincoln, made by the Ford company. Hhhhh, Lincoln was elected to Congress in 1846 and that was one hundred years before Kennedy was elected to Congress in 1946 and Lincoln was elected president in 1860 exactly one hundred years before Kennedy was elected president in –

Elvis, yelled Damian, stepping forward and gripping Elvis's shoulders, yanking him forward. Tell me.

Elvis made a roaring sound.

Stop it, yelled Roger. Stop –

Don't touch him, Damian, cried Jasmine.

When Damian released him, Elvis backed away and his roaring diminished. Damian looked at Jasmine as if seeing her for the first time.

This has nothing to do with you, he said.

Yes, it does, she told him firmly. He may have taken something from you, but you can't treat him like shit. You can't treat anyone like shit.

You like to get in the middle of things, don't you?

I don't –

Look at you. Don't you think my uncle is a little old for you? You're –

Damian, said Roger.

Fuck you, Damian, she said in a low voice. I didn't want to get in the middle of things. It was your mother who invited me here.

She could feel her eyes filling with tears, but she wasn't going to cry. Her voice was steady when she spoke. At least your uncle is kind to me. That's a lot more than I can say for you.

She turned to Elvis. Did you take the box?

Hhnnn, said Elvis.

You did? Where is it now?

There, he mumbled.

Where?

He pointed.

Elvis, said Jasmine. Where did you leave it?

On the sidewalk over there, he said, pointing. I opened the box and the jar fell and it went all over. He spread out his hands. But I didn't mean to make it fall.

Damian took off, sprinting, and Jasmine watched him.

Elvis, said Roger quietly. It's not right to take something that doesn't belong to you. You know that.

Elvis rocked from one foot to the other.

Come inside, said Roger.

But Elvis didn't move. He stayed where he was, rocking.

10

Then Damian ran across the road without looking for cars and found the shattered urn on the sidewalk with some ashes in a heap and some more scattered in a line like a comet's tail he held the box open and scooped handfuls of ashes into it along with the shards of the urn but he couldn't pick up all the ashes even when he swept them with his hands and they left a smear on the sidewalk when he stood up and went back across the road over the front lawn to the house taking the porch steps two at a time leaving the door swinging he was still shaking as he went inside and up to his room stuffing his things into the knapsack and rolling up the crumpled drawings of Jasmine and taking the car keys from his mother's purse in her bedroom maybe he should leave a note but what would he say and instead he went downstairs and out the front door he could hardly breathe as he opened the car door and got in clutching the box setting it on the seat beside him and tossing his knapsack and the drawings on the floor then he backed the car onto the street under the spreading branches of the chestnut tree he didn't care if they saw him leave he drove quickly up one street and down another thinking of how they'd been in the kitchen together Jasmine with her arms around Roger and Roger running his hand through her hair but seeing her like that was the same as a cleaver chopping a slab of meat on a board and he wondered what they were doing now he circled back to Roger's and parked the car on the street where he could look through the pendant-shaped chestnut leaves no way of knowing what they'd been doing whether it had been a long time or a short time but then the screened door banged and Jasmine called out good night

9

as if nothing had happened she came out to the sidewalk with her bicycle in the dark then into a pool of street light and he could see the shape of her legs under her skirt and her hair swinging as she walked it made him want to run to her put his arms around her and she'd hold him close and kiss him but she made him angry he didn't want her to hold him close and kiss him and he sat in the driver's seat crying looking at her through his tears she brushed something from her face a mosquito and glanced behind her down the street there was still time and he opened the door but she'd already begun to ride away with a reflector shining one weird red eye just above the rear wheel of her bicycle and at the convenience store at the end of the street she turned the corner and sped away with her light flashing in front and he couldn't change anything and maybe it was the last time

8

he'd see her the tears came down his face and he couldn't stop them he couldn't get back to what went before because it had all changed when his mother said his father wouldn't be coming back he was sitting on the bed in his room picking at the chenille spread and he saw he could stretch the loop as long as a noodle but what will he do Damian asked he won't have a house to live in oh he'll find an apartment his mother told him Damian could see a large framed picture of himself on top of the bureau he was in a rocking chair with his feet sticking out in front and behind him a window that wasn't a real window and a tree in the window that wasn't real either and he was holding a stuffed bunny with soft fur but they'd only given it to him to keep him quiet while they took the photograph

1

and then they'd taken it away he thought of his father leaving in the orange taxi as the snow fluttered down his father who hadn't finished the story about the dragon he's gone back to Vancouver his mother said his mother and sister are there she reached over and put her hand on Damian's because he was pulling at another strand in the bedspread you know sometimes people get confused so they do rash things but he didn't finish the story Damian said twisting the loop of chenille he went away she said as if she hadn't heard him because he had to go but you know we'll be fine the three of us together we'll be fine

6

Damian started the car again and slowly drove along the street turning at the convenience store there was his mother walking with her head down because it had begun to rain and she didn't look up as he passed he almost stopped but he had to do one thing then another if he could do each thing carefully it would be all right he wouldn't say goodbye to anyone he was shivering but it was hot hotter than before his hands clenched the steering wheel he was perspiring strange to be hot and cold at the same time he drove to the Hydro Control Dam above the Falls he knew he was done with it and all he wanted was to walk out of his life into the first pattering of rain he heard no thunder and there was no lightning but it rained hard streaming down the windshield as he sat in the parked car

5

imagining the huge crouching shape of the Control Dam by the river he recalled how happy he'd been when his father lifted him up to put him on his shoulders and the pieces of a puzzle had been far below on the floor how easily things vanished how swiftly his sister had gone too as if she had not lived it would happen to him he thought of Lisa putting his hair in pigtails all over his head and his mother laughing he heard the tumbling sound of his mother's laughter as though she were next to him he curled up in the driver's seat and when he woke the rain had stopped and there was a breeze several times he fell asleep his dreams vivid and fleeting night passed he didn't want it to end

4

yes he did and now he could see the grey struts of the Control Gates with hundreds of herring and ring-billed and great black-backed gulls wheeling up and over and down he fumbled among his things and got a card out of his wallet glancing at it before dropping it on the passenger seat he got out of the car unfastened the kayak from the rack and took it down he hefted up the boat and went along the path everything was clear to him a car passed and splashed up water as it went he felt the light spray but he didn't want to be seen carrying a boat at this time of night or was it morning he could feel the river going past as he walked to the place where the trees grew sparsely and the rocks were jumbled on the bank there was no fence he'd been here before and he knew all along he'd do it like this but he wanted to see the first of the light in the sky even if he had to wait for it

3

he worked his way down the bank testing each rock because they were slippery after the rain and at the bottom he wedged the kayak between the rocks where it was half hidden by a screen of sumac he could make out the turbulent water then he went back for the box fitting its flaps together so it would keep all the broken things inside he was tired when he reached the yellow boat it was too noticeable it was colourful as a toy in a sandbox he shifted it out of its hiding place and stowed the rattling box with its fragments as far as he could under the sturdy cross-ribs at the bow it would be hurled out into the river but wasn't that the point he found a sheltered place out of the rush of water and this was where he pushed the nose of the boat into the river he could feel the pull but not as much as he thought and he knew he'd be able to shove off without difficulty there were several ducks with four brown ducklings protected from the river swirling past just a few feet away he pulled up the boat's rudder because it didn't matter how the current took it

2

he was prolonging it perhaps he should say something
some kind of prayer he hunched over the boat his fingers
grasping the coaming it had begun to rain again drench-
ing him and he shivered as it came down fiercely when it
stopped a robin sang out maybe an omen the trunks of
the sumacs dark and graceful against the moving water
and a few drops fell from the slender leaves in a flash of
amber the light increased imperceptibly so it was impossible to tell if it was fading or growing but then the dimness
turned to gold the first sunlight broke through a ragged
part of the cloud he looked up to the east and then at the
Control Dam before passing the boat hand over hand
onto the river and time wasn't outside he could feel it
through his body his head his hands his bones his skin

1

the strong river rushing rushing rushing through him –

DAMIAN PUSHED THE KAYAK away from the bank and, through the sumacs, watched it float, tipsily, over the water. Orphaned. He went back to the car and got his wallet, knapsack, and drawings; he put the keys in the glove compartment. When he turned around, he couldn't see the boat on the river. Maybe it had already gone over the brink. Maybe it was falling. By now the ashes would have become one with the water. He walked along the path by the river. He'd done what he'd come to do. His feet moved ahead, but he could feel things collapsing. His body, a house of bone. Soon he could rest. It took a long time to walk to the bus terminal. A woman and a man, sitting by the wall, talking, as the man divided a chocolate bar into pieces. No, he said to her. You can't look – you have to shut your eyes. He put a piece of the chocolate bar on her tongue, and it seemed to Damian that darkness rushed into her mouth at the same time. Toronto, said Damian, at the counter. No, just one way. The kayak floated gaily down the river, tropical yellow on the grey water. He could have gone with it. By now the box had been thrown out of the boat; the box flaps pulled open by the force of the water, the urn shattered.

Niagara Falls to Toronto. That's $28.76. Man behind glass, an insect. Leaves at 7:10. The ashes had spilled into the river. Shards of urn, like bone, turned over and over in the water. The man stroked the woman's closed eyelids. The ashes were part of the water too, now, flickering in it, part of the chloride, mercury, phenol, phosphorous, a brilliant taint of water, pouring from Lake Erie into Lake Ontario. Mmmm, she said. He put another piece of chocolate in her mouth, then another. She laughed each time he did it, and he smiled as she ate it. Then he kissed her; she was loose in his arms, letting him taste the sweetness on her tongue. Damian went outside to wait for the bus because he couldn't look at them. Once, there had been a green moth, with wings like doll-sized sails, dying on the screen of the back door. He'd put his finger up to the screen, on which the creature was hanging, limply, but not so close his finger touched it. The moth didn't move. Then, as he watched, it twitched weakly. Or had the air moved its wings? It was the first time he'd seen something die, but the moment came and went and he didn't catch it. A moth, dying. A soft band of purple all along the top of the wings; markings that looked like eyes, and antennae, feathery and delicate. The wings themselves were green and transparent, thinner than the thinnest silk, shot through with morning light as it hung on the screen. He'd never seen anything so beautiful, but it had been dying. Ticket? You got a ticket? The bus driver ripped off part of his ticket and handed the receipt to him. It was snowing the morning Damian's father left. The cabbie thumped the trunk shut, so the shadows inside the trunk would stay there, together with the red suitcase and the old brown one with the straps. Tears on his father's face. Can't stay here, a man said, leaning over Damian in the bus terminal in Toronto. The man's breath stank. He could have buried the green moth, but he didn't want to think of putting heavy earth on top of those wings. So he left it and by evening it was gone. Can't stay here, repeated the man. Security'll come. You gotta go. It might have blown away after it died, because he couldn't find any trace of it when he looked outside. The man had a chain around his thick neck, tight, so it pressed against the flesh. He said that his name was Yvan, like Yvan Cornoyer, one of the greats. In 1972, Cornoyer passed the puck to Paul Henderson with thirty-four seconds left in the game, so they scored the winning goal, and *that* was a great moment. No great moments any more, but *that* was a great one. Yvan used to have a pet rat called The Terrible, but The Terrible had died. He laughed; he had a missing eye tooth. He took Damian to the mission on Spadina Avenue, but it was full, so he took him farther. Around they went, and down, like two small creatures caught in water as it swirled them past the rocks. Yvan found him a place in a hostel and gave him a peace sign when he left. Be cool, man. There was a smell in the hall of the hostel, but it wasn't the same as the sharp, acrid smell of the stained urinals. It had the thick sea smell of eelgrass. On the door of Damian's room was a plastic-covered placard explaining the rules. Block letters, tilted and pressed close together. A lost and found box by the door of the hostel's office, filled with unmatched shoes. The eelgrass washed along the shore, that in-between place between high tide and low tide, where there was always a thick, musty smell of salt. Death came to the beach every day. Usually it was so small no one noticed – a crab, the remains of a lobster – but sometimes it was larger. One of the shoes in the box was a child's black patent leather shoe with a strap and a sparkling fake diamond clasp. There had been the kid who had been diving with his friends, and the other one who had been hit from behind by a Sea-Doo. There was the man who'd had two vials of Ambien in his knapsack, one empty, one full, who had walked into the water, up to his knees, his thighs, his waist, waiting for the cold water to take his sleeping body out to sea, as far as Georgeville, on the other side of the cape, where a twelve-year-old found it. The clasp on the shoe glinted, mysteriously, in the box. When he was turned out of the hostel in the morning, Damian went to lie down under a tree in a park. Children in a wading pool. A body could be washed into shore; it could be rolled back and forth, as the tide pulled away. Sometimes the children in the wading pool screamed. Lengths of eelgrass over the white skin of a drowned man's legs. And on the beach, higher up, the eelgrass was matted, woven together, in long scrolled patterns. Here and there were jellyfish, purpled and shiny, and flattened into round, gelatinous disks, like organs taken out of the body: a liver, a heart, strewn here and there. He didn't like it when the jellyfish were in the water, because they stung him. They usually came in July during a spell of slow, humid heat, but they were gone by early August. Jellyfish thronged the water like blooms and died on the sand, with the eelgrass in strands over them, the way hair falls over eyes. He left the park and went to the terminal on Bay Street, taking a bus out of the city. He didn't care one way or the other that he was running out of money. Inside the bus it was cool, but it was very hot when he got out. Waves of heat, making the road look fluid as he walked from the Bowmanville bus terminal to the truck stop by the highway. The Fifth Wheel had full-service fuel islands, parking for more than one hundred rigs, drivers' lounge and showers, a forty-nine-room motel, a restaurant featuring an All-day Breakfast, Daily Buffet & Weekend Brunch, and, in the parking lot, near one of the fuel islands, the softened pink mess of a strawberry ice cream cone, melting. It was harder to swim when the jellyfish were in the water. They came in droves. In the gift shop, Damian fingered a miniature tiger with a bobbing head as people washed into the shop and out of it, swirling around him. He was hungry; he would have eaten the sweet, pink ice cream lying in globs on the pavement. He would have fallen to his knees to eat it. The glossy mass of a dead jellyfish on the sand. I'm going as far as Trois-Rivières, said the driver, his moustache like a grey-white brush above his lips. I'm not supposed to pick up anyone, but you don't look so good. So what am I gonna do – let you die of heatstroke? When he turned the steering wheel of the eighteen-wheeler he used both arms to do it, pulling hard. Where you from? Halifax. You sick? No. Eat something. Eat that bag of Cheezies, kid. I'm not sick, said Damian, opening the bag of Cheezies. The world was darkening slowly. Lights flashed at the side of the road. Red, yellow. My name's Greg, said the driver. That's my father's name, said Damian. Well, Bob's your uncle. What? Damian's father had taught him about fireflies. It was June, and they were in the backyard, watching as the night air lit up, closed, lit up again. They're talking to each other, Damian's father had said. Look, there's one now. This one's talking to that one over there. The way I'm talking to you. Damian's face in the truck's passenger window, pale, in a black window, through which passed a gloss of red and white light from a gas station, yellow brilliance from a U-Store-It. Aria of lights, passing through him. Well, you look kinda sick. You had trouble with your girlfriend or something? asked Greg. I had a girlfriend, I guess, said Damian, until I – Lisa had looked at him with her clear hazel eyes, judging him, the needle still in her hand, as she embroidered a flower on her jeans. Now he felt the needle under his skin, stitching it. Shit – you ran away from her, didn't you? Greg laughed. And now you're kicking yourself. Lisa pulled the thread taut, and Damian felt it glide through his flesh and stop. Then he felt it again. The thing with women is you gotta understand them, Greg said. That's the thing. Most guys don't even try. I buy roses, you know, on Valentine's Day. I buy roses on birthdays, anniversaries, Christmas. Always the same, always a dozen. And red, not pink or yellow. Red. I take her out to a steak house. I treat her like a queen. That's the way she should be treated. Greg took down a photo from a clip on the sun visor. Her name's Angela. Damian looked at Angela's curled brown bangs, the soft cleft in her chin. She's a great gal – Angela, said Greg. What's your girlfriend's name? Jasmine. You love her? Well, said Damian. No ifs, ands, or buts about it, said Greg. You love her, she loves you. What you need to know about fireflies, Damian's father told him, is that the male does a kind of aria in lights – an entire light song. But the female only flashes once. I don't think she wants anything to do with me now, said Damian. How does he know which one is the girl for him? his father said. It's a case of timing. So many beats in the darkness, then just one beam of light, like a voice. Oh, there you are, she says, lighting up. It's a two-way street – that's what I figure, Greg told him. If you're good to her. Remember what I said, kid, Greg said, as he dropped him off. Remember it. Damian got a ride to Cabano, then a ride to Edmundston in Jean-Marie's pickup truck. He remembered everything Greg had said, waiting half a day by the side of the road in Edmundston, watching the smoke from the mill plume into the air, filling it with a noxious smell. Jean-Marie had given him two rolled cigarettes, an old pack of matches, and a package of beef jerky. Had he slept? Had Jasmine slept, far away from him? The sky was white, the heat was white, and even the smell of the pulp mill was white. Had he dreamed? He could taste it in his mouth: cloudy, thick, and almost sweet in its sourness. He smoked one of the cigarettes and afterward he felt sick because he hadn't had enough to eat. He lay down by the highway under a tamarack tree with his head on his knapsack, and even with his eyes closed it seemed there was an intricate contraption hovering above his face, a finely made miniature palace. He put his hand up to touch it, but he couldn't find it. Oh, there you are, said Damian's father. He could hear the logging trucks passing on the Trans-Canada Highway. There you are, there you are. How soft Jasmine had looked when she held the candle between them. Her face, her skin, her eyebrows, her eyes, gazing at him. The candle, fixed in the little dish, divided the world into light, into darkness. You love her? Damian turned his head. In the ditch, the clover swayed. Some of the flowers were purple, some were blackened and dead. Damian, *stop*, Jasmine said, but he didn't want to stop, because if he'd stopped, he wouldn't have been able to go all the way through her body. She wanted him to stop. He didn't stop even when her head began to hit the wall each time he shoved himself inside her. Both of them were sweating, and it wasn't easy to keep a firm grasp on her hips. He heard his own body against hers. Slapping. He groaned as he came. Smoke filled the air above him, grey against white, making itself into Jasmine's body high in the air, where it

212

hung, suspended. She'd turned away from him and curled up on her side of the mattress, without saying a word. There she was, light as cloud, with her back to him. It was hard to breathe. Damian was on his way home, away from her. I treat her like a queen, Greg said. That's the way she should be treated. Damian would go to the beach at Cribbon's, where there were wild rose bushes on either side of the path. He wouldn't go near the cottage. Lisa might be there, sitting on the couch, asking him why he'd taken so long. He'd go straight to the beach, where water would shimmer, in its coolness, over his thighs, his waist, his chest. There would be a familiar, almost savoury, smell of kelp and eelgrass. One arm would slide into water, then the other, and the ocean would be pearl-grey, calm and quiet. It would be easy, slipping into it. He didn't need a Sea-Doo; he didn't need vials of Ambien. He'd swim as far as he could, to the east, as far as the blue of Cape Breton. In a fringe of spruce near the water there would be one crow, another, then a frenzy of crows. High up, much higher than the crows, would be a single bald eagle, cutting silently through air.

Victorian

HAIR   BRAIDED
WREATHS   PICTURES

&

JASMINE BLAKENEY

5934 STANLEY STREET   NIAGARA FALLS, ONTARIO   TEL. (905) 555-1007

THE SKY WAS A FRESHLY WASHED BLUE, and the air was cool, much cooler than it had been the day before. Two men came to the front door of a little bungalow on Stanley Street. One fiddled with a hangnail on his thumb. His cheeks were slightly flushed and he had a neatly trimmed moustache. The other was older and less self-conscious. There were wrinkles around his eyes, and his dark brown hair was beginning to turn grey at his temples. Both were dressed in uniform.

The older one, Bob Rieker, had done this kind of thing before, but it was the worst part of his job. The only good thing, he thought, as he knocked, was that he'd had two cups of strong coffee that morning; this helped, though not much. He knew that Warren Sangster, the young police-man next to him, was hoping his inexperience might not be apparent to the person who came to the door.

Rieker rapped hard on the door a second time, and now they could hear someone unlocking it.

Good morning. Jasmine Blakeney?

A purplish-haired young woman faced them at the threshold. He flipped open the leather wallet that held his identification and the younger policeman did the same.

We're with the Niagara Parks Police, said Rieker.

The woman tightened the belt of her terry-cloth robe. Jasmine, she called. Couple of cops here to see you.

She scrutinized them.

So what'd Jasmine do? she asked. Rob a bank or something?

No.

Another young woman came along the hall in bare feet, smoothing her sundress.

He won't tell me what you did, Jas, said the purple-haired woman, drifting away from the door.

Jasmine Blakeney? I'm Constable Rieker and this is Constable Sangster. We'd like to ask you a few questions, if you don't mind.

I don't mind, she said.

Do you know someone by the name of Ingrid MacKenzie?

Damian's mother, she said blankly. Yes.

Have you spoken to Ingrid or Damian this morning?

Why? she asked. What's happened?

We have reason to believe that Damian is missing, Rieker said, thinking how she was about the same age as his daughter.

Missing?

A jogger saw a car, a car with a roof rack, parked near the Hydro Control Dam early this morning. She also saw a yellow boat, which she described as a kayak, going down the river toward the Falls. She thought she saw someone in it, a man, but she wasn't positive. She contacted us early this morning. She also contacted the *Niagara Herald*, unfortunately –

What are you saying?

We're just conducting an investigation at this point, he said, as casually as he could. We'd like to find the owner of the car that was abandoned. It's got Nova Scotia plates and the owner is Ingrid Elizabeth MacKenzie, from Halifax. Halifax police have been to her residence, but there's no one at home. What we need to know is whether she owned a kayak – there's a roof rack on her car, but no kayak.

Yes, she said. No. It's Damian's kayak. Are you saying that he could have – I don't think – no, you must have the wrong person.

We're just trying to find out more, he said quietly.

She made a moaning sound and backed against the wall. Tarah, she cried.

The purple-haired woman came and put her arms around her. Oh God, she said. Oh shit.

There was a card on the passenger seat of the car, Rieker continued. He held the card away from him because he needed his reading glasses.

Victorian Hair Wreaths & Braided Pictures, Jasmine Blakeney, 5934 Stanley Street – He looked up from the card. You're Jasmine Blakeney, aren't you?

She didn't answer, and her friend, still holding her, nodded for her.

All I can say, Miss Blakeney, is that a car has been abandoned and a kayak is missing. That's as much as we know. Rieker wanted to be out of the dark hallway, out in the clean morning air again.

His partner pulled out a pencil and a small coil-bound book.

You're Tarah? he said.

Yes.

Maybe you can help – do you know who else Damian has been in contact with since he's been here? he asked. Do you know where he's staying?

I know he was staying with his uncle, said Tarah. Damian and his mom were both staying there. Roger Hock – something.

Hockridge, said Jasmine. On River Road.

He noted it in the book.

What are you going to do? asked Tarah.

We'll be in touch as soon as we can, said Rieker.

Their shoes made crisp, authoritative sounds as they went down the steps. The younger man got in the car, but the older man paused with his hand on the door handle and looked back at Tarah, still holding Jasmine in the doorway. Then he got in the car too.

What Bob Rieker hated was telling the mother, who'd said nothing at all. She'd just closed her eyes and put her hands up as if to shield herself. Then she'd gone quickly out of the kitchen and down the hall; he heard her going up the stairs.

That left the blind guy, sitting there crying like a child. He imagined the worst, right away.

Last night Damian was upset, he said, wiping his face. There was just no reasoning with him. His sister died less than a year ago, and last night he couldn't find the box that held her ashes. His cousin had taken it – my son. And Damian was just beside himself. It's all my fault.

It's not –

I should have gone after him. I should have made it right. God, I wasn't there for him. Once, you know, I said something to him. I said that he should do it in the middle of the night, because they'd slap a fine on him otherwise. I told him that. He must have got the idea from me.

Do what in the middle of the night? asked Rieker.

He was going to toss his sister's ashes in the river. I never imagined he was thinking of anything like this.

Would you say he seemed depressed?

No, he was angry. He was angry with his cousin. He was angry with all of us. Not so much depressed as erratic, capable of anything. Poor Ingrid, he added.

The boy's mother?

Yes.

It reminded Rieker of the time his grandmother had died, and how his father had told him, carefully, as if there was a way to say the words without making them hurt. But it had hurt. He'd run upstairs, away from his father, and cried in the bathroom with the door locked, lying on the cold tiles of the bathroom floor, looking up at the round, shiny underside of the sink.

What could Rieker have done? He wasn't the kind who had ever reached out and held another man, but something about this man's crying made him want to.

Oh Lord, cried the blind man, rocking back and forth. Oh, Damian.

We don't know anything yet. We're just conducting an investigation.

But he took the kayak and –

The man couldn't finish. He pressed his hands to his forehead, drawing them down his face so that Rieker could see the inside of his lower lip for a moment. It was ruby red.

No one at the Control Dam saw him? he asked.

No. A jogger, a female, said she saw a kayak going toward the Falls – it was above Table Rock. But she was looking through the trees and it wasn't completely light.

Will you tell me as soon as they find the boat? As soon as they find anything at all?

Yes, sir, we'll let you know just as soon as we know anything more. We'll certainly let you know.

What surprised Rieker, and also made him feel foolish, was that the man cried tears. They ran down his face until his cheeks were wet. The man was blind, yet he cried tears, just like anyone else. For some reason he found this unexpected, like the time he had seen a thin slash across his dog's paw, made by glass, and the beads of bright red blood that sprang from it. He'd been stupidly surprised by the red blood, which was so like his own.

After the two policemen left the big house on River Road, they went and got themselves a cup of coffee at Tim Hortons. It was only ten o'clock, but it seemed as though they'd put in a long day already. Rieker drank his doubledouble, but he had a headache. He knew he had to look as if this kind of thing was all in a day's work, because Warren, who looked like he was still hanging on to his mother's apron strings, was watching his every move. At some point, this kid would have to do what Rieker had done, and he'd have to do it well, but he'd also have to make it seem as if he'd done it many times before.

Rieker rolled up the rim of the paper cup to see if he'd won anything, got up with a sigh, and tossed the cup in the trash. They'd go back and do up the paperwork. He'd eat his sandwich with light cream cheese and turkey that Moira had made for him. But this business of the boy had made a black hole in his day.

Jasmine circled around the kitchen aimlessly, tears running down her face. She turned to the wall, leaning her forehead against it.

Oh fuck.

She struggled to think of what to do next. Her thoughts were very slow. She sat down at the table, looking at the steaming brown liquid in the blue cup. Tarah had made coffee for her. Jasmine could hear, distantly, the sound of a shower in the bathroom, and she concentrated on the sound.

Tarah had held Jasmine and talked soothingly to her. But finally, she said she had to go to work, because she was two hours late already. Would Jasmine be all right? And Jasmine had nodded.

Milk. She needed milk for the coffee. When she got up and reached for the handle of the refrigerator door to get the milk, she saw Damian standing in the doorway, tall and loose and sleepy. She closed her eyes and when she opened them, he was gone.

They'd got it wrong. Those policemen. The jogger.

Yet she could see a yellow boat, bright as a bird, tipping over the edge. It tipped and was gone.

She splashed cold water from the kitchen sink on her face and stood alone in the dim room. She picked up the phone and dialed. Her mother answered, and Jasmine imagined her on the brown sofa with the handmade blue-and-chocolate-brown quilt folded neatly over the back. She spoke softly, in that breathy voice that was so familiar.

Hello, Mum, said Jasmine, putting her hand to her eyes to stop the tears.

Sandra, said her mother. It's so early in the morning. Only Esther Pavlovich phones so early. The rates are better after six in the evening.

I know.

What time is it there?

I don't know.

Well, it's not yet nine here. Do you want to call again after six in the evening?

No, Mum. I just wanted to hear your voice.

Oh, said her mother. Well, here it is. My voice, I mean. If you hadn't gone off to God-knows-where you'd be able to hear my voice more often.

Mum –

Do you need money?

No – no, I'm fine for money. Jasmine was staring at the clock. Was it ten o'clock or two o'clock? She couldn't figure it out.

Sandra? Are you all right? It sounds like you've been crying.

No, I – How are you and Dad?

We're fine. This cat of yours has been acting strangely. Didn't you say you were going to take it?

Yes. I'll take her the next time I come home.

Well, that'll be Christmas, said her mother. I don't know if I can wait that long. Some days I think it's that cat or me, and both of us won't fit in the same house. She's ruining the curtains.

The curtains, repeated Jasmine.

The new ones from Sears. Are you all right, Sandra? You don't sound all right.

I'm –

You're still working? asked her mother. Are you taking your vitamin C every day? You are? Well, are you pregnant? You're not phoning to say you're pregnant, are you?

No, I'm not pregnant.

Well, you're probably low on iron, because girls always are. And you have to be careful there. It's not like here. People take advantage of you in places like that. It's really no place for you to be –

You've said that, said Jasmine.

You could come back here. There's always your room here – we haven't changed a thing, except that I made a new valance for your window. It's pink and white, like the bedspread.

Is Dad all right?

Other than being cross with you, he's as fine as a person can be who's on blood thinners.

Tell him I called. Jasmine leaned her head back; she closed her eyes.

I'll tell him. Remember to take care of yourself, will you?

I love you, Mum.

Yes, dear, I love you too. Next time call after six in the evening, all right?

Yes, Mum.

She put the receiver down slowly, thinking about the cat. She saw Spats, the grey cat with the white paws, and her father's large hand holding it by the scruff of its neck. Spats had peed on the living room rug. She remembered how he'd chucked the cat out the door, but it righted itself even as it fell, so it landed perfectly. And then she'd run outside to comfort it. That was what she wanted now, she thought, to hold her cat in her arms and feel it purring. She wanted her old dog too, but Queenie was gone.

She still had her hand on the phone. Then she picked up the receiver again and dialed a number.

Roger? Oh, Roger – I'm sorry, I can't do this. I can't talk.

Jasmine.

I can't talk.

Wait –

It was several days before the policemen returned to the house on Stanley Street.

Jasmine was lying on her bed staring at the ceiling when she heard the knock at the door. She hadn't been able to sleep for two nights, and now she was exhausted. But the knocking at the door persisted and after a while she got up, buttoning her jeans, and went down the hall.

May we come in?

She opened the door wider and the two officers stepped inside the house.

Miss Blakeney, said Constable Rieker, the kayak has been recovered. It was pulled out on the American side. It's been identified as the one belonging –

Don't, she said, putting a hand up to her forehead. Please don't.

Rieker looked down at his shoes.

It's only the kayak they've found, he said.

She couldn't take in what he was saying.

It's just the kayak, he repeated.

She couldn't speak. She'd been thinking about it for days, and now he was saying it.

Was it a yellow kayak? asked Jasmine.

Yes. The mother – Damian MacKenzie's mother – identified the boat. Both the car and the kayak were released into her possession.

But have they found –

Have they found the boy? He spoke gently. No.

But —

It's been three days. What you should know, and what I've told the boy's mother, is that if indeed he went over the Falls, and he may not have done that, but if he did, you should know that the body may not be recovered.

Not recovered? She could hear her voice quavering.

If he was in that kayak, chances are his body was caught behind the Falls in the plunge pool. That's why I say it might not be recovered.

Her eyes filled with tears. Oh, she said, as if she could hardly get the breath to say it.

But we haven't closed the books on this, you can rest assured. We'll let you know as things unfold.

She stared at him.

Will you be all right? he asked.

She made a gesture, as if to ward them off, and closed the door behind them when they went away. She leaned against it.

She slid down the door onto the brown carpet.

His body in the plunge pool. His beautiful body. His long hair, released from its braid, like the hair of angels. She could see it fanning around his head as he was swept up by the water in the plunge pool, swept down. Around and around went the body, pale and almost translucent in the water. How was it possible?

No, it didn't mean that he was dead. He might still be alive, walking around, breathing in and out.

The water would peel the flesh from his bones, like a glove from a hand. How long would it take? Eventually the bones would ride that circuit, up and down, over and over. His ribs and spine, his skull, the bones of his arms and legs and feet. How long would it take a body to decompose? How long before he was nothing but bone?

But nothing had been confirmed. Nothing was certain.

Yet the darkness came over her, bearing down hard, pressing the air from her lungs. She put her hands to her face as she cried, for a long time, hardly making a sound.

Daredevil's Kayak
Found in Whirlpool

NIAGARA FALLS, N.Y. – A daredevil's kayak (upper right) was recovered from the Niagara River yesterday afternoon. Jay Adonis, a visitor from Egypt, New York, was the first to spot the boat.

Initially, it was not clear whether the kayak could be retrieved, since it was caught in the Whirlpool. But several hours after it was sighted, a jet boat roared out to pick it up when it came within 150 feet of shore. It was then handed over to Canadian authorities.

A jogger caught sight of the kayak just as it went over the Falls at about 5:40 a.m. on Wednesday, August 3rd. "I saw a flash of something yellow out of the corner of my eye and I realized it was a boat. I don't know what that poor guy was

227

thinking when he did it," said Melissa MacLean, of Niagara Falls, Ontario.

To date, a body has not been found. But a man from Nova Scotia, Damian MacKenzie, disappeared on August 3rd, abandoning a car near the Hydro Control Dam above the Horseshoe Falls. It is feared that he made a rash decision to brave the Falls.

"Going over the Falls in a boat of this type is the equivalent of crashing into a brick wall at 100 miles an hour," remarked Capt. Jim Rossi of the Niagara County Sheriff's Marine Unit. He responds to calls like this more than a dozen times a year, but summer is the peak period. "Some people jump off the bridges, but more often they're hypnotized by the Falls, and throw themselves over," he explained. "A great many are suicides, of course, but a few think they can defy death. And there's just no way they can survive."

"From what we understand," Rossi commented, "this particular individual went over the Canadian Falls without being detected by Niagara Parks Police."

Ten million people descend on Niagara Falls each summer, and most are content to photograph their families or friends in front of the picturesque backdrop. But a small number of sightseers are lured to their deaths by the siren call of the Falls.

"As far as I know, this guy was a drifter," states Gordon Samson, proprietor of the Ornamental Hand Tattoo Arts. "He came in here once or twice, but he seemed kind of down in the dumps."

Samson also believes that MacKenzie was in possession of small quantities of marijuana, and that he may have been under the influence when he embarked on his fateful trip over the Falls.

THE MAN FINISHED WIPING his telescope. He was afraid there was moisture inside the lens, but as he finished polishing it with a soft, dry cloth, he saw none. The next day he'd spray the tripod with WD-40. He took the telescope outside on the deck, but instead of looking through it, he sat down on one of the deck chairs and gazed up at the night sky. There wasn't really a need for a telescope on a night like this. He could see Cassiopeia with its zigzag of diamond points; he always looked for it at this time of year. When he leaned back with his arms behind his head he could see the whole panoply of constellations. How far away they were, and yet how close, giving off light from thousands of years, or millions of years, before, a light that came from enormous distances. These thoughts gave him pleasure, though he couldn't have said why.

The dog came and put his heavy head on the man's knee. He wondered what he'd do without this dog, but he didn't think he would get another because he'd never have one that loved him the way Max did. He reached forward and stroked the dog's head, and Max wagged his tail so it thumped against the other chair.

The man got up and walked to the far side of the deck, where his running shoes had been drying in the sun during the day. As he picked them up he glanced at Heinrich's place at the top of the hill. There was a light on. He said he'd check on the house while Heinrich made a trip to Stuttgart, but Heinrich wasn't due back for another couple of weeks.

He stood for a while thinking about it, slapping the shoes together to get rid of the sand. It could be a break and enter. It could be teenagers up there shooting heroin, or it could be someone starting a fire in the living room. This last thought goaded him into action, because he thought of the time Heinrich had spent working on the hardwood floors. He put the shoes on a deck chair and opened the sliding door to get the flashlight that hung on a hook just inside.

Come, Max.

It was very dark on the beach, but he found a ridged track that he followed until it curved away, and then he clambered onto the rocks. Holding Max by the collar, he climbed the steeply inclined hill and by the time he got to a cluster of birch trees near the house, he was out of breath. Heinrich had made a bench here for his second wife, Jutta, so she could look out at the ocean, but she'd never used it. She was a good dozen years younger than he was, and she'd never really taken to Nova Scotia; she preferred their house in Lanzarote, in the Canary Islands. So it was local kids who sat on the bench sometimes, swinging their heels.

He stood with one hand against the smooth, papery bark of one of the birches. When he swept the flashlight back and forth, he could see battered beer cans under the seat, and he reminded himself to collect them in the daytime. Somehow the thought of Heinrich building this seat for his wife, and his wife never using it, struck him as sad. He went up the hill toward the house. It had the best view for miles around, and many times he had sat with Heinrich on the deck, not talking much, but simply gazing at the slate-blue ocean.

The dog went on ahead, perhaps drawn by the smell of an animal, and the man came to the top of the rise where he could see the light in the living room. Whoever was inside was enjoying that light. He went forward, and at first he simply saw the bulky shapes of the furniture, the red leather couch with the woven throw that Jutta had bought in Thailand. He remembered how he'd visited once, when the red leather couch had been new, and how happy Jutta had been, spreading out the throw that she'd bought in Bangkok to show him how well the colours matched. Near the couch were the bookshelves, full of books written in German, and the table and chairs, hand-carved in Togo.

He went up onto the deck, moving as softly as he could. Although he was much closer now, so he could see the tassels of the throw from Thailand, the glittery threads in the pillows at either end of the couch, and the polished hardwood floor, he could not tell who was inside, if indeed anyone was there. But then there was a small movement that caught his eye. On the other side of the couch, close to the fireplace, someone was lying on the floor. He waited, and Max followed him onto the deck, claws clicking on the wood. The man reached out as the dog came close; he gave the dog a firm tap and Max sat down obediently, quietly.

Finally the intruder got up, moving lazily, nonchalantly, as if he owned the place. His blond hair was pulled back into a braid, and it was this that made the man start a little.

He'd seen him before. He'd seen tears on this face. How could he forget that moment? Yes, of course, it was the same boy, though his boyishness was nearly gone. But what was he doing here? The man moved back so that he was hidden by the shadow. There was the low noise, the beginning of a throaty growl, from the dog. He patted the thick fur at the dog's neck to calm him.

The boy lifted some crumpled papers and took them to the table, where he studied them, one at a time. Then he turned them over. The man gazed at his face; he hadn't recalled the boy's features exactly. Anguish changed a face, he thought, and he'd first seen the boy when his sister had died. He was very good-looking. His mouth, not unlike a girl's, was full and sensuous, though his face was that of a man: his jaw was angular, his brows dark, and his hair shone brilliantly under the light.

Much would be forgiven this boy because of his beauty. The man thought of his own son and sighed, and perhaps because of this he could feel himself becoming more lenient. He knew the boy had been devious in order to break into the place – he was sure Heinrich didn't know him – but he wasn't angry with him. He was filled with curiosity, though, and without thinking he knocked on the French doors. The boy ducked. He left the papers on the table and slipped down behind the couch. There was, amusingly, the man thought, a bare foot showing at the base of the couch, but it was drawn in as he watched.

He knocked again. He waited, and then it occurred to him that the French doors might not be locked. He turned the handle of the left-hand door.

Stay, Max, he commanded in a low voice.

He opened the door and stepped inside. Hello, he said.

There was a regular *tock, tock* from the grandfather clock.

This is Heinrich Kaefferboch's house, said the man, because he wanted to invoke Heinrich's presence. Did you know that?

No, of course the boy didn't know that. The man stood looking at the painting above the stone fireplace. He always did this. Heinrich would go to the fridge and get him a beer, but he would stand at this same place each time, as if to pay homage, and Heinrich would return with the cold beer in one hand and a hand-blown glass in the other, and pour it for him slowly, letting the honey-coloured liquid run down the inside of the glass.

The painting was about five feet long and three feet wide, showing fields in the evening, perhaps in autumn, with a darkening sky. In the foreground, blown by the wind, several fires fanned up in ruddy orange and yellow-gold, with smoke feathering into the air. At the brow of a hill was a small, bunched-up tree, an apple tree gone wild, its dark branches formed into claws by the wind. He liked the thought of evening fires in such a forgotten landscape, with fields going on and on into blue-blackness. It haunted him, and made him feel almost tender. He wasn't always aware of paintings, but this one was different, and it made him want to keep looking at it.

That's a fine painting on the wall above you, said the man. I don't suppose you've noticed it.

Silence.

It wasn't the smartest move, he went on, breaking in here. It's a good thing I came, instead of the Mounties. It's probably a good thing.

The boy got up abruptly, rushing forward as if he meant to tackle the man, who moved quickly out of the way.

He hit the French doors instead. If the way the boy slammed into the doors hadn't hurt him, if he hadn't fallen down, the whole thing would have struck the man as absurdly comical.

Are you all right? he asked, bending over the boy. He helped him to the couch, surprised at the thinness of the boy's body. You've never played football, have you? That's not the way to –

I saw the painting, grunted the boy.

How long have you been here?

He shrugged.

Days? pressed the man. Weeks?

The boy turned his face away. I don't know.

You've heard me coming in and out?

It was strange that the man hadn't seen traces when he'd come in before. What did you eat? he asked. Did you gnaw on the furniture?

The boy laughed.

The man went into the kitchen and opened the cupboards: several boxes of chicken noodle soup packets, canned tuna, canned peaches, tea, hot chocolate, one box of English water biscuits, white sugar in a cork-topped container, cinnamon sticks, salt and pepper in their shakers. Not much of anything. Only the things Heinrich had left there. He went back into the living room, and it crossed his mind that the boy might not recognize him.

What's your name? asked the man.

Damian.

Damian. From the Greek – it's a Greek name.

It was clear Damian didn't care where his name came from.

Anyway, Damian, you should come with me. I think you could do with a good meal.

Damian didn't move from the couch.

You all right? asked the man.

Yes. I shouldn't have taken a run at you.

No, probably not.

Damian sat up.

You sure you're all right?

I don't know. Yes.

Do you have a few things? A sleeping bag?

The boy didn't look well. His face was gaunt and there were blue shadows under his eyes as if he hadn't slept. He appeared to move lazily, but perhaps he had no energy.

He got up now, taking the papers from the table to the kitchen and stuffing them into the garbage, and the man could see how his dirty clothes hung on his frame.

Shoes? Sweater? asked the man.

He collected his sweatshirt and sandals, tossing them into an old knapsack.

Is that everything?

Yes.

The man went back into the kitchen. He checked the stove, switched off the light, and came back into the living room.

Damian was by the door, looking at him.

Do you remember me? the man asked.

You're the one who helped me, aren't you? When my sister died.

Yes.

What's your name?

Raymond.

Raymond. Damian's lips curved up. From the Greek.

From the German.

Oh, from the German, said Damian wryly.

They went out into the darkness together, after Raymond turned out the lights. He'd come back the next day and find out how the boy had got in.

They went across the lawn, a lawn that needed cutting, Raymond noticed, and Max trotted behind them. The leaves that had fallen on the grass looked like phantoms, pale in the darkness. They passed the bench Heinrich had made for Jutta, and the stand of slim birches; stones clattered on the rocks below as they made their way down the steep path. Raymond used the flashlight, but the circle of brightness illuminated only a few things and made the night seem darker all around, so he switched it off. Max had bounded on ahead, but now he returned to his master, jostling him.

No, Max.

Soon they reached the shelves of rock where it was easier to gain footing. Damian walked along easily and jumped down onto the sand on the far side.

It happened right over there, Damian said as they walked.

They stood together listening to the small sounds of the water against the sand.

I couldn't do much, said Raymond. To help, I mean.

Damian didn't move. Raymond shifted his gaze and looked up at the shaving of moon. What a tiny thing it was. He thought of his telescope and reminded himself to take it inside. And then, abruptly, he remembered the girl's face, with that look of the dead: that look of having gone so far away she couldn't be called back. Cecily had looked the same.

I often wondered what had happened to you, said Raymond.

You did?

Yes.

It made me a little weird.

It would have made anyone a little weird.

Damian went ahead, and Raymond walked briskly to catch up.

When they reached the house, he showed Damian the shower and offered him soap, shampoo, and a clean towel. It was a blue one, with green leaves and nodding lily-of-the-valley flowers that Cecily had always saved for visitors. He made up the guest-room bed with yellow sheets and folded an extra blanket at the bottom of the bed because the room was on the north side and tended to be cold. He put out a pair of old trousers and a long-sleeved green T-shirt that had *Notre Dame Fightin' Irish* emblazoned on it. Then he went into the kitchen and poached some eggs. He put bread in the toaster and the little jar of raspberry jam and the ceramic pot of honey on the table. It was the kind of thing he might have made for breakfast, but it was good, comforting food.

When Damian came into the kitchen he had rubbed his hair dry and it hung over his shoulders in damp ropes. He smelled of soap and shampoo, but there was something feral about him. He was wearing the long-sleeved T-shirt, a relic from Raymond's alma mater, which was too big for him.

Here's a plateful to keep you going, Raymond told him.

Thanks.

Damian ate with ravenous speed, as if he expected the plate would be taken away from him before he finished. But a person's hunger was a private thing, and Raymond faced away from him, turning on the kettle to make tea.

They sat up for a while that night. Damian drank his tea, and Raymond put some music on the CD player: *Waltz for Debby*, one of his favourites. He leaned back in his armchair and shut his eyes, half-sleeping, half-awake. Damian fell asleep on the couch, and Raymond didn't wake him later, when he got up and turned off the CD player, patted Max's head as he slept on the rectangle of rug that was his own, and got the extra blanket from the guest bed. He put it over Damian as he slept, though how anyone could sleep on a couch like that was beyond him. Then he went back and got a pillow, but he couldn't put it under the boy's head without waking him.

In the morning, Damian was still asleep on the couch – his hand drooping so the fingertips touched the floor – when Raymond got up and made his usual breakfast of toast and coffee. Damian didn't wake when the coffee bubbled through the coffee maker, nor did he wake when Raymond went out the door and slid it shut behind him. Max trotted out at the same time.

Raymond realized he'd forgotten about the telescope, which had been left outside all night. But it promised to be another good day, which made him think that the fall would be mild. He raised his hands over his head and stretched his back. The dog had already gone down the steps and was racing across the beach, after something, perhaps another dog.

Max. Here, Max.

The dog wheeled in its tracks and ran back to him.

Good dog. Get a stick.

They went up the hill together and stopped at the top to look down at the dark blue water and beyond it to the headland. There was a jutting red-brown cliff topped by spruce, and farther northwest were the hills around Cape George, with the trees on the distant slopes beginning to be tipped, here and there, with yellow and crimson. A few colours blazed among the dark green spikes of spruce, and he found himself wanting to stay for another couple of weeks, watching the colour flame through the woods.

He checked each room of Heinrich's house, and saw that things were untouched for the most part. Damian must have slept on the red couch, because none of the beds had been disturbed. The window in the bathroom was unlocked when Raymond checked it – Damian could have come in here and jumped down on the toilet. The floor was a little dirty. In the kitchen, there was nothing to show that anyone had occupied it. The tuna cans had been cleaned and put in the recycling bins in the mud room. The garbage in the kitchen was stuffed full of the papers Damian had thrown out the night before, but Raymond took them out.

They were drawings, much crumpled drawings, of a slim, pretty girl. The expression on her face, her dark hair, the quality of her skin, and the way her body was modelled and shaped by lights and darks so it seemed real – all of it was drawn with deftness. But it was her eyes that caught him, because they seemed to hold the light. She could have been looking at him. There was some luminous quality about this girl, some grave, indefinable sweetness in the way she'd been drawn.

He put them on the floor in the living room, shifting the table out of the way, so he could see them better. Damian had drawn the girl from one angle and then another, as if he had walked around her, stopped, made a drawing, then walked around her a little more and stopped again. Here she was from the front, then from a three-quarter view, then from the side, so her face was in profile. There was one from behind, showing her buttocks and strong, lean legs. There were eight drawings in all, and in each one the girl's features were consistent, and recognizable, even though in several there was less detail in the rendering of the mouth, nose, or eyes. Yet it was as if Damian saw that this girl was not just one person, but many. He'd seen all the way through her to some transparency within, as if she were made of water, not flesh and bone.

Raymond rolled the drawings up and put them under his arm. He latched the French doors from the inside and went out the front door, locking it behind him. Then he slid the key under the stone owl in the garden and went down the hill.

JASMINE FOUND ROGER in the backyard working in the herb garden. She propped her bicycle by the back door and walked across the lawn to the garden. He was taking out some of the mint, which had grown raggedly wild through the oregano, basil, dill, and thyme. His hands fingered the mint plants and moved underneath to uproot them, pulling hard.

Hello, she said.

Jasmine. He sat back on his heels. How've you been doing?

The heaps of uprooted mint lying on the grass filled the air with a strong, pungent scent.

Oh, not good, she said. Nothing's certain.

That's the trouble.

It makes you go around in circles. She bent down and picked a mint leaf. You think if he's dead, why did he do it? On the other hand, you think if he's alive, why did he do it? Where did he go? But if he went and – her voice broke.

She crushed the mint leaf and let it drop. She tried to gather herself.

If he went and killed himself – I don't know. Do you

think he saw us and jumped to conclusions? Maybe I should have said something –

You're not to blame, said Roger.

We could have set him off. Anything could have set him off. He's like that, she cried.

Roger had a hat made of heavy cotton with a floppy brim and a cord that hung down to his neck. It made him look old. Jasmine wanted to take it from him and hurl it to the grass.

How could he do something like this?

I don't know, he said, poking at the heap of mint aimlessly. Maybe it was an accident. Maybe he just wanted to throw Lisa's ashes on the river and have done with it.

Do you really think it was an accident?

No.

Do you think he was in the boat?

I can't say, Jasmine.

Sometimes I think I'm losing my mind. It must be awful for Ingrid – how is she?

Not good. He grunted, yanking a root. She won't come out of her room except to make a cup of tea and eat a couple of crackers.

I'd like to see her.

You would?

No, said Jasmine. Yes.

She won't bite you, said Roger. She might not answer the door, though. She's in pretty rough shape, he said. I guess it's to be expected, but it would be good if you could rouse her.

People should go around howling when things like this happen, don't you think? Why don't they go around howling?

I don't know.

That's the kayak over there, isn't it? Jasmine stared at it.

The kayak lay beside the carriage house. The yellow plastic had been bashed in near the bow, and it was covered with scratches and one blotchy, rust-coloured stain, but it was intact.

Yes. Ingrid won't let me get rid of it.

Jasmine turned away and started to sob. Oh – I can't stand it.

Come here, kiddo.

No.

But he found her and put his arms around her. He waited until she stopped crying and stepped back from him.

Fuck, he said quietly, what was that kid thinking?

He wasn't thinking, said Jasmine. Or at least, he wasn't thinking about any of us.

She went into the house. It had been such a short time since she'd been there, but so much had changed. Here was the large kitchen with the table and chairs, the pantry stocked with soup cans and jars of pickles, the leafy greenery outside the window. She left her flip-flops by the door. It was as if she were in a church; she didn't want to make a sound. As she went up the stairs, she noticed the snake skeleton hanging from the light fixture, fine bones bristling from its spine.

From the top of the stairs, she could see the butterfly cases half hidden in shadow at the end of the hall, and it reminded her of the time she'd stood there, talking to Damian. No, she didn't want to think about that.

She wasn't sure she wanted to see Ingrid, but something compelled her to go down the hall to the closed door and knock on it.

Ingrid, she called.

Something dropped on the floor.

Ingrid.

There was a sound of someone walking to the door, and then it opened.

Jasmine. It's you.

Ingrid's face was frightening. It was grey and completely without expression.

I came to see you, said Jasmine.

Why? said Ingrid blankly. She left the door open and vanished into the room. I won't be any good to you.

Jasmine stood at the threshold.

Come in, said Ingrid. If you're still there.

The room was dark because the blinds had been drawn, but ladders of light showed through. Jasmine entered cautiously. There was a faint, cloying scent of perfume. Roses, she thought, but not real roses. On the floor were a few scattered pieces of clothing: a blouse, a T-shirt, a white sweater.

Oh, where to sit? said Ingrid. Just throw the things off that chair.

There was a suitcase on the chair and Jasmine put it on the floor. Ingrid was sitting on the edge of the bed, her white hair hanging down, uncombed. She wore a lacy camisole and gym shorts. She hadn't cared at all what she put on, Jasmine thought. She was past caring.

You don't mind if I lie down, do you? Ingrid asked.

No.

Good. My head is better if I lie down. Things don't fly around.

Are you all right?

Ingrid laughed. Then she stopped. She lay with one arm above her head and the other hanging slackly off the bed.

I'm all right if we don't talk about Damian, said Ingrid. I can't talk about him. You start, Jasmine. Tell me something.

Jasmine was silent.

Anything at all, Ingrid prompted. I spy, with my little eye, something that is –

I've been thinking of my grandmother's house, said Jasmine. My Ukrainian grandmother, my mother's mother.

Strange.

What?

Strange that I might not be anyone's mother's mother. What was her name, your mother's mother?

Aleksandra, but people called her Sandra.

Ingrid put her hands up in the air as if to study them. She dropped them. Aleksandra. And you were thinking of her.

She's dead.

So's mine. My grandparents, my parents – Tell me about your grandmother's house. Describe the kitchen.

The kitchen?

Yes.

It was a big kitchen, a farm kitchen. It had green tiles on the floor with splatters of red on them. And rag rugs my grandmother had made. There was a small tin shelf above the sink, said Jasmine. On the shelf was a miniature Virgin Mary.

She stopped. Do you really want to hear about this?

Yes, about everything in that kitchen. Tell me everything.

Jasmine considered. Well, at Easter, my grandmother put two decorated eggs, ones that her friend Mrs. Kolowsky made, on either side of the Virgin Mary. They were red and yellow and black. Inside the egg on the Virgin's left I used to imagine an entire world, with waving grass and horses and a farm in the distance. The sun was always coming up there, and the sky was always pale blue, and the horses whinnied and cantered in circles. I thought of this as the Eastern Egg. And inside the other egg, the one on the Virgin's right –

The Western Egg.

Yes, inside the Western Egg I imagined the sun going down over some European city, a city with an onion dome rising up in the middle. But that egg broke. Mrs. Kolowsky waxed and painted another, but it couldn't replace the one that broke. That's what I remember best. The Easter eggs.

And your grandmother, what did she look like?

It was best to humour Ingrid, thought Jasmine. She closed her eyes, trying to focus on her grandmother.

My grandmother had long, white hair. She braided and coiled her hair into a bun at the back of her head. My grandfather said that she'd been the sort of woman who made heads turn, but I didn't know what he meant. I was little, and he had to tell me that heads didn't really turn; it was in a manner of speaking, and then he had to explain what in a manner of speaking meant. After that, I imagined people's heads turning the way sunflowers do, as if my grandmother was the sun.

Ingrid had shifted her head to look at Jasmine, a hint of a smile on her lips. Sunflowers.

Yes.

My grandmother was tall, said Ingrid. She carried herself as if she had a book on her head, and when she sat, she sat like a lady, gracefully, always with one hand under her to keep her dress from wrinkling. She had a dry sense of humour. And she knew about things; she knew about the quality of crystal, or whether a sherry was good or not so good. She also knew four languages, Spanish and Portuguese and Italian and French. And she painted miniature watercolours – the smallest things. Elizabeth Victoria. I'm not the least bit like her.

But you carry yourself that same way, as if you had a book on your head.

No, she was queen of her own small kingdom. I used to be terrified of her.

Ingrid laughed.

I was terrified of you, said Jasmine.

You were? Well, Roger says I drive people away.

But you made that cake for me. You were the only one who remembered my birthday.

That was a fiasco. I'm sorry.

I did come here – to the house. I came for some cake. I guess you knew that.

That was the night all hell broke loose. Oh, God, she said. I don't know if he's dead or alive. She covered her face with the pillow.

Jasmine waited, but there was no sound under the pillow. Ingrid, she said. *Ingrid.*

Ingrid removed the pillow.

Jasmine held herself so tightly that her fingernails dug into the skin of her arms.

It's not your fault, Ingrid said bleakly. *Oh,* she cried. We can talk about grandmothers and Ukrainian eggs – but it's horrible. Isn't it horrible?

Yes.

But you're cool as a cucumber.

No, said Jasmine. I'm not. I can't tell whether I'm awake or dreaming. I keep thinking of – I keep seeing Damian. He's standing by the fridge. Or he's sitting in front

of me, drawing. I don't know how people keep their balance
through something like this.

They don't, said Ingrid. No one knows how to do it.

But you've been through this.

No, I haven't been through *this*. I went through something else. I went through something that was clear from
the beginning, but there's nothing clear about this.

There's no way of knowing, is there?

No. And the gods are hungry. They want more and
more and more – they want our days and nights.

Jasmine could see the gods as if they were in the room.
They leered out from the corners.

I've had such nightmares –

So have I, murmured Jasmine.

And I've been taking pills that Roger gives to me. But
he won't give me the whole bottle. No doubt he thinks I'll
do something.

The blinds made a sound as if a deck of cards were
being shuffled.

You can raise those blinds, if you like, said Ingrid.

Jasmine got up and raised them. Afternoon light
poured into the room.

Ingrid blinked. Oh, it's too much.

Do you want them down again?

Yes, I think so.

Jasmine lowered the blinds.

What did you say before? asked Ingrid. Did you say
Damian made some drawings of you?

Yes.

He's very good. My grandmother was an artist, but I
told you that. That's where Damian gets it from, but he
hadn't drawn anything in almost a year.

He did a few drawings of me, said Jasmine, but nothing he was happy with.

Ingrid was quiet for a while, until Jasmine thought she'd gone to sleep. But then she spoke.

When you first heard about him disappearing like that – what did you do?

I don't know. I can't remember all of that day, just bits of it. I called my mother. I didn't tell her about Damian, but she asked me if something was wrong. She asked if I was pregnant.

Are you pregnant?

No.

I don't know if that's good or not good, said Ingrid. I just don't know. Do you want to be pregnant?

No. It wouldn't be good for me. It wouldn't be good for anyone.

Jasmine looked at the things on the floor. A pink towel. A thin white sweater with a missing button. A flower-printed sheet that had fallen off the bed.

You're wise, said Ingrid. For being nineteen.

Jasmine didn't want to be pregnant, but she was thinking that there was nothing inside her. Nothing the size of an Easter egg. Nothing that would grow until it was the size of a fisted hand, until it was as large as an outstretched hand, until it was the size of two hands.

I wouldn't say I'm wise, Jasmine said.

Do you love him?

Damian?

Yes.

I don't know if I do.

Ingrid sat up and rubbed her face with her hands. It was an unfair question, she said.

Jasmine listened to the blinds making their soft clatter.

Jesus, Ingrid moaned. *Jesus.* She rocked back and forth on the bed.

Ingrid, said Jasmine gently. She went over to the bed and sat down beside her, afraid to touch her, even though Ingrid was crying hard now.

I'll go, said Jasmine.

No. No, don't go. Not for a while.

Okay, I'll be right here.

Jasmine slipped down to the floor and rested her back against the bed. She closed her eyes. She smelled mint; it must have been because she'd crushed the leaf between her fingers out in the garden. The sharp, wild scent comforted her.

What Sandra had liked best about staying at her grand-mother's house was getting up early and eating breakfast at the old pine table. Once, in spring, she had stayed there, and in the morning her grandmother made her golden pancakes with thick, sweet syrup. She had also made sausages and put six of them on her granddaughter's plate, but Sandra had put three of them back in the frying pan.

Aren't you eating anything? Sandra asked.

Her grandmother didn't answer. Her face looked older than Sandra had ever seen it, perhaps because her hair was down, and her skin had the transparency of paper held to the light. She leaned across the table and stroked Sandra's cheek. So young, she murmured.

Not so young, said Sandra. Sixteen.

Sixteen, repeated her grandmother. I lost a baby when I was sixteen.

You did?

It died.

Did you miscarry?

No. She was four months old. She died in her sleep. And I – I was very unhappy. She pointed out the window to the garden. That rose bush – do you see it?

Yes.

When we came here and I started a garden, I planted that rose bush. For her, for that baby.

The room was still and warm. Jasmine opened her eyes drowsily and got up. Ingrid was sleeping, one hand under her face. She had drawn up her knees, and lay curled on the bed.

Jasmine went out of the room and closed the door behind her.

RAYMOND HAD WAKENED EARLY and walked with Max as far as he could along the beach before coming back to stand on the rocks and look out at the water. How much this morning was like the others during the past week, each one flaring like the tip of a match, but now he could feel a kind of glory passing out of his reach.

He poured Damian a cup of coffee and set it down.

The boy's long blond hair, taken out of its braid, fell over his shoulders. It was a wealth of hair, streaked through with light and dark so it was honey-coloured in shadow, and radiant, especially now, with the sunlight coming through the glass door and falling on it. But there was something about him that wouldn't be disclosed, even if he'd wanted to disclose himself. It was apart from his looks.

Raymond recalled his first sight of Cecily when she'd been running down the steps near the fountain at the university. Her hair had been flying behind her, that fine hair. She'd smiled at him briefly and raised her tennis racket, going past. She'd been wearing white, and her legs had been tanned. Her socks had yellow cotton bobbles on them. It surprised him now that he knew her young self and her aging self, and all the different selves she had been in between. Her particular beauty had caught him, over and over, and it had become more ethereal to him as she'd grown older, as if veils were being lifted.

Damian sipped from his full mug. Raymond thought this was what it might have been like if Peter hadn't been ill, that he might have sat together with Peter, here in this house, drinking coffee and talking. They could stay and watch the leaves changing outside, now that it was early September, and tell each other they didn't have to go back to Halifax just then. They could wait another day, another couple of days.

I've been thinking about my sister, said Damian.

Must be hard to think of her, said Raymond. His words sounded flat, even to his own ears. Hard to imagine that someone's gone, he added. Really gone, I mean. It's not as if the dead can answer a question you have about a place in the Florida Keys, for instance.

What?

Oh, it's not important. It's just that I couldn't remember the name of a place we went once. I remember standing next to my wife and looking out across the ocean. I was fifty-three years old, eating an ice cream cone and thinking how happy I was. I didn't want to forget anything about that moment.

Yes, I know. It's strange – I can't see Lisa's face any more.

That's the first thing to go.

And the way she moved her hands. Her laugh. I hear it sometimes, but only if someone laughs the way she did.

That time in the Florida Keys, Raymond said, I wanted to keep everything close. The breeze lifting the hairs on my arms, gulls circling, a plane's contrail, the salt smell, the sound of a jeep. The way Cecily's hair fell over her forehead.

He took the milk from the table and put it back in the fridge.

Sometimes I don't think I should be alive when Lisa is dead, said Damian.

Raymond came back and sat down, trying not to look alarmed. He rubbed the place on his right knee where he'd once been hit by a baseball bat, taking his time as he thought of the right words to say.

You have to think of what you can accomplish by living. And it's true that two wrongs don't make a right.

Platitudes, Raymond thought. All he could offer was a dusty shelf of platitudes.

Damian spilled the contents of his mug as he set it down. Shit. A pool of dark liquid was spreading across the table, and he wiped it up with the dishcloth. I could have been a better brother.

It's not who we *could* be – who cares about who we could be? We're loved for who we are. Raymond spoke quickly. I went through all of this when my wife died.

But how could you allow yourself to indulge in, well, to indulge in –

In being happy?

Yes.

Better to indulge in being happy than to indulge in suicide, don't you think? And, you know, your sister would have wanted you to be happy.

Well, anyway – it's over.

Over?

I met someone this summer.

Raymond studied him.

I thought – I don't know what I thought, but I messed up, Damian said. I didn't treat her very well, and then I left because she –

You left?

I just got on a bus and left. I couldn't think straight, what with my uncle –

Does she know where you are? Does your uncle?

No.

Does *anyone* know?

No.

Damian, they'll be frantic with worry. You have to let them know where you are.

Damian went and stood by the glass door and put his hand against it. He looked out at the light flecking the water, glittering on it. It was the beginning of fall, but it was still warm. If he went barefoot on the beach, the sand on the surface would be warm, though the sand under it would be cooler. A boat skimmed by, a white motorboat, and it made him think of July and lemonade and picnics. Once there had been a time of July and lemonade and picnics.

I could have done something, he said. But I didn't get there in time.

Cecily's last day was in spring. A chilly day with a wind from the north. The pear tree was in bloom, but because the wind had started up, there was a wedding of white, faintly pink blossoms outside the kitchen window. Some of the petals scattered in the light wind, and lay, delicate and pale, on the grass, which seemed vividly green after the rain they'd had in the night.

Raymond had made grilled cheese sandwiches that

day. He'd chopped wood and piled some in the mud room, in neat stacks, the way he always did. He'd put kindling there too. He was thinking of how much Cecily liked fires, though she hadn't been out of their room in more than a week. It was possible she'd let him carry her down to the chair by the fire.

The home-care nurse paid a visit just before ten o'clock in the morning; she checked Cecily and then came down to the kitchen. He offered her coffee, but she refused politely. She'd covered the grey in her hair with an auburn dye, though it was plain that her hair had lost its colour underneath. She was getting over a bit of a cough. Her name was Mary Lynn, and she was at least fifty pounds overweight, and getting bigger, even though she went to Weight Watchers religiously and lived on iceberg lettuce and celery and cherry tomatoes, and never ate a thing after six at night. For the love of God, she'd said. Iceberg lettuce and celery and cherry tomatoes. How could a person *not* lose weight?

She filled out a form on the kitchen counter. You'll want to watch her closely today.

She's worse, isn't she?

Mary Lynn didn't lift her eyes to meet his gaze. It'll be soon.

How soon?

It might be hours, or a day – it might be longer. Sometimes people hang on for a few days. Do you want me to stay for a bit?

No. It'll be all right.

She collected her things and put on her winter boots, which she wore even though it was spring. The door closed behind her with a decisive sound. He watched her through the window in the mud room; she lit a cigarette and stood in the driveway by her car, smoking. He went back into the kitchen and switched on the kettle, fatigue coming over him in a wave. He'd spent too many nights without a decent sleep, thinking Cecily would die, especially now that she was not being hydrated, now that they weren't doing anything for her constipation. They were just keeping her comfortable. That's how they put it. But Raymond still tried to give her water with a sponge. He couldn't bear to think of Cecily dying of thirst.

Finally he heard Mary Lynn's car – she had some problem with the starter – and waited until he couldn't hear it any more. He switched off the kettle. He didn't want tea. No, he'd make a fire instead, and then he'd bring Cecily down and warm her in front of it. He made the fire, washed his hands, and went upstairs, slowly, dreading what he'd find, though surely not much could change in a half-hour. Sometime he would climb these stairs and he would find her dead.

He unhooked the tube that fed morphine into a butterfly on her arm and took her out of her bed, though she wasn't aware of it, and, cradling her in his arms, went downstairs to the fire he'd made. He sat in the armchair with her body in his lap, and he cried. She had no idea he was crying. Some of his tears fell on her neck and he wiped them away. She was light as a cat against him. If she slept, perhaps she didn't feel pain, or maybe pain went through the transparency of sleep so that it was always there. He didn't know. He could smell the burning wood in the fireplace; it crackled occasionally, and once it snapped quite loudly, but nothing bothered her. She breathed noisily. Though he'd put balm on her lips, they were cracked and dry. He held her body close to him and her pale feet, swollen, hung down as if they didn't belong to her. He studied her arches, the curved line of each instep. There was a smell of wood burning. There was a smell of dying, though it was probably something he imagined. He knew it was something he imagined.

There was also a scent of almond soap. A neighbour had brought over a basket of soaps – watermelon, almond, and apple spice – and he'd chosen the almond. He'd washed her that morning. He'd started with her face and worked his way down her body. Her thin arms, her fore-arms, her wrists. Her stomach with the sharp pelvic bones on either side, and her thighs, legs, and ankles. He did all of this gently, with a basin of warm water and a washcloth, and then he towelled dry each part of her before moving on to the next part. He rubbed lotion into her dry skin after he was finished.

When the fire died down he took her upstairs and put her back on the bed, covering her up as quietly as he could. Her eyes flew open and she looked at him, without seeing anything. Something lodged itself within him, because it was her look, and yet it was not her look. It was the look of death. Her eyes seemed darker than they'd ever been. They bored through to the realm of death, which she could see and he could not.

She died at 5:22 in the afternoon. Perhaps it had been 5:20, because he hadn't looked at his watch until after he closed her mouth. There was one dragging, rattling breath from her, as if she'd been emptied out inside. Her mouth was open, and it made him afraid, because now there was darkness within her mouth, and it was deep and black.

259

There was the sound of a crow, and then another crow. He reached to close her mouth, but his hand trembled. There was no way to shut out the brazen noise of the crows. He tried to think of what he ought to do next, and he glanced at his watch, trying to figure out the time. He couldn't read the little golden hands on the face of his watch: the minute hand and the hour hand. What were they trying to tell him? That he was alone. He sat on the bed, looking out the window. All that was left was a blue rectangle of sky, and below, where he could not see them, were the pink tulips Cecily had planted around the birch tree.

What happened with your sister was an accident. Raymond cleared his throat. It was a terrible thing, an accident – it wasn't your fault.

It was my fault.

You didn't turn that ATV on. She turned it on. She took it onto the beach. She happened to have an accident.

Damian shrugged.

Here, Raymond said, going to Damian and taking him by the wrist. He opened the door and they both felt the cutting wind, though it was quite warm. Raymond stepped through the door, holding Damian's wrist. He was old, but he was strong. He took Damian down the steps, across the sand.

It reminded him of leading Peter by the hand when he was a boy. When had he let go of him? He could see the child, excitedly bending to scoop up handfuls of sand and getting up, hooting, to skip beside him. Raymond had been at the centre of his son's universe. Raymond, from the German, meaning protector. Meaning guardian.

Damian twisted his wrist lightly out of Raymond's grasp and walked beside him.

They came to a shallow ditch where a stream of water intersected the beach. It didn't look like the kind of place where someone could die.

When Damian found her she was face down in the water. Her hair was wet, but he could see the dark strands and the paler ones, floating out from her body in long, serpentine strands. Her body was splayed under the machine. Damian sloshed into the shallow stream toward her, breathing hard from running. He couldn't lift the ATV, and he didn't try. He managed to turn Lisa's head with his clumsy hands, raising it out of the stream. Water dribbled from her mouth. He felt the weight of her head as he held her, as he cleared her mouth, and breathed into it.

It wasn't happening. It couldn't be happening.

Time went backward. Lisa's face came out of the stream, blind with surprise. Water streamed away from her as she was drawn up swiftly, loose as a rag doll, into the seat of the four-wheeler. It jerked and righted itself, shuddering, and jolted into motion, taking her back across the sand. It shone in the light.

She was withdrawn as if something was pulling the four-wheeler with a magnet, back to where Damian had parked it in front of the cottage, after taking it off the trailer on the back of the car. The keys came out of the ignition, and Lisa sat still for a moment looking at them in her hand, before she got off the seat and walked around the four-wheeler. Swinging the striped beach bag out of the rack, she moved away from the vehicle to the cottage. She went backward and when she came to the steps, she sat down on them. The sun was on her hair as she fiddled, thoughtfully, with the keys.

Damian made a shallow dive, a brief arc, backward to the rocks. Water sprang from his body, gleaming, as he returned to where he'd been standing.

The two of them had been outside on those rocks the night before, and Lisa had cried, as if someone had slapped her. No one had slapped her, but she was crying. She called him a son of a bitch. It had nothing to do with Trevor, she cried, but it had everything to do with Damian wanting to control her life. He'd always wanted to be in charge of her life, trying to play the part of their father, but he wasn't their father.

Anger was drawn back into their throats, and they stood, awkward in the silence. Lisa left him there by himself, as she walked back to the cottage. He hadn't been looking at her; he'd been scuffing pebbles off the rocks into the black water below. *Plink, plink.* It was stupid, how things went.

Night unreeled into the day before, each hour folding into the hour preceding it. Lisa wasn't coming into the cottage with her knapsack, she was leaving. Damian turned to her as he locked the cottage door with the key their mother had given them. He saw Lisa getting back into the car, long hair caught back in a ponytail. Going away from him. The sound of the car door: not opening, but closing.

Raymond put his hand on the boy's arm, but after a moment he took it away. Let's go back, he muttered.

Damian was standing next to a man he hardly knew.

The water was the same as it had always been, slowly coming in, slowly going out, making a soft, hushed sound. He wanted to lie down on the sand and let it all slide away from him, but it wouldn't slide away. He knew it wouldn't. It was there in the morning when he woke up, and it was there when he went to sleep. It would always be there.

I keep waiting for something to feel different, Damian said.

For what to feel different?

I don't know.

You'd like to get outside yourself. But you can't.

I made her cry. The night before she died, we had an argument.

You're torturing yourself – it's going to make you crazy. I'm positive that a single argument wouldn't have changed anything for your sister. Sure, she might have been angry, but she'd have forgiven you if she could have. It's not your sister who needs to forgive you.

Who, then? asked Damian, bewildered.

DAMIAN WASN'T EXPECTING his mother to answer the phone. He was expecting Roger.

Mum, he said. It's me – it's Damian.

There was a pause.

It's me.

Raymond was tapping his pipe into the palm of his hand.

Damian put down the receiver slowly. She hung up, he said. I guess I should have expected that.

Raymond put the ashes from his pipe in the hollowed-out rock that served as an ashtray. You dropped out of sight and didn't tell anyone, he said, taking new tobacco from the tin and tamping it down in the bowl of the pipe.

What should I do? asked Damian.

Give her some time, and try again.

Raymond's briar pipe, which had been his father's, was the one he liked best. It had an elegant little bowl and a curving stem, and when he smoked from it he thought of his father.

She didn't think it was me, said Damian.

She's probably been beside herself with worry. Raymond

264

lit a match and danced it across the surface of the tobacco, drawing on the pipe at the same time. It's a shock.

He got the pipe going and sat back, imagining Damian's mother receiving the call. Perhaps she sat down and ran her hands through her hair, or got up and wandered around her kitchen before sitting down again.

When Raymond and Cecily brought Peter home from the hospital, he wasn't himself, though they'd been assured that his medication was back on track. Once they were home, they took him up the stairs to his room, where he sat down, heavily, on his bed, eyes closed. He didn't help to take off his clothes, except to extend his arms when he was coaxed, or to stand so his jeans could be taken off. His face was smooth and blank as a stone.

You're crying, Cecily said softly to Raymond.

He needs his pyjamas.

She got them and handed them to Raymond. She touched Peter's arm, but there was no response.

What have they done to him? she whispered.

I don't know.

Ray, he's cold. We should get him in the bathtub – get him warmed up.

She ran the water in the tub and came back to help Raymond take him into the bathroom. He was big and awkward, and they had to move him as if he were asleep or dead. This thought wouldn't dislodge itself from Raymond's mind. They sat him down on the edge of the tub, but Raymond had to roll up his own trouser bottoms to the knee and step ankle-deep in the hot water. The tap was still running. He got Peter into the tub, and finally got him to sit down, head bowed, with his legs stretched out in front of him. Cecily went to make up the bed, leaving Raymond and Peter alone.

The light in the bathroom had always been other-worldly, like the depths of a forest. It was the reflection of the mint-green tiles, and it tinted Peter's fair-skinned body pale green. His legs, underwater, were thin. There was dark hair on them, but it was sparse. It was curious how the threadlike hairs waved a little in the steamy bathwater, as though they weren't part of a body at all, but had small alien lives of their own.

Are you warmer now? asked Raymond.

Nothing. Nothing at all in Peter's eyes.

Raymond got up and dried the breakfast dishes when Damian phoned a second time.

It *is* me, Damian said.

Raymond finished drying a mug, a bowl, a plastic container.

But I didn't. I didn't. I'm sorry –

Raymond set things out on the counter as quietly as possible.

I'm at Cribbon's, said Damian. No, not the cottage. I couldn't – You mean you'll come? You'll come all this way?

Damian looked at Raymond.

No, I'm at a different place. Yes – yes, it *is* me. Wait, I'll let you speak to the person I'm staying with. Raymond – his name is Raymond.

He passed the receiver over to Raymond.

Was that Damian? asked Ingrid.

Yes, said Raymond.

Are you sure?

He's right beside me here.

And he's fine?

Just fine.

But we thought – we thought he was –

You're welcome to come here and see him for yourself.

It's what? Mid-morning? she asked. I'm not going to waste time trying to get a flight. I'll drive straight there. I'll leave now and that way I can be there around midnight, well, give or take – do you mind if I come? Wait, you're at Cribbon's? We used to rent a cottage there. It's the place where – the place –

Yes, my house is at Cribbon's, next to the old Boyd farmhouse. But flying might be easier for you.

The one beside the Boyd's, the one with the green trim, yes, I know that house. You don't mind? I won't be able to see the green trim in the dark, though, will I? Oh God, Damian. Let's see, I'll bring something – what should I bring? I'll bring some apples. We've got corn here – I'll bring corn on the cob. Do you like corn on the cob? I'll bring some.

Yes, but –

My name's Ingrid, she added. Just so you know who I am.

Ingrid, said Raymond, think about flying here. You could fly from Hamilton. You're in Niagara Falls? That's a very long stretch of driving.

Yes, but I can't wait.

Well, it's pretty lonely and it's exhausting. Stay overnight somewhere. Stay in Edmundston if you can.

I can't wait; I wouldn't sleep at all. Would you tell me your name again? I'm sorry, I've forgotten.

He told her.

Do I know you? she asked.

I don't think we've ever met.

But are you sure it's my son? Are you sure it's Damian?

Yes, it's Damian.

Raymond got Peter out of the tub and stood face to face with his son. What sort of storms went on in his mind? Raymond wondered. His body was not flaccid, it was firm. His penis hung between his legs: pinkish, pendent, and his pubic hair was dark and curled, but rather sparse. His hips were narrow but well-proportioned, and there was the slightest bit of extra flesh around the middle. Raymond had the same slight fleshiness.

He bent down to dry Peter's feet and ankles with the towel, working his way up the legs. The calves were firmer than he expected. He dried the thighs and the chest, and turned his son around, gently, so he could dry his back. He passed the towel over the nodes of the spine, each one a hidden stone. He rubbed Peter's hair, and the scent of the shampoo emanated from him. Clean and dry. Raymond helped him into his pyjamas, buttoning up the shirt.

Cecily came back and stood at the door, watching. Do you think he'll sleep?

He won't have any trouble sleeping.

They spoke in whispers, Raymond noticed. He took Peter to the room he'd had since he was a boy. Cecily turned on the lamp by the bed, the one that Peter had never wanted them to change. It gave off a warm, golden halo of light. There were hockey players skating around the shade after an elusive puck. Cecily drew up the sheets and blankets once Peter was in bed.

Goodnight, dear. She kissed him on the forehead.

Raymond turned off the lamp and they went down the hall to their own room, where they undressed without speaking and got into bed. For a time, both of them lay side by side, her thigh touching his. He felt desperately lonely, despite her nearness. Finally he heard her soft, breathy snoring, though it was hardly more than a murmur. He heard her inhalations, her exhalations. His heart was beating quickly, and he couldn't seem to make it quieter. He couldn't calm down. What he forced himself not to think about was how, soon, they would take their son out of the house where he'd grown up and settle him somewhere else, probably in a group home, where other people would take care of him. Each time his mind moved around the edges of that thought, tears came to his eyes. It was not to be borne.

It had been a long time ago, but the thought of Peter stayed with Raymond after he spoke to Ingrid on the phone. It stayed with him as he mowed the small lawn and raked it, as he weeded the little flower garden that was filled, once again, with Cecily's gladioli, day lilies, and roses, just as if she were still there. As if she'd come around the side of the house to put away the gardening tools in the shed – there, there she was – with that large straw hat on her head.

All day Raymond had been busy, and he kept finding things to do in the evening. Now it was past midnight, nearly one o'clock, but he didn't want to rest, and he didn't want to sit and read. Damian had fallen asleep on the couch, his head against the worn curve of the armrest. His mouth was open. Max was tucked into a warm place by his legs, his heavy head on Damian's thigh. It might be a long time before the boy's mother came. She'd be in the car; she'd probably put cobs of corn in a bag and slung it in the backseat, and now she would be wide awake, driving along a dark highway.

Raymond rose quietly and went to the door, taking his warm jacket from the hook. The keys jingled in the pocket, but not enough to rouse the two on the couch. He slid the door back and went outside.

The woman would come to meet her son and stay the night, and Damian would go away with her, and that would be the end of it. What would Raymond do? He'd go to Halifax, straight to the group home where Peter lived, and they'd have tea and misshapen cookies studded with orange and yellow Smarties. There would be a little conversation, initiated by Raymond. Then he'd go away.

He had walked along the path to the beach without paying attention, and now he stood looking up at the sky. It was aflame with rose-coloured light, and there was a band of pale green below. He watched the aurora borealis move and shift in the darkness, like the skirts of a flamenco dancer. He'd seen it several times before in October, but not in September: it could have been a gift or an omen. He wanted to show someone.

After the fifth treatment, when she tired easily, Cecily spent her mornings in the living room. Wrapped in the moss-green mohair blanket, she spent hours looking out at the ferns that had begun to poke up their heads in the rock garden. There were books beside her on the table, but she rarely picked up any of them. It was spring, and the last of the snow had melted away in the hollows. Chickadees and slate-coloured juncos lighted on the birdfeeder, snatched a few seeds and flew away.

Raymond had been about to take her some tea one morning, but he'd paused between the dining room and the living room. She'd changed; she was so much thinner. Her hands rested on the green blanket, and the sunlight fell on them. He'd put on Bach's *English Suites* for her, and it was clear and concise, yet sprightly too, like a curled fiddlehead. She would not live long. He realized this, and he could not make himself go forward. He could not go and give her the cup of tea. It didn't matter if he lavished her with all the love and kindness in the world, she would still disappear.

She turned, with the cautiousness of people who are ill, and smiled at him. He didn't trust himself to speak, but he set down the tea and sat beside her. She reached over and he took her hand in both of his, wordlessly. She moved her hand inside his, not restlessly, but gently. It was as if she was trying to say all that could not be said. They stayed like that, her hand inside his two hands, until a raven in the white pine made a series of rasping croaks that sounded like steel wool rubbed against the inside of a pot.

He released her. She picked up her cup of tea and drank.

It seemed a long time before Ingrid arrived. Raymond went back to the house and made himself a cheese sandwich after the northern lights faded completely. He sat in the armchair, dozing, until he heard the car just after three o'clock in the morning. Max heard it too and jumped down from the couch, but Damian didn't waken. Raymond went outside with Max, who promptly leapt up on Ingrid when she got out of the car.

Down, Max, said Raymond sternly. Down.

It's all right. She held out her hand and he took it. I'm Ingrid.

You made it.

Yes. Can I see him? Is he here?

He's just inside, sleeping.

I want to see him. I won't wake him – I just need to know that it's him.

They went up the stairs to the deck, where they could see Damian through the sliding door. She stood still, gazing at her son, fast asleep on the couch. The room was illuminated by the light from the reading lamp.

It *is* him, she whispered. He's so much thinner. It's been weeks, you know – it was early August when he disappeared.

Max made a low moan and scratched at the door; Raymond opened it and let him inside.

I can't go in, she said. I'm so angry. I can't.

You'll be all right. He closed the door softly, with Max inside and the two of them outside. Max sat down, looking at Raymond with his head cocked inquiringly.

No, I can't. I'm afraid of what I'll say to him – it was awful not knowing. You've no idea. You can't imagine.

No.

I'll – do you have any cigarettes? Not that I smoke. I don't smoke.

I just smoke a pipe. But come inside; you're shaking.

Yes, you're right. Look at that.

Here, come inside. We don't have to wake him.

He put his hand out to her and she took it, stepping into the room. She was tentative, as if any movement she made might break the spell, but then she went forward and sat in the armchair. Her whole body was alert and tense, and her

272

hands gripped the armrests of the chair, though she sat with apparent calm.

Raymond filled the kettle and plugged it in, but none of these slight movements, with their accompanying noises, wakened Damian. Max's claws clicked on the kitchen floor as he followed his master out of the house.

When Raymond came back from the car with Ingrid's big canvas bag, she was sitting in exactly the same posture. He unplugged the kettle and made some tea, putting sugar and milk in a cup without asking what she took in it. He set it on the table near her, where she could reach it. She looked up at him, hardly noticing, and turned back to Damian, stretching out her hand as if to touch him, but her hand stopped in mid-air before she drew it back, and Raymond studied her. There were wrinkles around the corners of her eyes, which, like her son's, were fringed with long lashes. Her nose was finely moulded, and her lips were full, though there were lines around her mouth. Her hair was silky and white; she had drawn it back into a ponytail. He could see how she must have been when she was young.

I don't want to wake him, she murmured.

She wasn't drinking her tea.

Have you eaten? he asked.

She shook her head.

He motioned for her to come to the kitchen, and she got up quietly. Raymond heated up some carrot soup that he'd made the day before. It was still all right, he thought, and he put it in a blue pottery bowl and took it to the kitchen table. Ingrid sat down, put her hands around it, and inhaled the steam.

Oh, he said, I forgot to get you a spoon.

He was a little flustered. When had a woman last set foot inside his house? He got the spoon and gave it to her.

Thank you.

I have some twelve-grain bread if you'd like.

No, thank you.

She said thank you the way a girl might say it.

This is very good. It's good by itself. She glanced at Damian. I can't stop looking at him. I can't believe it. I'm still shaking.

Raymond didn't know whether to sit or to stand. He felt clumsy.

Does he have any idea what he put us through?

I don't think so, said Raymond.

I have to call Roger. And I'll have to call Greg. The expression on her face changed swiftly. I'm furious, you know. I'm furious and I'm relieved. Imagine having no idea what happened to your son, and thinking – thinking day and night – that he might have committed suicide. And then he's in front of you, right as rain.

He wasn't exactly right as rain when I found him, said Raymond. He wasn't doing so well.

What do you mean?

He seemed sick. He was weak, physically. And distant – I couldn't reach him.

He hasn't been himself since his sister died.

But he was troubled in a way that –

In what way?

She looked so childlike and trusting that he hesitated.

Troubled in spirit and mind, thought Raymond, recalling Peter. I'd go easy on him, he said gently.

But to think he was alive and I didn't know – we didn't know.

Raymond saw that she'd eaten only half the bowl of soup. Her hand, holding the spoon, was trembling.

She smiled at him. I'm elated, you know, and a bit giddy. You'll have to excuse me.

It's all right – you have reason.

When he was born, he was so small, she said. Well, I suppose he was the right size and everything. He was even long for a newborn; I think he was twenty-one inches long. But to me he was so small, and so perfect. He still had some white, cheesy stuff on his skin – vernix, I think it is – though the nurses had cleaned him. They'd swaddled him in white flannel, striped with blue at the edge. I remember that clearly. He was the size of a loaf of a bread.

I remember that. With Peter.

You have a son?

Yes.

Then you know what it's like. That moment, at the beginning of things. It's as if you can see further.

Yes, he said. Yes.

It's not like anything else. She put the spoon up to her lips. Oh, I'm so tired – I'm not making sense. I can't explain it.

It makes sense.

I thought there would never be another moment like that again.

She stopped speaking for a long time; she ate her soup. It was no longer hot, but he didn't offer to reheat it for her.

Those sorts of moments, really, you think you've lost the capacity for them, she added.

He extended his hand to take her empty bowl.

Thank you very much, she said.

Well, soup like that is easy to make.

No. She put her hand on his arm without seeming to be aware she was doing it. I can't tell you. To be given something back, something like this, well, I can't begin to tell you.

He didn't know what to do with her gratitude. Just a minute, he said. He went down the hall to his bedroom and returned with a roll of papers under his arm.

I want to show you these.

He moved the soup bowl to the counter and spread out Damian's drawings in front of her.

Damian did them?

Yes. I, well – I got them out of the garbage. He'd thrown them away.

That's her, exactly. It's Jasmine.

You don't have enough room there, said Raymond. Try putting them on the floor.

Ingrid got down on her knees to examine them.

It's hard to say what it is about them, said Raymond. It's not just that the drawings are good – they're very good.

She came to the last drawing and then went through them again.

It's rare, said Raymond. That kind of gift.

He *is* very good. I know.

She looked across at Damian. He'd always go to my husband, Greg, she said. He'd go to him when Greg was angry, and hold him around the knees, because, you know, Greg and I quarrelled a lot. Once Damian gave him a picture, with a yellow house and popcorn trees and a purple sky, and on the back he'd written, I love you, Daddy, in purple crayon. I remember looking at Greg then, and his eyes were so soft. I know he nearly stayed with me because of the kids. It wouldn't have worked, but he nearly stayed.

Raymond helped her gather up the drawings.

I've lost a husband, a daughter, she said. I nearly lost Damian. That's almost my entire family. She sat back on her heels. You have family; you know what I mean.

My son's in a group home – he can't live on his own. And my wife died of cancer some time ago.

Oh, I'm sorry.

Would you like these drawings?

Yes. I would, thank you. She smoothed out the drawings. I used to draw, way back when, she told him. I used to draw and paint. Nothing like this, of course, but it would take me into another world.

I used to play the saxophone.

Did you?

It was a long time ago. I used to think I could be really good at it. But whenever I listened to Charlie Parker or John Coltrane – early Coltrane, especially – I knew I would always be *trying* to be a musician. They were great. They made it seem as though they weren't trying.

You could go back to it, she said.

He looked wistful.

You could go back to making something, she said. That's the thing, isn't it? You have a choice about it. Oh, goodness, I'm talking too much tonight.

It's all right. I don't often talk like this.

She rose, letting go of the drawings. Look, she whispered. He's waking up.

Raymond busied himself with the drawings, rolling them up. He put the elastic around them, left them on the table, and went out, because the two of them needed to be alone. Once he was outside he realized he'd forgotten to take his warm jacket, and that he didn't really want to go to the beach with Max. He'd been out already, but he couldn't stay in the house. He walked down the beach to the rocks, pulled up the hood of his fleece sweatshirt, and lay down, even though it was cold, and colder still when he lay on the rocks. Max nosed around him, licked the side of his face once, and then slipped into the darkness. There was only the sound of the water lashing stone.

The aurora borealis had completely vanished from the sky. He could see the Big Dipper clearly; all the stars seemed to have grown sharper in the darkness. Just hours before, there had been mysteries hidden by the coloured, shifting veil of lights, but now it had all changed.

INGRID SET DOWN THE COOLER and blanket at the top of the bluff. Down on the beach, Damian was standing where the water laced his feet with white. The ocean gradually deepened to dark blue beyond a string of large, mottled rocks, and it was here that a straggling line of four cormorants nearly touched the surface with their wings as they flew along.

Damian waded into the water up to his thighs.

God – it's *freezing*!

He flung himself forward into the water, swimming parallel to the shore, and Ingrid lost sight of him behind a cluster of rocks.

Don't be silly, she told herself.

He was nowhere to be seen, even when she went quickly down the rough, sloping track to the beach. She was gripped by panic.

Damian. *Damian.*

There was no answer. Then she saw him swimming back, his arms moving powerfully through the water.

This was what it was like, she thought. Always the fear. But here he was, trying not to lose his balance on the slippery stones as he worked his way back through the shallows. He teetered, caught himself.

What?

Ingrid shook her head. He retrieved his towel and they walked along the stony beach and up to the bluff. She unfolded the blanket and spread it out.

I spoke to Roger this morning on the phone, and I also called your father. They both want you to call them – they have some things to say to you. She smoothed out a corner of the blanket. Have you talked to Jasmine?

No.

He towelled himself dry. He bundled up his jeans and sweatshirt, and went to change farther up the bluff.

You can't leave it like that, Ingrid persisted, when he returned. Jasmine has to know you're all right. She was so torn up –

I can't talk about it.

But, Damian, you have to tell her. She thinks you may be dead – we all did. It's terrible not to know.

Let me do things my own way.

He twisted the wet towel.

She waited for him to speak, but he didn't, and she opened the cooler. She closed it, shaking her head. Then she opened it again and busied herself with its contents.

There, grapes. And cheese. What else did I put in here?

What happened with Elvis – Damian began. All I can say is that when I finally found him, I could have strangled him. And then Jasmine and Roger. I went a little crazy. But seeing them like that –

Like what?

I saw Jasmine with Uncle Roger. They were in the

kitchen and he was holding her. She kissed him. I guess thought – I don't know. I still don't know.

Damian, Roger would never – she's just a girl.

Ingrid looked at him and then at the package of blue cheese in her hand. She stared at it as if it were a rock from Mars.

Maybe she was upset about something, she said. Maybe he was comforting her. You're his nephew, Damian. He wouldn't do anything to hurt you. Anyway, he's always been a one-woman man, and that woman went out of his life long ago.

Damian chewed thoughtfully on a piece of nut bread in his left hand. He had a slice of cheese in his right. He took a bite of bread and then a bite of cheese, and Ingrid watched, amused, as he shifted from one hand to the other.

I was mad at all of them, he said. And I thought Elvis had broken the urn on purpose. Those ashes all over the sidewalk – I don't know what happened to me.

Elvis wasn't doing it to be malicious. He's not capable of that. For days after you disappeared, he wouldn't talk to us. He wouldn't even play his guitar and he loves that guitar. I can see why you'd be angry with him, but Damian, you shouldn't blame him.

He lay back on the grass.

There's some cranberry juice, she said. And glasses – let me find the glasses.

I guess I was a shit with him.

Ingrid drew the glasses out of the cooler, taking two of them out of a plastic sleeve. Everyone's a shit at some point or other, she said pragmatically.

He laughed.

281

stopped pouring juice.

he word *shit*. It's like fuck. You never say

aid experimentally.

e to just say it, the way you say apple. Say apple.

w say fuck.

uck. She burst out laughing.

No, you just can't do it.

Ingrid gave him a glass of juice and poured another for herself.

But Jasmine's another story, he said. I can't see that she'd want anything to do with me.

She came back to see me after they said you'd gone missing, said Ingrid. It was a comfort to have her there.

You must have talked about me.

We did, but we talked about a lot of things. You'd like to know what we said about you, though, wouldn't you?

He ran a hand through his damp hair. No.

I'd say Jasmine is angry and confused, she said. And she has a right to be.

The light seemed to catch on everything around them. It was tangled in the dead petals still on the wild rose bushes, in the lacy leaves of the chervil, in the asters, in the flat pinwheel tops of the Queen Anne's lace, in the plumes of goldenrod, and in the grass, which was dry and golden. And there, again, was the cool onshore breeze, riffling the surface of the water below and touching the grass on top of the bluff so it swayed.

She needs to hear from you, said Ingrid.

Ducks, raggedly forming a V-shape, flew southward. The swallows had already gone. There was a kind of urgency in the air, but the sun, warm on Ingrid's skin, lulled her. She looked down at Damian, lying beside her on the blanket with one arm shielding his eyes, and the other arm extended, fingers holding the glass of cranberry juice, ruby bright, on the uneven ground. His hair, not yet dry, was exactly the same colour as the grass.

Raymond lowered the screen out of its frame carefully and propped it against the side of the house. There was work to be done and he hadn't been attending to it. Ingrid and Damian had gone off for a picnic that morning, and as soon as they'd driven away, he wished he'd gone with them. They'd asked him, but he thought he'd be in the way. They would be back in the afternoon, and the following day they'd leave for good; Raymond knew it was bound to take something out of him, even though Damian had only been with him a few days.

The only solution was to work. When he worked, he got into a quiet rhythm that made him content. He'd done it a lot when he was younger. Manual work meant that he could turn things over in his mind, but not too rigorously. He'd done a fair bit of cabinetry work back then, and it had given him satisfaction to see the gleaming walnut surface of a captain's table after he'd varnished it, lovingly.

He'd get the screens down and then do the storm windows. As he went around the house, he saw places that needed caulking, but he hadn't done it. Next season, early, he'd get new windows. But one of the screens didn't want to budge. He'd undone the hooks and wing nuts, and now he gave it a bang with the palm of his hand, hard, on the right side, until it loosened so he could pull the screen out and set it down. He should have finished this business of the storm windows, but he'd put it off.

It was helplessness, he thought. He took out the next screen. He hadn't been able to do anything. It had happened with Peter first, and then with Cecily. He hadn't been able to protect them, and that was his job, wasn't it? It was his job. He took the screens over to the shed where he stacked them, tidily, against the wall, beside the old lawn mower. Whether he could look after Peter by himself, he didn't know. The very idea made him feel uneasy, because he was not a valiant man. He thought of how difficult it had been after Cecily died; Peter had been in the group home a long time by then, but Raymond had been so lonely he almost brought him back home.

He retrieved the screens on the opposite side of the house, and when he returned to the shed, he stopped. The shed door had swung open to show its dim interior, its hoes and rakes. He was afraid of dying in a way that Cecily had never been. She'd gone into it gracefully, but he didn't expect he'd do the same. He wished that they could tell him, that Cecily could tell him what to do. How should he prepare himself?

Max came tearing out of the wild roses, looped around once, and crashed back into the bushes. He was chasing a soft brown hare. Raymond saw the alert tips of its ears, its light, bounding movements, the way the tail was dark above and white below. He took the last of the screens inside and shut the door of the shed. He'd do the caulking in the afternoon, and the next morning he'd put the storms up, but right now he wanted a good bowl of soup and a piece of toast.

It was when he was heating up the soup that he thought of Ingrid. He thought of her face when she'd arrived, and he stirred the soup, thinking of what she'd said. How had she put it? That large moment, she'd said. He remembered holding Peter for the first time, how he'd been overcome with love as he gazed at the miniature fingers and toes. The skin, soft as the lining of a hare's furred ear. Oh, he was getting maudlin, he thought, getting out a dish for himself and ladling the soup into it.

It had been a large moment, so large that he hadn't been able to quite grasp it at the time. It was a moment lit with the radiance of first things. But how strange it was, he thought, with the soup bowl in one hand and a slice of toasted twelve-grain bread, dripping with butter and honey, in the other, that it was similar to the moment when Cecily had died.

He hooked his foot into the chair leg and pulled it out from the table. Sitting down, he bowed his head over the soup. He thought of Peter's starfish hands, and the strength of that infant grip around his own finger. He'd loved him from the time the nurse had handed him the newly cleaned, pink-faced infant, wrapped in warm cloth. She'd shown him how to hold a newborn and smiled at him. He'd been the one to give Peter to Cecily, as if it had been his gift to her, rather than hers to him. And he'd sat beside them as Cecily had held Peter for the first time, marvelling. Everything had been new to them. It had changed them, so they were no longer two. There was a third, powerful thing between them, and it was not just this child, with the imprint of the forceps still on the side of his face. It was more than that. Cecily was crooning to Peter, touching his newborn face. She wasn't aware of it yet, but Raymond could see it plainly. It made her more of who she was.

Ingrid and Damian walked up the track, which gradually ascended through spruce, bayberry, and wild rose bushes, up to a headland. Signs were posted at the edge of the cliffs, warning about the danger of going too close to the edge. The two of them kept close to the edge anyway, because they could get a better view of Cape George on one side and Cape Breton on the other, with the smooth blue ocean between. Several uprooted spruce trees, tilting in different directions, were suspended halfway down the cliffs. All along the sand below were fallen rocks, like pieces of a giant's vertebrae; the land was eroding badly and would keep eroding, because of fierce winter storms that pared away the coast each year.

So much had happened, thought Ingrid. And it wasn't as if she was finished with grief. There was more, and then more after that. But there were times, like today, when she could look at it steadily. It was as though it was spread out in front of her: the eroded debris, carved by the tide, and the paler blue of the shoals together with the dark blue beyond, and the horizon, far out, that marked the limit of ocean, except that it was no limit at all.

Are you all right, Damian? she asked.

Yes.

You're sure?

He nodded.

She didn't press him further. It was enough just to walk beside him, along the track with the ocean on her left and a dark pond, filled with cattails, on her right. They came to the highest point of land and stood, entranced. To the east was another beach, extending in a curve as far as Pomquet Beach, which lay in the distance, and to the west, far off, was the brow of another hill, densely covered with spruce.

The beaches formed an unbroken necklace of sand that joined each of the hills and headlands from Dunns Beach as far as Pomquet Point.

When Lisa died, I felt as though someone had thrown an axe into me, said Ingrid. I'm always going to feel it, and you're always going to feel it.

He nodded.

Ingrid felt her throat tighten. A parent is not supposed to outlive a child, she added. She dropped her eyes to the ground, where she noticed wild strawberry flowers close to the earth, stars hidden in the grass.

She loved life – Lisa. She loved it intensely.

I know, said Damian.

Ingrid dug her hands into her pockets.

That was all that could be said.

Ingrid drove Damian to the bus terminal in Truro in the morning, before going home to Halifax. A light covering of fog burned off as they came to New Glasgow, and by the time they reached Mt. Thom, they saw the slopes on either side were touched with red and gold.

It hadn't been easy saying goodbye to Raymond. All three of them were awkward, and then Damian had forgotten a sweatshirt and had gone back for it, and Raymond wanted Ingrid to take a jar of honey that a friend had given him.

Will you stay here much longer? asked Ingrid. She'd rolled down the window to talk to Raymond.

No, he said. I'll go soon.

I don't know how to thank you.

Don't thank me, he said gruffly. He leaned down and spoke to Damian. You take care of yourself.

I will, said Damian.

As they drove away Ingrid could see Raymond in the rear-view mirror, standing alone at the side of the road. Then the morning fog obscured him.

While drinking coffee with Raymond that very morning, in the early hours before Damian got up, Ingrid mentioned Ralph LeBlanc. She'd hardly given Ralph a moment's thought in years.

Ralph LeBlanc, she'd told Raymond, came from a place called Paradise Hill in upstate New York. For a while he lived in Niagara Falls, and then he went to Maine with his uncle. He had black hair and he was tall, taller than anyone else she knew. There was a huge, winding tattoo of a python on his left arm. It went all the way around his left arm in a spiral. He used to lift weights in his uncle's garage, summer and winter, and he was so strong he could easily murder someone. He never minded the cold, and he said that anyone who minded the cold was a chicken shit. He had the power to do something out of the ordinary, but he wound up slowly destroying himself, and the police caught him, probably because he let himself be caught. Probably because he thought anyone who ran away was a chicken shit.

What did he do? Raymond asked.

He burned down a house with another man, she said. There was someone inside, and he got out, but he had to be treated for smoke inhalation. Much later on, I heard Ralph was up for armed robbery. Maybe I shouldn't be telling you all this. You'll think less of me.

No, I won't.

It was strange, you know. We'd have bonfires on the

beach at Lake Erie. Mostly it was harmless, but sometimes Ralph would build up the fires so much we had to back away because they gave off such intense heat. We used to drink vodka straight out of the bottle, and when it was done Ralph would throw the bottle away. I remember the way the bottle would shatter and little pieces of glass would fly out from it.

Ingrid thought of the time she'd turned to Ralph without thinking and caught hold of his arm, the muscles like thick rope. He'd set fire to the brush by the side of the road and the fire was too close; it was dangerous. She could feel it coming back to them where they stood on the gravel shoulder. The others had gone farther up the road to the bend, where they huddled together, laughing. They weren't looking back at Ingrid and Ralph.

The fire went through the underbrush and then it came back. She could taste the smoke. It had a heavy, sickening taste. It caught a young, slender birch and shot up through it, through the canopy of green leaves. It caught the leaves, and burned them, so they were brilliant, flickering things. In a moment they would be hanging, dead. It burned the tree through and went on to another, brushing from one to the next.

Ingrid had put her arm on Ralph's because she was frightened, and then she drew away. He pulled her to him. He pulled her close and kissed her hard on the mouth. She remembered it clearly. She remembered the smoke, and the feel of his body, and how she had relaxed a little, as he'd held her, his mouth against hers. He hadn't let her go.

She could feel him pressing against her. And, abruptly, she wanted him to stop; she didn't like the scent of the cheap stuff he put in his hair. She didn't like the smell of his

Player's cigarettes. All of this was mingled with the acrid smell of the smoke from the fire – the fire Ralph himself had set – and it made her sick. She yanked away from him, flinging her hair over her shoulders, and walked up the road to her friends.

Ingrid, he called.

She didn't turn back, but she knew something had passed between them.

I loved those fires, she told Raymond. I loved everything about them. But then Ralph wanted to start fires up on the escarpment, and that was different, because there was no way of stopping them. We'd watch a dead tree go up in flames, exploding. It wasn't quite real. It was terrifying, but there was nothing like it. I craved it, but I was afraid of it. And this is what I didn't realize until much later: I was like Ralph. I mean, how was I so different?

You loved him?

No, she said. It wasn't that. I didn't love him. And I didn't admire him; in fact, I pitied him later on. His life had gone off the rails. It was just that I recognized something in him.

Don't you think, he said, don't you think there's so much that's wild in all of us? I don't mean grief, though that's wild enough. I mean –

Most of us live half asleep, she said. And then there are some people who don't live that way. They're all lit up and they don't know what to do with it.

The bus was already there when they arrived at the terminal in Truro. Damian went inside and came out with his ticket in his teeth as he hoisted his knapsack on his back.

He took the ticket out of his mouth. Bye, Mum.

You've got teeth marks on it.

I know.

Take care of yourself. And let me know how you are. You *will* let me know how you are, won't you?

Yes.

I love you, Damian.

She kissed him fiercely and stepped back, bumping into a woman who was waiting to get on the bus.

Oh, she said, flustered, I'm sorry.

He got on the bus and sat on the side where he could see her. He waved. She waved until the bus pulled out of the terminal and turned the corner.

She walked to her car and got in. There – the maple tree across the street was bright red. She put the key in the ignition, but didn't turn it; she couldn't take her eyes off the tree, vibrant with the last thing it could do before winter.

When she was young she'd painted a small canvas, an oil painting. She'd liked it when she finished because it was riotous with crimson. It was the colour she'd liked, more than anything. It had been one of the few things that she'd saved, but then she'd misplaced it somewhere along the line. She recalled it vividly as she gazed at the maple tree.

She held so many people. She held Greg, even though he'd left her, and she held Lisa, living and dead, and she held Damian. She held Roger and Elvis, and even Marnie. She held Ralph LeBlanc. It was her life. It was her life and no one else's.

IT'S RAINING HIPPOS AND ELEPHANTS, said Elvis, coming in, his hair plastered damply against his head. Bruce says it's raining hippos and elephants.

Elvis unsnapped the buttons on his raincoat and took it off, holding it out in front of him. He hung it on a hook beside the door, where it dripped into puddles on the cushioned flooring, and then he took off his boots and put them side by side on the mat. One wasn't lined up exactly with the other one, and he adjusted it. He straightened up and looked around the kitchen, first at Jasmine, then Roger, then Tarah. They hadn't said anything. He saw they made a triangle, standing there in three different places. Three points of a triangle. A = Jasmine, B = Roger, and C = Tarah. ABC made a triangle.

Ingrid left here right away, said Roger. She drove all night. That's what I've been trying to tell you.

Holy shit, said Tarah. Holy *fucking* shit.

It wasn't a mistake? asked Jasmine. Are you sure it wasn't a mistake?

No, said Roger. Damian was there – alive and well – when Ingrid arrived.

292

But how is that possible? I just don't understand.

Elvis liked to look at Jasmine even when she didn't look at him and even when she was A in a triangle. He felt warm, the way he did after he ate chicken broth, because Jasmine was there and Jasmine hadn't been there for a long, long time, now that Damian had gone away. She glanced at him and that made him feel even warmer, so he had to put his hands up to his wet face and wipe it. She didn't say hello to him, but that didn't matter.

He took his Mickey Mouse Thermos to the sink and rinsed it out and put his zip-up bag in the recycling bin. Usually after he did this, he went upstairs and lay on Roger's bed with his legs wide apart and listened to the *Elvis '56* CD with Roger's CD player and earphones, but now he stood rocking from his left foot to his right, uncertain of what to do next. He wanted to go upstairs and lie on Roger's bed, and he wanted to stay in the kitchen where he could look at Jasmine, but Tarah was looking at Jasmine too, and Roger wasn't talking, and they didn't seem to want to move out of the triangle where AB = AC. If Elvis replaced Roger, he would be B and there would be a direct line from A to B. But Roger was making his own small triangle inside the triangle with his left leg and his right leg and the one he called his seeing leg. They didn't look happy. A was not smiling at B and B was not smiling at C.

I have a joke, said Elvis.

It's true, Jasmine, said Roger. It *is* true.

How can it be? He was gone so long – he was gone for weeks. And now he turns up?

I know, said Roger gently.

Elvis wanted to say something about Jasmine so she would look at him, the way she looked at Roger. But they hadn't laughed at elephants and hippos.

So I'm the only one who didn't know? said Jasmine. You knew, and Ingrid knew, and –

I've only known a couple of days. I'm sorry. Maybe I should have called you before. I thought Damian –

You're right, maybe you should have called me.

Ingrid said that he'd been through a bad time of it.

A *bad time* of it?

Yes.

I have a joke, said Elvis.

It sounds like he's doing just fine, she said. That's what it sounds like.

What's pink and lies at the bottom of the ocean? You won't get it.

He's alive and well, said Roger. That's the main thing.

That was the joke. What's pink and lies at the bottom of the ocean?

That's nice for him.

Not now, Elvis, Roger told him.

But it's good. It's a good joke. Bruce told it to me and he laughed when he told it to me. He said it was a dumb joke, but he liked it anyway.

I thought you should know, Roger said. But Ingrid said Damian wanted to talk to you himself.

Oh, *right.* It doesn't look like he's going to do that. That would be hard on him, wouldn't it? Since he's been through a bad time of it.

It's Moby's dick, said Elvis. Get it?

Elvis didn't want to see Jasmine's eyes go all shiny and bright. He didn't like it when her voice went high and then went low. He wanted to make her laugh. He wanted to put his whole body against her whole body, but he wasn't allowed to because she was the girlfriend of Damian Benjamin MacKenzie, May 31, 1987, Halifax, Nova Scotia.

Tarah moved over and put her arms around Jasmine.

Elvis was hungry, and they hadn't listened to his joke.

He stepped between Roger and Jasmine holding on to Tarah. There was no triangle any more; there was only a line from B to CA, so it didn't matter if he went between them. He got a can of asparagus soup from the cupboard. He got the can opener and the pot, but some of the other pots fell over when he got out the pot he wanted, and Roger made the sound he made when he was cross with Elvis. Elvis knew how to make soup, though, and he was hungry. He didn't want to eat macaroni and cheese again, even though he knew how to make that too.

They hadn't laughed at his joke.

He opened the can carefully and put the creamy liquid in the pot, but he put the pot on the stove with a bang. It was a louder bang than he meant it to be, and droplets of asparagus soup flew out of the pot and landed in a pattern all around the burner. It had to be wiped up. He hadn't turned on the burner yet, and now he lifted the pot, undecided.

There was a front left burner and a back left burner, and then a front right burner and a back right burner. It was like arms and legs. Left arm, left leg. Right arm, right leg. He put the pot down on the right leg burner and turned the right leg burner dial to five, which was in the middle. He would have to stir it and he got the wooden spoon out of the large ceramic frog above the stove, where the spoons and ladles were kept. They'd told him at the workshop that if he got confused he just had to do things slowly and in order. Everything had an order. He had to follow the right order, but right now he wished he could have ice cream and not soup. He'd rather have ice cream. He'd rather have ice cream and cake with lots of swirly white icing and pink and yellow roses on the top and Elvis Presley's picture right in the middle and Happy Birthday Elvis in pink icing. That's what he wanted.

Maybe they wouldn't be angry and he could tell them the other joke that Bruce had told him. The one about the seven dwarves and the penguins.

And so all this time Damian's been safe and sound in Nova Scotia?

Yes –

Well, fuck him.

Elvis stirred the soup. He didn't like it that Jasmine's voice wobbled. He stirred the soup faster because it was bubbling, and that meant it was time to take it off the burner, but he had to remember to turn off the right leg burner too and not turn on another one when he did it. He had to do it right. He used the blue-and-white-striped pot holder to lift the pot, which he put on the coaster on one side of the stove. He was doing everything right. He didn't need the pot holder, though, because the handle wasn't hot, so he left it on the stovetop and went over to the counter. He had to walk between B and CA again as he did this, with the pot held out in front of him. He kept holding it while he got a white bowl out of the cupboard. Then he put the pot down in the sink and the white bowl on the counter, so he could spoon the soup into it.

Oh my *God*, cried Tarah. The pot holder.

He turned around. Tarah made a sudden move and Elvis lunged forward. He got to the stove at the same time she did. He reached for the blazing thing and so did she. He let go. Someone shouted his name. She held it with the tips of her fingers. It was the pot holder. He saw Tarah hold it for a moment before she took a couple of quick steps, as if she were dancing, and then she threw it into the sink. She did it so rapidly that it was hard to follow. She pulled him over to the sink, but there was pain in his hand, and now she was running water in the sink, so it made a hurrying, rushing sound. A fast white sound. Roger shouted. They told him to follow the order of things when he got confused. But there was no order. She put his hand under the tap and the cold water ran over it, and ran over it, and ran over it, making a rushing sound that he felt in his hand.

Is he all right? Roger was asking. Is he all right?

Yes, said Tarah. He's fine. He's shaking. But you're fine, aren't you, Elvis?

I'm okay, he said, but the pain was still bright. He watched the water, the way it came out of the tap and poured over the place on his hand.

God, Tarah said, staring out the window at the rain. What a day this is turning out to be.

She kept his hand under the tap, though Elvis could have held it there by himself. She held him by the wrist, hard, but not too hard.

She hadn't said Elvis's name, but he waited, because he was sure she would say it. She was going to talk about the pot holder. The pot holder had gone from being a clean, blue-and-white-striped thing to being a blackened, soaked thing. He could feel something. It banged around in his chest. It was his heart. Roger had told him that. He kept looking down at the pot holder that lay underwater in the sink. It was a square. His heart was banging around in his chest.

Tarah left the tap running over Elvis's hand and turned away from him.

It's not a bad burn, she said.

Maybe butter would help, said Jasmine.

There's ointment in the upstairs cupboard, Roger told her. That would be better. And there's a roll of gauze in the left-hand drawer by the sink, if you need it. Does he need it looked at?

No, said Tarah. It'll be all right.

Jasmine got the ointment. Tarah turned off the tap and then she dried Elvis's hand with a towel, but Jasmine was the one who put the ointment on it. It was Jasmine who held his wrist now, not Tarah. The ointment felt good.

Things go wrong, said Tarah. Why do things just go wrong?

She rubbed the darkened tips of her fingernails against the palm of her other hand. Oh shit – what's the time?

It's nearly six.

Oh fuck, fuck, *fuck*. I was supposed to meet Matt – and it's raining and I'll get all wet.

She left.

Jasmine, said Roger. This is a shock – it'll take a while for it to sink in.

It's not a shock.

Ingrid said Damian was coming here. She put him on the bus in Truro – he should be here tomorrow.

Good for him. If he's coming here, I'll be gone.

If he's coming back it's because of you, Jasmine. It's because he wants to see you.

Why would he do that?

Because he –

Don't say he cares about me.

He does.

Right. Well, I don't want to see him. He screwed up my life. He screwed up all our lives. And then – what do you know? He turns up.

Roger sighed.

You're angry with him, she said. You are. I know you are.

Yes.

So why would you welcome him back with open arms?

Because.

Some kind of prodigal son *shit*, she snorted.

Jasmine, don't.

Don't what? Don't turn cold and heartless? What kind of a guy does something like that and then expects to be welcomed back with open arms? Tell me. Tell me, because I'd really like to know.

Roger didn't say anything.

I'd like to know, she said.

I can't speak for him, he told her.

No, you can't.

Maybe I shouldn't have told you.

You didn't say anything about this to anyone, said Jasmine flatly. I don't know anything. As far as I'm concerned, he's still missing. Okay?

Roger went tapping out of the kitchen. *Tap,* step, *tap,* step, *tap.*

Now Elvis was alone in the kitchen with Jasmine. It was nice to be alone in the kitchen with her, together and alone, with the sound of the rain on the window. She unrolled a little of the gauze and stood looking at it. She held it up and looked through it at him and he grinned, because he could see her through it.

She took another look at Elvis's hand, as if she were figuring something out. There was a line between her eyebrows. She was the way she always was. She was Jasmine. A small white flower. Elvis was close enough to lean his whole body against her, but he didn't. He held his hand up for her. She asked him if she was hurting him and he said she wasn't. It didn't hurt at all.

I don't think gauze is a good idea, she said, and rolled it back up. It's probably better if the air gets at it. Don't you think?

He nodded, because she wanted him to do something. He could look at her all he liked and no one would say he was staring.

Do you want to sit?

He went over and pulled out a chair with his good hand.

Oh, she said, sitting down and looking up at him. I don't know.

She didn't say anything for a long time.

It makes me angry and it makes me sad and – oh, I don't know, she said. Why would Damian just go off like that? Why would he do it? Wouldn't it make you angry if somebody went off and left you?

Yes.

I don't know what to think, she said. I just don't know.

Don't cry, said Elvis.

Oh, Elvis.

Don't cry.

I don't know what to think. I don't want to see him. I want to see him and I don't want to see him. *Jesus.*

300

Elvis shifted his weight from one side to the other. The pain was in his hand, bright and then not bright, bright, and not bright.

They could hear Roger running water in the upstairs bathroom.

Anyway, she said. I'm finished with it.

Roger tapped along the upstairs hallway.

But sometimes I wonder what it could have been. Damian and I, together.

You and Damian getting married and having a baby.

Well, I wasn't thinking of getting married or anything. I wasn't thinking of a baby.

She got up and put the top back on the ointment. Then she took the blackened pot holder out of the sink, squeezed the water out of it, and put it in the garbage.

She leaned against the counter. You know, sometimes I think I loved him. Did I? And then I think I didn't love him, she added, in a low voice. But either way it hurts.

Like my hand. My hand hurts, said Elvis.

And now there's nothing to keep me here.

Are you going away?

She looked at him. I'll go to New York City and do all the things I've been wanting to do. I could make things out of hair. She looked around the kitchen. Chairs and tables and cupboards – whole rooms made out of hair. She laughed. They like that kind of thing in New York.

But Damian is coming back. Roger said so. And Damian's your boyfriend.

Not any more.

She took the garbage out of the bin under the sink and put the bag on the floor where she spun it around and made a knot in the top. Elvis watched her do it. She spun the bag around on the floor and made a circle in four squares of the floor.

I like babies, said Elvis. Bruce at the workshop – he has a baby.

Jasmine opened the door and tossed the garbage into the can outside.

I should go home, she said. I shouldn't hang around, but it's awfully wet out there.

She poured the rest of the asparagus soup into a container and put it in the fridge. Then she rinsed out the pot.

Bruce and Joannie named their baby Ethan, after an actor, said Elvis. The actor and his wife broke up. Joannie read it in a magazine and she said she was sad for him because he wasn't with his wife any more. So she called the baby Ethan.

That's a nice name for a baby.

She wiped the counter where some of the soup had spilled. She wiped the counter in circles; her hand went around and around. Then she went over to the stove and made a swipe around each of the burners.

Ethan has soft skin, said Elvis. I like the top of his head, but you have to be careful about the top of the head because there's a spot where the skull hasn't closed.

Jasmine stopped wiping the stove. She looked at him. You know things about babies, don't you, Elvis?

I like them. I told you. Ethan has three first names. Ethan Gregory Matthew Cook. Cook is his last name. It's Bruce's and Joannie's last name. He's not big. He's about the size of three cans of soup. Maybe four cans of soup.

Jasmine smiled. Three cans of soup.

He's gaining each week, Joannie says, but he's still not very big. When she weighs him she stands on the bathroom scales and weighs herself, and then she weighs herself holding Ethan and then she subtracts his weight from her weight. She weighs 139 pounds, and with him she weighs 153 pounds. So Ethan weighs fourteen pounds. We did it together. I helped her. She said her dressing gown probably weighed a ton because she usually weighs less. She usually weighs 125 pounds, but now she weighs 139 pounds, so she's not going to eat any more of those big chewy cookies with the chocolate chips in them.

And I helped her bathe Ethan after that, in a plastic tub that she put in the bathtub. She was going to put papaya bath foam in the water, but then she didn't because it might have given him a rash. It smells nice, that papaya bath foam. She washed his head with a washcloth and did his ears, but he didn't like it much. Ethan's got soft ears. They're small. I like his ears, and his hands. And I like his toes. But I like it best when Joannie wraps him up in a towel and hands him to me, and I hold him the way she taught me to, in the crook of my arm. I like that a lot. He stops crying then, because he likes me. Ethan likes me. I sing to him and he likes it.

What would you call a baby, Elvis? asked Jasmine. What would you call a baby if it were a girl, say?

Priscilla, he said. Or Lisa Marie, but I like Priscilla better, because it's a really nice name.

But you couldn't call her that, could you? It's too long. What would it be for short?

I'd call her Silly.

She laughed. Silly. A baby called Silly. She laughed and he laughed too.

Silly, he said, and she laughed again.

She put the scissors and gauze in the string drawer.

The rain's not coming down as hard, she said, closing the drawer with her hip. It's not coming down hippos and elephants. She looked out at the rain.

What would you call it? he asked.

What?

A baby.

If I had one, you mean?

Yes.

Sophie, she said. If I had a girl. Sophia means wisdom. Sophie. I like that name.

But if I had a boy I don't know what I'd call him.

You could call him Elvis because it's the name of the greatest star in all of music history.

The name of a star, she murmured.

They were together and alone in the kitchen, looking out at the rain. It was pretty, Elvis thought; it made shiny spatters against the glass.

THE BUS SWUNG INTO GATE FOUR at the Niagara Falls terminal and when it came to a stop people got out of their seats, waiting in the aisle or standing awkwardly with their heads craned to one side because of the luggage racks overhead.

Damian didn't get up from his seat on the bus. He'd caught sight of Elvis and Jasmine.

The sharp thorn of seeing her.

Jasmine had a big knapsack on her back that almost prevented her from bending to pick up a brown suitcase. It broke open as she picked it up, and a tumble of clothing fell to the ground: a drift of shirts, a robe, dresses, flip-flops, something white and lacy. It could have fallen open hundreds of times, clothes spilling out. Damian thought he could hear, far off, the water from Lake Erie flowing down the Niagara River and parting into the Chippewa and the Tonawanda, passing Grand Island and tiny Buckhorn Island, until it merged into one powerful river. But it was only the sound of another bus drawing away, expelling blue fumes as it went. Jasmine waved away the smell, got her things bundled together and straightened up, speaking quickly to Elvis. An edge of lace hung from the closed suitcase.

She was leaving, thought Damian, as he went down the steps of the bus behind an elderly woman. He could see whitened skin through her sparse grey curls. When the woman had planted both feet on the ground, in running shoes that were too large, she turned to him, smiling, and her eyes nearly disappeared into a face that was folded and puckered with hundreds of wrinkles.

There, thank you for bringing my cane, dear.

Leaving. Someone jostled Damian, so he couldn't see Jasmine and then he could, just over there, with Elvis. He slung his knapsack over his shoulders and went out of the terminal, where the air was crisp. Deep autumn blue. He went around the corner and stopped, putting down his knapsack and taking out a bottle of water and half a carrot muffin. He drank some water and put the bottle and the remains of the muffin away, hoisting up the knapsack again.

He hadn't phoned and now he'd come too late.

What could he possibly say? When he went inside, the terminal was dark after the sharpness of the light. He walked toward her slowly. He'd surprise her, coming upon her so suddenly; he'd probably frighten her. It would do more harm than good. She was trying to fix the clasp of the suitcase, but he could tell from a distance it couldn't be fixed.

Jasmine.

She couldn't hear him.

Jasmine.

Elvis saw him first. He didn't say Damian's name or his birthdate.

Damian's mouth was dry, which made it hard to speak.

Hello, Elvis.

Jasmine was holding the halves of the suitcase together. He could tell she was bracing herself by the way she held the suitcase, as if it were an animal that might escape.

So, she said.

She spun on her heel and walked away, still holding the suitcase together. A man coming out of the terminal held the door open for her and she smiled. His eyes lingered.

Damian stared at Elvis's unbuttoned shirt.

That's a new shirt, said Damian.

It's got snaps instead of buttons. See?

Elvis unsnapped the shiny blue shirt to his waist, so his pale chest was fully exposed, and then he did it back up again.

Your boat was on TV, Elvis said. Tarah saw it. They said you were a daredevil.

I'm not.

They said there's people like you every year.

Damian took out his water bottle and drank greedily from it.

Jasmine's going all the way to New York City, said Elvis. She's getting the bus.

Why? asked Damian.

Elvis put his hand up in the air, fist clenched.

If she was leaving, Damian didn't know what he could do to change her mind. He couldn't think clearly, because it was so strange that her life had intersected with his life, precisely, when they could so easily have passed one another.

Roger said you were coming. Elvis fingered the pearly snaps on his shirt. He said you were coming here.

Did Jasmine know I was coming?

Yes.

She knew I was coming today and so she decided to leave? asked Damian.

Elvis didn't answer.

Damian watched Jasmine inside the terminal, pressing against the ticket counter. She'd put down the suitcase and the knapsack. Her heels had lifted out of her ballet slippers as she leaned forward to speak to the vendor through the opening in the glass.

He wondered if it was the last time he'd see her, ever, if he'd remember only her feet lifting out of her ballet slippers, turning into tawny birds. She reached into her drawstring bag and her silver bangles slid down her wrist. Her hair fell in a dark swoop, dark against the yellow of her sweater, as he knew it would. She was so far from him, behind the door that people opened and closed as they went in and out.

She came to the door and held it open. Elvis, she called. Maybe you can go home with Damian. You don't have to wait for me to get the bus.

But I brought something for you, said Elvis. I've got something to give to you.

She didn't hear him, and he went inside the terminal after her.

Damian looked down at an oily puddle on the ground: blue-black streaked with purple and turquoise and gold. It had been a stupid idea, coming back. In the pool of oil, colours bloomed light years away from him, one nebula whirling into the next.

When he went inside, he couldn't find them. Then he saw them over by the fixed seats against the wall. Jasmine had some duct tape and she was busy wrapping it around her suitcase with Elvis's help. Around and around went her hand, unrolling the silver tape. When she finished, she cut the tape neatly with a pair of scissors, and took the tape and scissors back to the ticket vendor. Her skirt swung, showing her slender legs, as she turned away from the counter and went back to sit beside Elvis.

Damian went to them, putting down his knapsack and sitting where he faced them, one seat over from a woman in a green jacket who was combing her hair.

Jasmine was looking at her ballet slippers. One of them was scuffed and she bent down and rubbed it.

She sat back before speaking. We thought you were dead.

The woman sitting one seat over from Damian took out a small hand mirror and tilted it toward her face, peering into it.

Damian leaned forward, trying to find words. I'm sorry, he said.

Her face was closed; she wouldn't look at him. She crossed her legs; he watched one of the ballet slippers go up and down. One of the slippers clacked to the floor and she put it back on. For a moment he saw the arch of her naked foot and he thought of running his hand along it, of kissing it.

The woman had put the comb and mirror into her purse, and now she put up a hand to fluff her hair in the back. A thread of hair detached itself and floated away.

I'm sorry, Jasmine, he said again.

This time she met his gaze. You said that already.

What else can I say?

I don't know.

If you asked me to go to Montreal and get a – I don't know – a hat, he said, I'd go to Montreal and get you a hat. If you asked me to go to the Gobi Desert, I'd go.

The woman glanced at him.

I wouldn't ask you to do that, said Jasmine, concentrating on her scuffed shoe. Anyway, I don't want a hat.

What do you want?

I want you to tell me what happened.

I don't know what happened. I had to get out of here, so I did.

That's it?

I wanted to get so far away –

Far from me.

No. I wanted to get so far away that I couldn't feel anything any more.

There's no place you could have gone. There's no place like that.

I know.

Oh, she murmured. Oh, Damian.

You've been to hell and back – I realize that, he said, That's why I'm here. I thought – I guess I thought if I showed up, the words would come to me.

I don't think words would help. She couldn't stop moving; one hand was swinging back and forth. I don't think anything would help. You and I – we can't go on.

Her eyelashes seemed darker than before, fringing her eyes. Green, so green. He had to hold her gaze without looking away.

Don't, she said.

He had to lean forward to hear what she was saying.

Don't make it harder.

She's going to Buffalo, said Elvis. She's going to Buffalo, then Rochester, then Syracuse, then – I forget what's after Syracuse. And after that, New York City. She's going to be an artist in New York City.

Damian fiddled with a toggle before he hefted his knapsack up.

Well, he said. I guess there's nothing left to say.

He couldn't talk to her in this place. He could feel his eyes stinging.

There was no way to stop things from going forward. It made him feel desperate, and he walked away from her, pushing the door open. When he got outside he couldn't see because of his tears. A woman brushed past him on her way inside the terminal, and he moved away from the door. He started down the street without knowing where he was going, but it heartened him, when he glanced over his shoulder, to see that Elvis had come out after him.

Jasmine's leaving, said Elvis.

I know.

Damian, called Jasmine.

She'd come outside the building, where she'd put down her suitcase. She kept her knapsack on her back, but wrapped her arms around herself, around her sweater, as she waited for Elvis and Damian to retrace their steps.

A tree nearby had turned pale yellow, and it was almost the same colour as her sweater. She seemed to be examining the way the bright leaves overlapped one another, but she shifted her gaze and looked directly at Damian when he approached.

My bus is here, she said. But I can't keep this – Elvis, I can't keep this.

It's for you, said Elvis.

They stood together, awkwardly. She held out a photo-graph, but Elvis didn't take it.

Damian leaned forward and spoke quietly in her ear. She looked at him.

Please don't go, he said again.

I have to. She dropped her eyes.

Jasmine.

Inside, they heard the final call for her bus.

She looked up and met his eyes, and he knew some-thing had softened in her. He saw how she would look when she was old.

With stops in Buffalo, Rochester, Syracuse, Schenectady, Albany —

Elvis, she said. I can't take something like this from you. I'm honoured you wanted me to have it, but I have to give it back.

Elvis took the photograph and held it with both hands, looking down at it.

It belongs to you, she said. It's precious. She bent and turned her head so he would look at her. That baby is you. And he's named after the greatest star in all of music history.

Elvis smiled when she kissed him on the cheek.

She turned to Damian and threw her arms around him. She held him tightly.

Oh, Damian.

It was only for a moment, and then she let go and wiped her eyes. She picked up her suitcase, which she held with both arms, and the light flashed on the door as Elvis held it open for her.

The river spilled past the Control Dam and descended in a series of rapids toward the rusted hulk of the Old Scow and the scrawny, bent poplars on scattered islands, and kept tumbling around Goat Island, pouring over stacked layers of dolomite as it fell over the edge, offering up a great, feathery veil of mist as it roared to the river below. It was all wild, noisy turbulence below the Falls, but the *Maid of the Mist* plied the water: one boat pushed upstream, before slipping into a curtain of white, and another followed, with its hooded cargo of humanity. It strained against the rush of water, and then, like something sprung from a trap, it turned and vanished. As soon as one boat departed, another appeared.

In the distance, a line of figures descended the stairs to the base of the American Falls, miniature people disappearing into a dark maw that swallowed them whole. But then they reappeared, ascending to the top, keeping their video cameras hidden under plastic ponchos. They came from every corner of the globe: women in tunics, wearing veils, men with turbans, girls speaking German, tourists led by someone who spoke mutilated high-school Spanish, an elderly couple from Tokyo, a school band from the American Midwest, and four sisters from Weslaco, Texas, who went on a trip together every year. The ponchos were dry when people began the trek down to the base of the Falls and wet when they came back up.

They all came to look at the great Niagara. But the water rushed away from them, sweeping chaotically through the gorge, under the Rainbow Bridge, where the Honeymoon Bridge had collapsed, in 1938, because of an ice jam. It flowed downstream to the Whirlpool, pulling everything into it: part of a boat fender, a stick, a shredded piece of tire, a Coke bottle that bobbled, dipped, and shot free, only to plunge back down. On the observation decks, people watched the jet boats packed with tourists skidding out to the edges of the Whirlpool. Above them, the Spanish Aero Car moved along its cable and drew back again, a bright red spider making a filament in its web, venturing out and then returning. From there, the river shot through a confined channel, past the Devil's Hole Rapids, with the Niagara Parks Botanical Gardens to the west and the Devil's Hole State Park to the east. It tumbled under the Queenston-Lewiston Bridge, until it opened out below Queenston Heights Park, topped by the monumental, unblinking gaze of General Brock on his high column.

It was still a powerful river, but it had less vigour as it flowed toward Lake Ontario. It was here, rounding the last corner, unheeded by the golfers at the Niagara-on-the-Lake Golf Club, that it spent itself in an ease of blue, or the Shining Water, as it had been called by the Iroquois. The river became a lake, and the water moved east, around the many islands and islets of the Thousand Islands, before it was channelled into the St. Lawrence River. Northeast of Quebec City, long before it reached the Gaspé, the river broadened into a vast expanse that moved ceaselessly, losing all the names by which it had been known, as it opened out, opened wide.

ACKNOWLEDGMENTS

Thanks to the people at McClelland & Stewart – Jennifer Lambert and Ellen Seligman, in particular – for giving this novel a home. It was my great pleasure to work with Jennifer Lambert so closely during the editing process. Deepest thanks, as well, to the wonderful Anita Chong for helping so much, and to Heather Sangster, for her fine work.

To Jackie Kaiser, of Westwood Creative Artists – my thanks for such clear-eyed insights.

I am also indebted to Jennifer Glossop, whose assistance came at a crucial time.

* * *

A Nova Scotia Arts Council grant helped give this novel the start it needed.

I was able to spend brief periods of time at the Abbaye Notre-Dame de l'Assomption in Rogersville, New Brunswick, where several chapters of this novel were written. Warmest thanks to the community there, especially Sister Kate Waters.

Dr. Rod Michalko was an enormous help to me.

I am also grateful to the late Dr. George Sanderson.

For medical advice, I am deeply indebted to Dr. Leone Steele, Dr. Imogen Fox, and Dr. Patty Menard. Many thanks, as well, to Brian Kelly, a paramedic based in Guysborough, N.S., whose help was invaluable.

Special thanks to Chief Tim Berndt of the Niagara Parks Police for his patience with my questions. I am also grateful for the help I received at both the Niagara Falls Public Library and at the Lundy's Lane Historical Museum.

As always, heartfelt thanks to Janet Simpson, and my sisters, Jennifer and Sue. Loving thanks to Paul, David, and Sarah, who give me such encouragement. I could not have written this without you.